This book was designed and produced by Silver Goat Media, LLC.
Fargo, ND U.S.A. www.silvergoatmedia.com
SGM and the SGM goat are trademarks of Silver Goat Media, LLC.

Cover art: Kan Liu, *Truth and Honor* © 2016 SGM
Cover design: Travis Klath and Kristin Langerud © 2016 SGM
Author Photo: Tamara Weets © 2016 SGM

This book was typeset in Perpetua Silver by Cady Ann Mittlestadt and Aurora McClain.

ISBN-10: 1-944296-02-6
ISBN-13: (Silver Goat Media) 978-1-944296-02-5

A portion of the annual proceeds from the sale of this book
is donated to the Longspur Prairie Fund.
www.longspurprairie.org

Started by **KICKSTARTER**

Peter Fane is on Facebook, Twitter, and Instagram. Come visit for maps, art, and stories!

First SGM printing – March 2016, Fargo, ND. 1.0 – 150316
Printed and bound in the United States of America.

The Blind Dragon

A Tale from the Canon of Tarn

Peter Fane

SGM

This story is for Anna —
sister, friend, dragon rider.

The Kingdom of Remain spans all space and memory.

It is the Eternal Kingdom, the Silver Kingdom, an ancient sphere born of our love and our sorrow, our blood and our joy.

The Kingdom of Remain encompasses countless stars and minds. It has served our people for millennia. And we have served it in return.

The Kingdom of Remain is our place. It is our home.

The Kingdom of Remain is our legacy. It is our story.

It is the only tale we have worth telling.

The following events take place in the Third Year of Dorómy III, Founding Year 12,037.

Cast of Characters

House Dradón — The Ruling House of Dávanor

Coat of Arms — A white dragon rampant on a field of sky blue.

High Lady Abigail Dradón, The High Lady of Dávanor, a girl of 9 years.

> High Lord David Dradón, High Lord of Dávanor, assassinated by persons unknown, F.Y. 12,036.
>
> Master Roger Khondus, Master of Dragons, a Davanórian veteran.
>
> Master Bengamon Zar, Master of Arms, an Anorian veteran.
>
> Master George Boród, Master of Books, a scholar and healer.
>
> Captain Jenifer Fyr, Captain of the Guard, a warrior and poet.
>
> Captain Sara Terreden, dragon knight, Captain of the White Demons.
>
> Captain Erik Dyer, dragon knight, killed in battle, F.Y. 12,034.
>
> Captain Jessica Dyer, dragon knight and freeholder.
>
>> Anna Dyer, dragon squire, a girl of 14 years.
>>
>> Penelope Dyer, dragon squire, a girl of 12 years.
>>
>> Wendi Dyer, a girl of 5 years.
>
> Voidbane, a dragon, the largest on Dávanor, 64 paces long, jet-black, 104 years old.
>
> Nightlove, a dragon, the prized broodmare of House Dradón, 41 paces long, pure white, 339 years old.
>
> Lightdancer, a dragon, Sara Terreden's mount, 17 paces long, silver, 213 years old.
>
> Rocky, a messenger dragon, 14 palms long, 12 palms round, purple, said to be 146 years old, but could be older — or younger.
>
> Gregory, a messenger dragon, Master Zar's pet, 11 palms long, blue, 404 years old.
>
> A Dragon foal, 3 paces long, pure white, newly born.

House Fel — The Second House of Dávanor
Coat of Arms — A two-headed dragon in gold on a dark green field.
High Lord Oskor Fel, Lord of Dávanor; pretender to its throne.

> Halek Fel, Lord of Dávanor, a sickly young man of 26 years.
>
> Malachi Fel, Lord of Dávanor, a young man of 18 years.
>
> Philip Fel, Lord of Dávanor, a young man of 17 years.
>
> Irondusk, a dragon, the most ruthless on Dávanor, 58 paces long, rust red, 213 years old.

House Tevéss — The Third House of Dávanor
Coat of Arms — Three black swords crossed on a maroon field.
High Lord Gideon Tevéss, Lord of Dávanor, advisor to High Lady Abigail.

> Layne Tevéss, Lord of Dávanor, a young man of 26 years.
>
> Captain Floren D'Rent, Captain of the Guard.
>
> Captain Stephen Corónd, Master of Dragons.

House Dallanar — The Ruling House of Remain
Coat of Arms — Acasius's Star in silver on a field of high blue.
High Lord Dorómy Dallanar, Duke of Paráden and Ward of Káladar. The High King of Remain. Also known as "the Iron Lion," or — in loyalist circles — as "the Pretender," or simply "the Traitor."
High Lord Bellános Dallanar, Duke of Kon and Ward of the Tarn. Also known as "the Silver Fox," or — in loyalist circles — as "the High King," or simply as "the King."

> Michael Dallanar, the Dark Lord of Kon, the High General of the Tarn, and the wielder of the Vordan; a warrior of legendary ferocity, a young man of 20 years.
>
> Garen Dallanar, the Lord Librarian of Remain, Master of Spies and Finder of Secrets; a scholar and healer unmatched in the Realm, a young man of 17 years.

"As for the Kingdom's smaller Worlds, a Wise Prince will do his Utmost to secure first the Duchy of Dávanor. The Ferocity of Dávanor's Dragons is the stuff of Legend. The Zeal of its Knights, even more so. Trained from Birth into the Arts of War, the Fervor of a Davanórian's Sword is matched only by the Fervor of a Davanórian's Honor. For this Reason the Dragon Riders of Dávanor are rightly feared throughout the Realm: Nothing is more terrifying than a Warrior willing to die for his Word."

> – Katherine II, *The Canon of Tarn*, "Prolegomena to Imperial Tactics and Diplomacies." F.Y. 189

1

"Curse my eyes," Master Khondus growled. "This isn't right."

Anna Dyer stopped in her tracks and looked over her shoulder.

"Shall I wait, sir?" she asked.

Anna held a covered basket in front of her. It was woven from silvery reed and was just heavy enough to make her lean back against its weight.

"No." Master Khondus scratched at his grey stubble. "No waiting. Maybe I'm mistaken."

Anna nodded, but she was confused.

Mistaken?

When it came to dragons, the Master didn't make "mistakes."

2

THEY WERE IN the lower stables' largest birthing stall, on the western side of the High Keep. The stall was warm and smelled of straw, dragons, and blood. Two flickering lanterns, hung from wrought hooks on either side of the door, lit the scene with warm light. Straw lay knee-deep across the flagstones, glimmering like spun gold. Somewhere above them, on one of the Keep's ancient ramparts, a massive chain clattered, a flight ramp thundered open, and a dragon leapt roaring to the sky.

Anna started to ask another question, then thought better of it. She was fourteen years old. She'd worked in the lower stables since she was nine. And she'd assisted with over a dozen birthings. She knew what she was doing. At least she thought she did. She most certainly knew that the Master of Dragons didn't suffer fools. So she leaned her basket against her hip, hitched up her leather apron, and continued through the straw to Nightlove and her newborn dragon foal.

Nightlove was a big dragon, their finest broodmare. Her scales were ghostly white. From nose to tail, she measured over forty paces long and barely fit the birthing stall's length. She lay in the golden straw, her huge white wings folded flat against her sides, her long tail curled back at the stall's corner. Even under the lanterns' glow, her scales seemed to make their own light; she shone like the moon.

Nightlove's dragon foal lay by her hips, still covered in its bloody birth skin. It was barely moving, but it seemed fine. Its birth skin was completely intact, its limbs looked well, and it was a good size, about the size of a smallish horse, if you didn't count its long, serpentine tail. Not Nightlove's largest foal—not by a stretch—but hardly a runt, either.

Anna frowned and smoothed a lock of dark hair behind her ear. The foal had been late in coming, and the Master had been worried about that. But there hadn't been much birth blood. And that was usually a good sign.

So what's wrong?

What did the Master see?

Anna knelt in the straw, set her basket beside her, and put her hand on Nightlove's flank. At her touch, the big dragon gave a deep sigh. Her scales were smooth and very warm, almost hot to the touch.

Anna waited a moment to be sure Nightlove was comfortable with her presence. Then she took the cover off her basket, turned to the foal, and began removing its birth skin, starting with the foal's snout, peeling the slippery membrane away from its nose like a veil, dropping the slimy shreds into her basket. Beneath the birth skin, the foal's scales were pure white, just like its mother's. With a warm cloth, Anna wiped some blood from the foal's mouth, nostrils, and the nubs of its horns. It twitched and gave a wet snort. Its eyes were clamped shut. A silvery film glossed its eyelids and bits of gold straw stuck to its nose. Anna finished cleaning its face, then continued peeling the birth skin from the rest of its body, being especially careful not to bump its delicate facial scales or the fine hairs on its pinkish nostrils. When Anna pulled the birth skin away from its wings—wings that were surprisingly well-developed, she noticed—the foal began to murmur and coo, its white tail coiling in the straw as its crest and wings touched fresh air for the first time. It took Anna only a few more moments to finish.

"There we are," Anna whispered.

The dragon foal went still at her voice. Then it snorted and swiveled its snout toward her. Its eyes were still shut. Its tail quivered and its nostrils flared. A menacing growl rose from its chest.

"Easy there," Anna said gently. "Easy." She placed her palm on its forehead, applying calm, steady pressure between its eyes. The foal went quiet, gave a satisfied snort, and settled back against Nightlove's flank.

And then it opened its eyes. They were big, blank, and sightless. Like white, silvery moons. The baby dragon had been born blind.

3

ANNA LOOKED OVER her shoulder.

Master Khondus said nothing, but his eyes were dark.

"What do I do?" she looked back at the dragon foal.

The foal cocked its head at her, its big eyes wide. Then it cooed, like a question—a question posed specifically for her. Anna frowned. Like all noble-born squires of Dávanor, she'd worked with dragons since she was a child. But this was a question for which she had no answer.

Master Khondus stepped up, looked the foal over, then knelt beside Anna in the straw. He cradled the foal's white jaws in his scarred hands and looked into its face. The foal went still, staring back at the Master, unblinking, as if it could see. Master Khondus licked his thumb, wiped some of the silvery film from beneath the foal's eyes, inspecting it. Then he sniffed it, tasted it with the tip of his tongue, and frowned. He glanced under the foal's tail.

"Male." The Master shook his head. "Nightlove's getting older. And this is Voidbane's first siring in three years. Should've been more careful with them both. Great misfortune."

Anna nodded.

Nightlove gave a deep groan.

"There's a good girl." Master Khondus patted her huge side. "Good girl."

"Shall I open the window, sir?" Anna cleared her throat. "Some morning air, sir?"

"Wait."

Anna shut her mouth and waited.

For a long moment, the Master neither spoke nor moved. Finally, he put his hand on the foal's chest. His fingers were thick and calloused, his wrists and grey-haired arms permanently scarred by the tell-tale pattern of dragon gauntlets. His hand rose and fell with the swell of the foal's breath—up and down, up and down—the rhythm deep and strong.

Some years ago, Master Zar had told Anna a story about Master Khondus's great grandfather, the legendary Jonathan Khondus, and how that great warrior had subdued Voidbane, House Dradón's largest war dragon, with his hands and eyes alone. "No goad. No tools. No harness." Master Zar had nodded, his purple eyes sparkling. "Just knowledge, courage, and will. The reputation of Master Khondus's people is ancient—and well-earned." There was no family of Dragon Masters more respected on all Dávanor. That meant there was no family of Dragon Masters more respected in all the Kingdom. Master Khondus was more than a great captain of House Dradón; he was one of the great captains of the Realm.

Anna put her hand on the foal's chest, right next to Master Khondus's, careful to copy the Master's stance and position exactly. At her touch, the foal turned its white eyes to her, pointed its snout at her heart, and gave a wet little burp. More gold straw stuck to its snout. Anna reached to clean it off.

"Get the hammer," Master Khondus murmured.

Anna stopped short.

"Leave it outside the door. Make sure she doesn't see it." He tilted his head to indicate Nightlove.

Anna didn't move. The foal turned its nose to the Master then back at Anna again. It didn't blink. Its eyes really were *huge*, Anna realized. The biggest eyes she'd ever seen on a newborn. Silvery white and beautiful. They seemed to glow.

Like pearls.

Like huge, perfect, silvery pearls.

"Hear me, girl?" Master Khondus asked quietly.

"Yes, sir!" Anna saluted, crossing her fist over her chest.

But she didn't move. She couldn't stop looking into the foal's eyes. The foal returned her gaze, equally mesmerized, or so it seemed, something powerful and unspoken channeling between them.

Voidbane's first siring in three years, Anna thought. *Voidbane's son.*

The foal went still, cocked its head, then gurgled inquisitively. It butted its snout against her hand, demanding her attention. She made to stroke his nose, then stopped herself. She knew her duty. Master Khondus shook his head, stood, and smoothed his hair over his head, tightening the leather strap that held his grey queue.

"Get the hammer," he sighed.

"Yes, sir." Anna's mouth was dry. "Should I finish cleaning him?"

"Why?" Master Khondus asked, a faint edge to his voice.

The foal cocked its head at the change in the Master's tone. It seemed to consider for a moment. Then it hissed and struggled to its feet, muscular legs splayed and wobbly, sticky wings peeling from its chest. Gold straw stuck everywhere to its white belly. It tilted its head toward Anna for a moment, reared onto its haunches, and stepped unsteadily in front of her, turning to face Master Khondus as if it wanted to protect her. For a long moment, it stared at the Master. Then its eyes narrowed, it leaned forward, and it hissed savagely, pinkish-white lips peeling back to reveal a mouthful of fully-developed fangs. It was well over twice Anna's height, sitting up like that.

"Easy there, strong one," Master Khondus said, as if he was talking to a newborn kitten rather than a war dragon bred to kill. "All's well. See his teeth? Fully formed. He was late, but even so. Unusual. And look how he stands, look at his wings. *Easy* there, strong one. Very fine indeed." He scratched at his stubble. "More's the pity."

"Easy there," Anna murmured, gazing into the foal's strange white eyes. "All's well, strong one."

The foal turned to Anna and gave her a gentle head-butt. Then it yawned, licked its fangs, and grunted, settling back on its haunches. Nightlove rumbled, eyes closed with exhaustion, and turned her head over her huge shoulder, nudging the foal with her snout. Her head was almost as large as the foal's entire body. Her broad tongue touched at its scales, its wings, the nubs of its horns, its legs, and its nose. Her eyes cracked open. They were dark blue, like liquid sapphire, a striking contrast to the white of her scales.

The foal grunted and settled back against its mother's flank, still staring at Anna. Then it seemed to reconsider, flopped onto its back, took a deep breath, and stretched its hind legs straight into the air, holding them like that for a moment before twisting onto its side with a satisfied snort, its white tail coiling happily in the straw. During this entire maneuver, its eyes never left Anna's face. Not even for a moment.

Nightlove began to croon, her sound a deep, soothing flute.

"We can't wait," Master Khondus said, below the dragon's music. "If she bonds any further with him, it'll ruin her for months. Get the hammer. I'll show you how to do it. He won't suffer."

4

ANNA STOOD AND walked out of the birthing stall. As she left, she heard the foal gurgle as it struggled to its feet.

Then it cried out, as if in pain.

Crying for her?

She couldn't help but wonder.

Master Khondus soothed it with a word, but Anna's stomach knotted.

And now the hammer.

The hammer.

"The hammer," she whispered.

And she'd be the one to swing it. That's what the Master

had meant about "showing her how to do it." There was no doubt about it. In a way, she supposed, it proved the Master's faith in her. He knew she understood her duty. So she'd kill this beautiful dragon. Voidbane's son. Because it was blind.

She walked past five other stall doors, down the stable's central hallway, to the storage closet at its end. It was early morning, not even dawn. No one was around. At the end of the hallway, she opened the closet and went to the tackle cabinet at its rear. The cabinet's doors were decorated with panels of Anorian oak, each carved with a dragon rampant, their eyes inlaid with dark blue glass. When the cabinet doors were closed, it looked like the two dragons were rearing up to fight one another. The dragons' sapphire blue eyes reminded her of Nightlove.

She opened the cabinet. Training harnesses jingled. The hammer rested in the back corner, behind stacked buckets, crisply folded fire blankets, and neatly stacked rows of feeding tubes, training harnesses, starter goads, oil pots, cleaning buckets, safety lanterns, and other gear. She scraped the hammer out. Its iron head weighed a full stone, probably more. Its handle was almost as long as her leg.

How was she supposed to swing the cursed thing?

In her mind's eye, Anna saw herself hefting the hammer awkwardly to her shoulder, then swinging it with all her might, smashing the foal's fragile skull, the wet sound like an eggshell crushed under a boot. She shut her eyes and shook her head, trying to push the image away, but was rewarded with another instead: herself swinging the hammer, but this time *missing* her target, hitting the foal's side or neck or snout. A scream of agony. The foal's eyes wide with confusion. What had it done wrong? Had it made a mistake? The ultimate violation of trust.

Down the hallway, back in the birthing stall, the foal howled, its cry echoing the ancient vaults. Her guts wrenched.

During her five years in the Drádonhold's stables, Anna had seen dragon foals put down twice. Two times in five years. Each of those times, the newborn had been born into pain. And each of those times, Master Khondus had swung the hammer himself. It had been terrible to watch, but the foals hadn't suffered. Anna was certain of it.

After the second time she'd seen it, back in the High Keep's

27

library, Master Boród had told her the same thing. "That foal felt nothing, Miss Dyer." He adjusted his reading spectacles, looking at her over their gold wire frames. "But that's not the point, is it? The point is this: There are other stables, other high houses on Dávanor, where *any* imperfection is met with the hammer. But not here. So consider yourself fortunate. You've seen this twice during your tenure with Master Khondus. If you'd served elsewhere, you might have seen it five or six times a season."

But not here.

Not in House Dradón.

"Dragons aren't like men, girl," Master Khondus had told her later that evening, when Anna had brought it up again. "They don't ruin their dreams with silly vanities—what some fool might say about an off-center crest, a bent horn, a patch of dull scale. And they sure as spit don't care about land, title, or coin. They dream of nothing save their rider's love—her love of the air, her love of the flight, and her love of a good fight. Those are their dreams, girl. So those are the dreams we honor. In House Dradón, every dragon fights."

Every dragon?

Anna frowned. She couldn't get the foal's silvery-white eyes out of her head. The trust there. The unspoken faith. Her Father had been Voidbane's rider for almost two decades. And this foal was Voidbane's first siring in three years. Didn't her family owe the great dragon something?

She shook her head. She'd seen it done before. It was a simple task.

But it wasn't so simple, was it?

"Enough." She took a breath. "In battle, dragons die."

Of course they did. Impaled, burned, slashed, shot, screaming, falling from the sky, their last moments savage and brutal, with only the glory of future song to give solace.

But those dragons had had a chance to earn their glory in battle, a chance to serve their House and their rider, a *chance* to face the enemy.

Anna realized that she hadn't moved.

She was still standing in the storage closet. Staring into the tackle cabinet.

"I won't hurt him," Anna said to the stacked goads. "I'll do it right."

5

ANNA SHUT THE cabinet doors, closed the storage closet, and walked back to the birthing stall, holding the hammer in front of her.

From inside the stall, Master Khondus said to someone, "I warned your father of this."

Anna stopped short, just outside the door. Inside, Night-love snorted like a blast furnace, then growled with exhaustion. The foal hissed, its tail thrashing the straw.

"*We* are responsible, Khondus?" A young man chuckled. His voice was a light tenor marked by the heavy accent of Dávanor's far western counties, where the Kingdom's common tongue was taught late to children. His voice seemed familiar. "This is *our* fault? My father will find that interesting."

"No," Master Khondus acknowledged. "The fault is mine."

"Just so." The young man sniffed. "It is good for you to understand. I have always told my father that you need to understand these things."

"Your sense of humor is as sophisticated as ever, my Lord," the Master said.

"Huh? That is . . . uh? Of course. Very well."

Anna peeked around the door jamb.

Master Khondus was talking to a skinny, blond-haired young man. Anna recognized him immediately. It was Lord Layne Tevéss—the son of High Lady Abigail's chief advisor, Lord Gideon. Anna didn't know Lord Layne personally, of course. But she knew his reputation: a gossip, showoff, and lack-wit whose giant mouth was outweighed only by his tiny brain. The lordling was a bit shorter than Master Khondus and elaborately dressed in the dark maroon of House Tevéss. He wore velvet leggings, a maroon doublet of Eulorian silk, and knee-high boots of Abúcian leather, also dyed maroon. An ornate dagger, pommeled with a burgundy stone, swung from his belt on a gilt chain. As was the fashion of the elite in Dávanor's western counties, his ears were clasped in elaborate gold casings. Under the lantern's light, the dark jewels on his fingers shone like blood.

The dragon foal cooed inquisitively and turned to face her. Anna pulled her head away from the doorway.

Something's wrong.

And then—suddenly, in her mind's eye—Anna saw

Father's armored body lying on the cot in the upper barracks, saw the gaping hole in his breastplate, dark blood pooled on ancient stone, saw Mother's face blank with grief. Her father, dead.

Slain by traitors.

Killed three years ago during the rebellion—a rebellion led by House Tevéss and House Fel, Lord Gideon and Lord Oskor's murderous revolt against House Dradón's rightful authority.

Inside the stall, the dragon foal hissed savagely, feeling her tension.

Anna pushed the vision away, took a measured breath. If she dwelled on it, she'd get angry. And if she got angry, she'd get distracted and she wouldn't be able to do her work—or her duty.

And Father wouldn't like that.

The foal gurgled and cooed, its wet, baby noises making her smile in spite of herself.

And suddenly she felt better.

Calmer.

The foal sighed.

She scooted closer to the stall's door, cocked an ear.

"Yes, the fault is mine," Master Khondus repeated, patting the foal's side. "And mine alone."

"Which brings me to my purpose." Lord Layne cleared his throat. "You have new orders for this broodmare, Khondus. And I have decided that *I* will be the one to give those orders to you——."

"And since the fault is mine," Master Khondus interrupted him calmly, "the responsibility likewise belongs to me. This is what happens when a dragon is over-bred, Layne. This is what happens when we break our most sacred trust. It won't happen again."

Lord Layne paused, as if he didn't understand the Master's words. Then he sniffed. "My father says you can breed a proper mare once a year, easily. Twice, even——."

Master Khondus chuckled. "Your father knows as much about dragons as you do."

"Uh . . . . What do you mean by that——?"

The Master laughed good-naturedly. "It means: 'You and your father don't know anything about dragons.'"

"Uh——."

"Regardless," Master Khondus continued, "the obligation and the duty are mine, indeed. If I'd insisted on a more reasonable schedule, this kind of flaw would be near impossible. I never should've allowed the breeding. The mistake will not be repeated."

There was a long pause. Then Lord Layne laughed. "Oh, I see! Ha! Very good! I see. So *you* make these decisions now, eh, stable master? And to whom shall I deliver this important news? To High Lady Abigail, Duchess of Dávanor? The Silver Courts of Paráden, perhaps? The High Council of Lords? Someone, somewhere, will want to know that the great, *wise* Master Khondus now commands the business of House Dradón! The High King himself, maybe? King Dorómy will be interested to learn of your—."

Master Khondus chuckled, but his voice was serious. "Call Dorómy Dallanar 'king' in my presence again, boy—we'll have more than words. Keep your ignorant, treasonous talk to yourself. And you miss the point, again. I will speak slowly: a broodmare of Nightlove's age and configuration cannot be bred more than once every two or three years. Look at her for a moment, Layne. Just take a moment. Do you see how she gasps? See how she barely moves? These are signs. They are not good."

"I—." Lord Layne began.

"Maybe this will be easier," the Master continued patiently. "How will this dragon foal fly? Its eyes don't work. How will it fight? Think about it for a moment, Layne. Just take your time. Think about it."

Lord Layne paused, as if considering, then sniffed. "Your sarcasm is unwarranted, stable master. And you shall address me as 'my Lord,' or 'Lord Tevéss.'" He paused. "And yes, it is a worthless beast, to be sure. I have never seen one quite so . . . ungainly."

"Further proof of your ignorance. His form is near perfect. Strangely mature, but even so."

"Well, I . . . uh, that is to say . . . surely you do not think this blind worm can be of some *use?*"

The foal growled. Lord Layne coughed nervously and stepped away from it.

Master Khondus sighed. "She'll not be bred again, Layne. Not for three years. Maybe four. Take that to your father and be gone. You're dismissed."

"What? What do you mean by——? Now, hold on you . . . you wait just a moment——."

"And if you feel inspired to grow some brains," the Master said conversationally, "you'll keep your silly mouth shut when it comes to dragons, politics, and the war. Your family's loyalties are known, Tevéss—by everyone. And you know mine. Never forget: High Lady Abigail, House Dradón, and the duchy of Dávanor are loyal to High King Bellános—and always will be. Now, off with you. Work to do here."

"Huh? Well . . . uh. Maybe *you* are the one who does not understand *me*, stable master. As I was trying to say, I have orders. New orders. For you and this broodmare."

The Master laughed. "I take no commands from you, boy."

"You do today, Master. That is why I am here. Today, *I* give *you* orders. Nightlove has had a great honor bestowed upon her. She shall be bred in four weeks. Lord Oskor Fel and his entire entourage fly now from Felshold with the great Irondusk. They arrive in three days' time and shall stay some months as honored guests. My father has made Nightlove available to Fel's stable masters, and I have been given charge of the breeding!"

6

"LORD FEL COMES here?" Master Khondus asked. His voice was quiet.

The foal hissed.

Anna blinked, her face going warm.

It isn't possible.

Lord Oskor Fel.

The traitor.

House Dradón's most ancient foe, despite three years of false peace.

Her family's nemesis.

Here?

The dragon foal's tail thrashed in the straw, as if hearing her thoughts.

"Indeed!" Lord Layne rambled on, growing even more excited, oblivious to the change in the Master's demeanor. "And Nightlove will be bred to Irondusk. Those are your new orders. Ha! A symbolic act, of course, but still good cause for celebration. The joining of our two prized lines, at last. Even *you* can understand that. Eh, Khondus?"

The Master said nothing.

"Perhaps," Layne mused, "it is easier to understand this way: this breeding is a foretaste of the future union between House Dradón and House Fel. Does that help, great Master? My father has arranged it. Lady Abigail is very young, but everyone understands the need. The two great houses of Dávanor finally united! A just and lasting peace! Is that not cause for celebration?"

"She's nine years old," the Master said softly.

Anna wanted to look back into the stall, but she didn't dare. Her head spun. Her anger—her old dark friend—grinned at her from the shadows of her mind. The dragon foal growled.

"Come now, Khondus," Lord Layne said. "You look . . . well, you look *disturbed*. My father has arranged everything. Why the sour face? This should be a time of *merriment*. There will be grand parties. The great Irondusk comes! Lord Fel brings the whole of his entourage! Come now! Come! Of course, there have been some silly misunderstandings in the past, but that is all behind us now. There shall be months of celebration! A delightful surprise, eh?"

Master Khondus said nothing.

"Well." Lord Layne sniffed. "You should be grateful that I

am telling you at all, stable master. It will be a great surprise. Nobody else is to know. I tell you only out of courtesy."

Nightlove rumbled. The foal's growl was low and continuous.

Anna still couldn't understand it.

Three years ago, High Lady Abigail's father, Lord David, had quelled Fel's revolt at terrible cost. Now the same traitor who had defied their High House's just authority, the same traitor who had plunged all of Dávanor into war came with dragons and soldiers and arms to their High Keep as an *ally*?

It makes no sense.

The dragon foal snarled.

"That animal is not safe," Lord Layne muttered uneasily. "You . . . you are *sure* it is blind?"

"Who else knows of Lord Fel's arrival, Layne?" Master Khondus asked casually. "When does he come?"

"Ah. Well. I can tell that you are upset, Khondus. No pretending. The birthing has upset you. I understand. These things can be difficult. But you do not see how important this is. I know that can be unsettling. But a soldier of your age and experience should understand these matters. These stables and dragons are the property of House Dradón. House Dradón is ruled by High Lady Abigail. Lady Abigail is young, yes. But she and her advisors are expecting an important guest with whom alliances must be made. This broodmare is a part of a larger plan. She must be bred. Do you understand now?"

"When does Fel arrive, Layne?" The Master cleared his throat. "You say three days. You know that with certainty?"

"Well . . . uh, yes. As I said—he is to come two days after tomorrow. No one is to know. I thought I would come and tell you because—."

"Three days. You're certain?"

Lord Layne laughed out of nowhere and clapped his hands. "I have it! Ha! You will like this, Khondus. A good use for a useless beast! This blind animal will fly strangely, no? It will fly eventually? Its wings do seem quite strong. Am I correct?"

Master Khondus didn't answer. The dragon foal went silent, as if listening.

"Oh, I have a very clever idea. I love it! I want you to clean it up and feed it. Train it. Give it some basic . . . uh, maneuvers. You know. Prepare it for 'battle.' Fel and his men shall be with us for some time, I'm sure. Several months, at least. Lord Dorómy has sent Lord Oskor two great cannon from Paráden, to be offered to High Lady Abigail, symbols of Dávanor's peace and unity and all that. When the guns arrive, I am *sure* that Lord Oskor and the High Lady would welcome the chance to test the skill of their war adepts. A small, weird target would prove very challenging, eh? Am I wrong? Good *use* for a *useless* thing. Clever, eh? No sense to waste the beast for nothing. And I am sure that father will agree. Then we can all enjoy the sport. It will be the highlight of the celebration! And think on this, Khondus: It shall be better for the foal, too. It can spend even more time with its mother before it gives 'battle,' eh?"

Anna stared.

The lordling's idea for "target practice" was fool nonsense, of course.

But two great cannon sent to Lord Oskor by the Pretender King?

If it was true, then it was war—plain and simple.

What more proof of Oskor's treason do we need?

The foal growled.

Layne stepped farther away from it.

41

"Eh, Khondus?" he asked again.

The Master said nothing. Anna was tempted to look around the door jamb, but she resisted.

Lord Layne didn't speak again for a moment, but when he did, it was with a firmer voice. "Now, listen, Khondus. I am patient, but I shall broach no further insolence from you. Answer me. I command you! I come to you as your superior. I may not be some kind of famous dragon master or warrior or some such thing, but I do know a few things about these animals. House Dradón has long held the reputation for coddling the undeserving. That ends today. Do you understand, stable master? Garbage will be thrown out with the garbage, and that will be the end of it. If we can make sport of it, so much the better. Now, you will prepare this broodmare for breeding."

Anna's face went hot, her anger rising from the dark, and she was struck by the insane urge to walk into the birthing stall and smash the fool's face with the hammer. She'd forgotten that she held it; it seemed lighter in her hands.

The foal's growl deepened.

Lord Layne coughed uneasily and scooted even farther

away in the straw.

The foal's growl went deeper still.

Easy, Anna thought to herself. *Easy*.

The foal grunted and seemed to settle. Anna took a breath.

Lady Abigail was young, to be sure, but she was still trained. And Master Khondus, Master Zar, Master Boród, Captain Fyr, the other senior captains of House Dradón— they would never tolerate this blatant outrage.

Never.

The foal growled again, the sound even deeper this time. It sounded like a full-grown war dragon.

"You are *sure* this beast cannot see?" Lord Layne asked. "My plan will not work if it can see. The sport for Lord Fel——."

"You're confused, boy," Master Khondus said at last. His voice was quiet. "You have no 'plan.' And the dragons of House Dradón don't provide 'sport' for our enemies. The dragons of House Dradón bring our enemies one thing—and one thing only: death. There will be no 'games.' There will be no 'celebration.' There will be no 'breeding.' And there most certainly will be no 'union.' It will not happen."

Then the Master stepped to the doorway, snatched the

hammer from Anna's hands as if it were a strapping switch, and stepped back into the stall, hammer held ready to strike.

7

"WHA—*WAIT*?!" LORD Layne cried, seeing the hammer.

Anna followed Master Khondus into the stall.

Layne was backing away from the the Master, one palm up, the other hand fumbling for his dagger on its gilded chain. The lordling's feet tangled in the straw; he stumbled, almost went down, then righted himself gracelessly.

Nightlove growled, but she was too exhausted to move. The foal, however, had energy to spare. It hissed and rose up on its haunches, white wings spread in the darkness, blocking Lord Layne's retreat, its eyes mean, silvery slits.

"*Wait!*" Lord Layne squealed, suddenly not sure which way to go, not sure which direction was least terrifying: Master Khondus stepping toward him from the front or the white dragon foal blocking him from behind.

"We'll take you to Captain Fyr," Master Khondus said pleasantly, still moving forward, hammer ready. "See what she has to say about you and your father's little 'surprise.'"

"How *dare* you! How dare——."

"Funny." Master Khondus smiled grimly. "Your big mouth has been an embarrassment to our High Keep for three years—yet now, in a mere moment, it's become our savior. Had to come down and show me who was in charge, didn't you? Thank the Great Sisters for your pea-sized wits, boy. Kneel. Put your hands behind you."

"You wouldn't *dare*——."

"Kneel, boy. I'll brain you like the senseless pup you are."

The Master took a step forward, hammer cocked.

"*Stop!*" Lord Layne cried, and actually stamped his foot in the straw. "I am of House Tevéss! Halt! I am Tevéss! You cannot——! *No*——!"

But as Lord Layne cried "No!" he reached for his sleeve, pulled a hidden stiletto, and lunged for Master Khondus's neck in a single, fluid movement.

The maneuver might have worked. On someone whose profession wasn't war.

Master Khondus ducked, Layne's stiletto spearing over his head, and jabbed the lordling hard in the throat with his finger. Layne reeled backwards, eyes bulging, hands at his neck. Master Khondus kicked his legs out from under him, knocked him to the straw, and flipped him over onto his stomach like a trussed pig, pulling the lordling's hands behind his back and binding his wrists with a leather thong from the birthing basket. Then he rolled Layne back over, grabbed him by the front of his doublet, hauled him up.

"Through which pass does Lord Fel come?" the Master asked him calmly. "Which pass?"

Lord Layne wheezed and stared. His eyes had gone glassy; he couldn't answer. Master Khondus dropped him to the straw. The dragon foal leaned over the lordling, its fangs gleaming.

"Three days," Master Khondus said. His voice was calm, but when he looked at Anna, she saw that his eyes were black with rage. "We have three days."

The Master glanced at the foal. It was leaning farther over Lord Layne, wickedly licking its fangs. The lordling wheezed, legs churning, his eyes wide with terror.

Master Khondus turned to Anna. "We must gather Master Zar, Master Borónd, Captain Fyr, and our other captains. We need to tell our allies in the minor houses. Your mother must know, as well. Lord Fel comes——."

He stopped and looked at the dragon foal.

"Sir?" Anna started, following the Master's gaze.

"And our work isn't yet done here," Master Khondus said.

Her hands went cold, the understanding coming quickly. With everything she'd just seen, she'd forgotten why she'd fetched the hammer in the first place. The foal cocked its head at the Master for a moment. Then it turned to Anna and cooed, asking its question. She looked at it. Then looked away. Master Khondus nodded and set the hammer in the straw in front of her.

"We must take care of him now, girl. There's no time."

8

IN SPITE OF herself, Anna shook her head.

It wasn't supposed to happen like this.

Master Khondus was supposed to spare the foal after what they'd just learned, after what had just happened. She didn't know why, but the Master was supposed to realize that the foal should live.

She took a step backward, her head spinning. She had the

sudden urge to grab the hammer, run from the birthing stall, and throw the cursed thing over the nearest balcony.

Lord Layne gasped in the straw.

The dragon foal cooed.

What's happening?

Lord Layne groaned and managed to hiss, "My father will see your head on a spike, you old——."

Master Khondus kicked Layne in the stomach, and he shut up.

The foal tutted.

Master Khondus put his scarred hand on Nightlove's side and took a deep breath. He seemed suddenly tired. The big dragon sighed at his touch.

Anna suddenly remembered something Father had said to her many years ago: "Duty usually means obedience. But sometimes, duty can mean defiance."

Anna nodded. "Truth and honor, Master Khondus, sir." She snapped her heels together and crossed her fist over the leather apron at her chest. "We serve you, the High Lady Abigail Dradón, and her rightful lord and liege, High King Bellános Dallanar, the true King of Remain."

Nightlove growled. The foal stared at Anna for a moment, then hissed its agreement, reared up, and extended its wings, as if showing them off.

"I know what you want, girl." Master Khondus shook his head. "But it must be done. Walk him down to the last stall, away from her."

The foal was right behind her now, its head leaning over her shoulder. Then it opened its wings and slowly fanned the air. Hay stirred. The lanterns' orange flames guttered. Without warning, it leapt to an oak perch that penetrated the birthing stall's far wall. Its rear claws had fully spired. They dug into the perch, the wood crunching and splintering. It cocked its head, eyes glowing, as if waiting for Anna to speak.

"It's a pity," the Master said. "But it must be done. Bring him down. If he bonds any further with her, it could ruin her." He patted Nightlove's side. "We can't delay. These next days—these next hours—will determine the fate of our House."

"You're all *dead*!" Lord Layne hissed from the straw. "My father—."

Master Khondus kicked him again, much harder this time, in that soft spot right below the ribcage. The lordling coughed and doubled up, wheezing.

"I will care for him, sir," Anna said calmly.

She knew that it might sound childish. She knew she could lose her position. She knew that they had no time. But she also knew that her family owed this foal something. This was Voidbane's son. She would obey Master Khondus's orders, of course. But the very least she could do was try to convince him of another course.

"I will find a place for him, sir. Until we find his rider. I'll clean him and mind him when I'm off duty, sir. I'll do the extra work. I will pay for his food and bedding out of my own purse, sir. I can take him home to our farm. Any offspring of Voidbane will be welcome there. I know my Mother will agree."

"It's not your decision, girl," Master Khondus said gently. "Nor is it mine. *Nature* has chosen. We must honor that. He can't see. He can't fly. And he can't fight. He's strong, no doubt. Strangely so. But he cannot serve. Would you put your own momentary suffering before his lifetime in a cage? And what of Nightlove? Every moment they share now will make it twice as hard for her to continue. You know this."

The Master's words sounded like wisdom. They *were* wise. But it didn't matter. She wouldn't do it. And, she realized quite suddenly, she wouldn't let the Master do it, either.

She didn't know how, but this dragon foal would live.

From its perch, the foal growled, as if reading her thoughts. Lord Layne coughed. There was blood on his lips. He tried to speak, but gasped and coughed wetly instead.

"Forgive me, sir." Anna nodded calmly, but her mind raced. "I'm sorry, sir."

Sometimes, duty can mean defiance.

Was this what Father had meant?

"You've done no wrong," Master Khondus said. "If you didn't feel this way, *that* would be cause for concern."

Anna nodded with what she hoped seemed like agreement and looked at the straw. Her head spun.

Think!

But she felt paralyzed.

And it was starting to make her mad.

"Anna." The Master's voice was gentle. "Look at me."

Anna did.

Her face was hot.

It *cannot* die!

The foal hissed.

Her brain whirled like a black pinwheel. And she could feel the anger coming on now, stronger than ever, hungry teeth glittering in that dark corner of her brain. Great Sisters, she hated the feeling, and yet sometimes . . . . She shook her head to clear it.

"Anna."

It was hard to look Master Khondus in the eye.

The foal cooed.

Easy.

She looked at the foal. It seemed to look back at her—even though it couldn't see. Its silvery eyes glowed, as if looking into her heart. And, just like that, the dark pinwheel slowed. She took a deep breath. And it was gone. The foal gurgled. Everything would be alright.

"I understand how you feel," Master Khondus continued. "When I was a dragon squire, I stood in the very place you stand now. This very stall, in fact. There's nothing harder. And nothing I say will make it easier. I can only tell you what my father told me. Sometimes, we're called upon to do things that *must* be done, whatever the cost. We must be the strong ones, Anna. The duty is ours, or it is no one's. Do you understand?"

"Yes, sir. I'm sorry, sir. It doesn't feel like duty, sir."

"I know," Master Khondus said. "Sometimes, that's what duty feels like."

9

"Come here," Anna said.

The dragon foal looked down from its perch, its eyes glowing in the dark. Then it dropped to the straw with a muscly grunt and gave Anna a gentle head-butt. She started to smile, then cut it off. The foal furled its wings and flopped backward into the straw, as if waiting for its chest and belly to be rubbed. But it had landed directly beside Lord Layne, who promptly squealed, coughed, and twisted away in terror. Upside down in the straw, the foal turned its huge eyes to Anna, fangs gleaming in what looked like a demented smile—as if Lord Layne's squeaks and yelps were the funniest noises it had ever heard. Which, considering his age,

Anna supposed they were.

"Walk him down to the last stall." Master Khondus cocked his head at Nightlove. He held the hammer in one hand. "I'll be there in a moment."

"Yes, sir." She nodded.

And when the Master arrived, Anna realized, she and the foal would be gone.

But where?

Anna could barely understand why she was thinking like this in the first place. All she knew was that she felt *good* when the foal was around. That when she looked into its eyes, there was no more room in her head for that dark, hungry rage. Would Mother understand? In one sense, yes. Mother loved Voidbane almost as much as Father had. She might appreciate Anna's regard for the dragon foal, but she'd never condone direct insubordination. But still, Anna just felt . . . *better*. Better than she had in three years.

"Anna——." Master Khondus began.

Anna nodded. Her mind was made up.

We'll run.

Outside in the hallway, iron-shod boots scraped the stone pavers.

Anna and Master Khondus looked at each other, at Lord Layne, and at the stall door, almost in the same instant. Nightlove's sapphire eyes snapped open with a growl. The foal leapt back to its perch and stared down, eyes glowing. It sniffed once, hissed, and showed its fangs. Master Khondus changed his grip on the hammer so that it was ready to swing.

"Get behind me," he said.

Floren d'Rent, Guard Captain of House Tevéss, stepped into the birthing stall's doorway. He wore a jet-black beard that rode high on his cheekbones. His armored hand rested on the well-worn pommel of his broadsword. Behind d'Rent, five guardsmen wearing the dark maroon livery of House Tevéss stood at the ready. They wore short swords at their hips and round shields on their backs. Like d'Rent, they all wore steel breastplates. D'Rent also carried a firearm, an ancient revolver crafted of the finest high silver. The gun was slung beneath his left armpit in a leather shoulder rig, its grip worn with use. He was a big man, yet he moved with that weird smoothness taught in the Kingdom's best combat schools. A muscular night lynx. His dark eyes seemed to take everything in at once, flickering only a moment on Lord Layne, before settling on Master Khondus.

"Take these traitors!" Layne choked. "Take them! Look what he *did* to me!" He tried to show d'Rent his bound hands. "He *struck* me! They were going to take me to——."

"Shut up," d'Rent told him, not taking his eyes off Master Khondus.

Anna saw the Master ready himself.

"No need for further injuries, good Master." D'Rent smiled, seeing the Master's stance. D'Rent's teeth were very white against the black of his beard. His western accent was thick. He showed Master Khondus his palms. "We will go now together to Lord Gideon, yes? Put the hammer down."

"Come take it," Master Khondus said quietly.

Nightlove growled, grunted, and struggled to rise, but she was too weak and collapsed into the straw with a groan. The foal hissed, but uncertainly, its eyes wide.

Be ready.

The moment the thought entered her mind, the foal cocked its head and went perfectly still, as if preparing itself—as if it understood exactly what Anna was thinking. Its white tail hung straight down from its perch, a pale serpent against dark stone.

"We both know that he is a fop and a fool," d'Rent said, cocking his head at Lord Layne, not taking his eyes off Master Khondus. "But his father cares for him. And he is a High Lord, after all. Lord Gideon will hear you fairly, Master. House Tevéss and House Dradón, we are friends, no? There is no reason for anyone else to be hurt. No reason for this to . . . how do you say? *Escalate?*" D'Rent pronounced each syllable of the word carefully.

Master Khondus didn't answer, but his grip tightened on the hammer.

"*Take* them, curse you!" Lord Layne cried, wiggling in the straw. "Take them! Kill them! I *order* it! By my father's name, I *order* it!"

And then d'Rent's revolver was in his hand, and he was moving smoothly into the stall. He didn't act on Lord Layne's hysterical command. Rather, his move was calm and deliberate, the calculated action of a professional soldier ready for combat. His weapon was trained on Nightlove's head.

Three of his guardsmen drew steel and followed him. The two others blocked the stall's door, standing just outside it, swords and shields at the ready.

Anna had no weapon. But she could still punch and bite. From its perch, the dragon foal hissed. Anna set her jaw, her head clear. She wasn't angry. She was determined. It felt *right*. They were at war. This was the enemy. And she'd make House Dradón proud. Father had died in battle. Perhaps she would, too. She looked at Master Khondus's broad back. If she did, then she'd die fighting beside one of the Kingdom's greatest warriors.

"We are strong," she whispered to herself. She could feel the foal's silvery eyes on her. "This is *our* time."

Anna stepped out from behind Master Khondus, looked d'Rent straight in the eye, and said evenly, "Prepare to die, traitor."

"See! You *see*!?" Layne screamed. "Why do you *wait*?!"

One of d'Rent's guardsmen chuckled, ignoring Lord Layne completely. The other guardsmen seemed to relax a bit. But not d'Rent. He didn't smile. If anything, he seemed even more wary. His dark eyes were practiced and lethal. Behind her, Anna felt the dragon foal tense, its white presence a vibrating silver javelin in her mind, waiting to be launched.

"Calm that thing," d'Rent said, feeling the foal's energy but not looking at it, keeping his revolver trained on Nightlove's head. "I will put one in its mother's brain. There is still time, Master. Come with us quietly?"

"You *fool*!" Layne shrieked and kicked in the straw, rolling, coughing, trying to stand.

The foal reared back, wings spread, took a huge breath—and burped a cloudy puff of silvery smoke.

D'Rent's revolver swung up and locked onto one of the foal's eyes.

"No!" Anna yelled and ran straight at the gun, arms waving like a lunatic. "Me! *Here*! You coward! Me! *Me*!"

And then she was staring into the black bore of d'Rent's weapon. She stopped in spite of herself and looked into death.

Time slowed.

Master Khondus grabbed Anna's shoulder and pulled her back just as d'Rent fired. The shot was impossibly loud. Anna's ears rang. Master Khondus grunted and staggered back. Something wet spattered Anna's cheek. But the Master was still moving forward, still brandishing the hammer. Nightlove bellowed. The stable shook. The big dragon tried to stand, collapsed. Layne squealed. On its perch, the foal rose to its full height, white wings wide against the darkness. D'Rent adjusted his aim and fired. The foal snapped its head back with preternatural speed, the bullet sparking off stone. D'Rent adjusted his aim once again and Anna dove straight at him crazily, arms wide and waving, doing anything to get in front of the gun. The foal took a deep breath, snout pointed at the ceiling. D'Rent knocked Anna back with a fast slap, aimed. But the foal was already dropping its head, fangs wide, wings spread. It blasted d'Rent with silver-white fire—neck craning, eyes clamped shut, flame roaring from its mouth. But d'Rent wasn't there. He'd already dropped to his side, rolling toward Lord Layne fast as a cat. The three guardsmen behind him weren't so lucky, however. They took the full force of the foal's discharge and were instantly burning, screaming, and running frantically into each other, swords dropping mindlessly to the straw. *Not trained to war with dragons?* Anna thought, a weird glee rising up in her mind. Her lip was bleeding. And she loved it. She reached for one of the guardsmen's swords. "Back." Master Khondus grabbed her by the collar and pulled her behind him, moving once more for d'Rent, hammer ready. The guard captain was up on one knee, his arm on fire, aiming at the foal, correctly assessing the most serious threat even as Master Khondus closed. Night-love roared. The stable thundered. The two guardsmen at the door looked like they wanted to enter, but they dared not face the dragon foal's flame. Layne screamed. D'Rent fired. Again the foal seemed to anticipate the shot, its neck whipping sideways, the bullet punching through the membrane of its right wing even as it craned its head to the ceiling, taking another breath, its head coming down, mouth yawning wide. Master Khondus saw the foal's intent and threw himself sideways. For d'Rent, however, there was nowhere to hide. Beside him, Layne shrieked, legs churning in the straw. The foal blasted them both full on, plastering them back into the floor, silver-white flames funneling flesh from bone. D'Rent dropped his pistol, raised his hands as if to fend off the dragon fire, lips and beard crisping and melting, white teeth flashing in a molten skull. Layne squealed once and went silent. And still d'Rent's three guardsmen burned. Two were down, but the last one ran in place with tiny steps, his voice a kind of mad gibbering. One of the guardsmen outside dove into the room and knocked his comrade to the ground, trying to tamp out the flames. "Run!" he shouted to his mate outside the door. His partner made to turn, but Master Khondus rose on one knee and hurled the hammer, striking the turning guardsman on the back of the head; dropped him like a stone. The foal swelled on its perch, wings spread wide, took another huge breath, and hit d'Rent and Lord Layne one more time for good measure, the force of the blast knocking them across the floor smack into the far wall. Then the foal turned its attention to the two living Tevéss soldiers at the center of the stall, cocking its head, staring at them inquisitively. The Tevéss guardsman who'd come in from the doorway had managed to put out the fire on his friend. He now rose to his knees, his sword held uneasily before him. The foal's wings slowly fanned the air. Cinders swirled. The stench of scorched straw and charred flesh was everywhere. Amidst the blazing straw, D'Rent and Layne burned. Nightlove stretched, calmer now, savoring the heat and the smell of battle. Smoke billowed. The foal seemed to be waiting for something, its silvery-white eyes wide, staring at Anna.

"Traitors!" the Tevéss guardsman finally shouted helplessly, his voice cracking. "Treachery!"

"*You* are the traitor, soldier," Anna shouted, her mind roaring. "We know your plan. Understand?"

The man stared at her. Clearly, he did not.

"We know!" Anna pointed at him, her finger aimed like a thunderbolt. "*We know!*"

The foal leapt from its perch and landed with a grunt in front of the guardsman. The man screamed. The foal looked at him for half a moment, cocking its head. Then it casually bit the man's head from his shoulders, tossed it out the birthing stall's door, and started in on its dinner, gnawing on the man's spurting neck, oblivious to the burning straw around it.

"And so die *all* who break their word!" Anna cried.

"Anna," Master Khondus said gently.

Anna blinked. A blood stain had appeared beneath Master Khondus's right armpit, but it wasn't large.

"The fire, Anna," he said. "I'll lock the outer stable door."

The foal looked up at her, as if awaiting a command.

"No." She shook her head at it and took a deep breath. "You did well."

The foal grunted and shoved its snout back into the bloody hole it had made at the top of the guardsman's corpse. It seemed to be eyeing d'Rent and Lord Layne hungrily, even as it feasted.

"Anna," Master Khondus repeated, "the fire." Then he hurried out of the birthing stall, pausing a moment to finish the Tevéss guardsman he'd downed outside the door with a boot stomp to the throat.

Anna blinked, and things came back into focus. In front of the door, everywhere on the far side of the stall, the straw was burning fiercely. Somehow, she hadn't really noticed it. Their enemies were dead and—despite the smoke and flames—Anna felt like she could breathe for the first time in three years.

10

STAYING LOW, ANNA ran and pulled several wool blankets from their shelf on the near wall, calmly laying the thick fabric over the fire. The smoke stung her eyes, but she was able to get the blaze under control. Master Khondus returned just as she'd finished tamping out the last of the flames.

The Master set the hammer down, saw that the fire was entirely out, then opened the shutter of the stable's small window to let in some air. A large crow sat on the window sill. The Master shooed it away, came back, and took a knee beside Anna. He glanced at the feasting foal then inspected Anna's face and arms and torso.

"You hurt? Looks like he split your lip. Your eyes?"

"The smoke, sir. It's fine." She looked at the bloodstain below his armpit. "You're injured."

"Don't mind that. Look at me."

She did.

Master Khondus took her chin, turned her face toward the window's light, and brushed a lock of dark hair from her eyes. He took a clean cloth from his pocket and cleaned her face.

"You all right?" he asked gruffly.

"Yes, sir."

"Good." He cleared his throat. "Now, attend. We've got less time than I thought."

From its place on the guardsman's chest, the foal burped, settled back on its haunches, and showed Anna its bloody fangs—its meal complete. Then it snorted, unfurled its wings, and leapt to its spot beside Nightlove where it turned three times in a circle and lay down, nose on its tail to watch her— or seemed to watch her, she had to keep reminding herself. Nightlove took a deep breath, closed her blue eyes, and licked the foal's face clean. The foal sighed, but its eyes stayed open. Even as Nightlove cleaned it, the foal tracked Anna, as if observing her every move.

Master Khondus raised an eyebrow. "Looks like we've got a war dragon on our hands."

11

"YOU MEAN HE'LL live?" Anna asked, all caution gone.

"How can he not?" Master Khondus scratched at his stubble. "Regardless, we'll attend to him later. Right now, we move."

Anna's heart soared and it took everything she had to keep a lunatic smile off her face. The foal grunted and cocked its head at her. Of course, Anna knew the foal's rider wouldn't be her. Couldn't be her. She was too young by two years.

But that didn't matter. The foal would have its chance.

"Let me bandage your side, sir." Anna grinned. "Can't win wars with open wounds."

Master Khondus's eyebrow arched at Anna's expression. "Very well. Hurry it up."

Anna stepped out of the birthing stall, knelt by the Tevéss guardsman that Master Khondus had killed outside the door, and removed the soldier's belt; it had not been damaged by the fire. She returned to the stall and tore one of the sleeves from her tunic to use as a pad for Master Khondus's injury.

"Master Borónd will have a healing cordial in the library," Anna said.

"No time," Master Khondus grunted. He turned and knelt in front of Anna. "Bind me."

Anna pulled Master Khondus's shirt up around his neck. D'Rent's bullet had plowed a furrow through the muscle just under his right armpit. There was some blood, but it didn't flow. Anna tended the wound with a clean cloth, using some warm water from one of the buckets they'd used for the birthing. As she did, she saw other scars on the Master's back. At least two other bullet wounds, three other punctures, and a raking gash that ran from shoulder to hip that only could have come from a dragon's claw.

"If Layne spoke true," Master Khondus said as Anna cleaned him, "then Lord Oskor, Irondusk, and House Fel make their way to our High Keep this moment. When they arrive, they'll make some announcement. Some 'new alliance.' A 'new treaty.' But what they really want is a bloodless coup. Maybe they'll leave Lady Abigail on the throne. Maybe they won't. Either way, Lord Oskor will settle for nothing less than complete control of our forces, our dragons, our High Keep, and—most importantly—our High Gate."

"A sneak attack." Anna nodded, pushing the cloth hard against the Master's wound.

"Yes." He winced. "When Lord Oskor arrives, he'll be supported by Lord Gideon. Between House Fel and House Tevéss, we'll be hard pressed. House Dradón may control Dávanor's best dragons, but against their combined forces we're badly outnumbered. Also, if Oskor and Gideon do indeed have the support of Dorómy Dallanar, if Fel has received two great cannon from Paráden, then any advantage we might take from our fortifications will be reduced. But did

Layne speak true?" He glanced at the lordling's burnt corpse.

"We'll find out soon enough," Anna said.

The injury was about as clean as she could get it. From its place beside its mother, the dragon foal grunted. Anna ripped her torn sleeve in half, folded the clean piece three times, and held it against the Master's wound. She looped the guardsman's belt over Master Khondus's shoulder, then tightened and latched the belt. The dressing wasn't the best she'd ever done, but it was clean, dry, and would serve.

"My thanks." Master Khondus nodded, stood, and tightened his queue in its leather strap.

He looked at her. "Regardless of how accurate Layne's information is, we must move against Lord Gideon and the forces of House Tevéss here in the High Keep now—before Lord Fel arrives."

"Yes, sir," Anna said.

Battle is coming.

The foal raised its head and hissed approvingly.

Master Khondus nodded. "And we must move before Lord Gideon or one of Lord Oskor's other spies can learn what's happened here." He cocked his head at the bodies and slaughter. "We're lucky. If it was later in the day, this would already be discovered. You'll hide everything, Anna. Keep the weapons separate. Feed Nightlove and the foal. Then slip over to the upper barracks. When you arrive, go to Sara Terreden—you know her, of course."

"Yes. Captain Terreden just took command of the White Demons."

Master nodded. "Tell Terreden what's happened here. Then tell her to pass word to our riders. They must ready themselves for battle. On my signal, and on my signal only, Terreden is to release Voidbane. Then she must seize and imprison every House Tevéss rider lodged in the upper barracks. She must do it quietly, and she must do it with as little violence as possible. Lord Gideon is a traitor, but our men will still have friends among House Tevéss. Perhaps some Tevéss riders will remember their oaths and be swayed to our cause, but this will never happen if there's needless killing. The Tevéss dragons also will need to be separated and cloistered, until we can be certain of their riders' loyalty, or lack thereof. I'll sound the summoning gong in the eastern tower when I'm in position with Captain Fyr and her guardsmen to move against Lord Gideon. The moment the gong sounds, Terreden must execute her orders."

"I understand." Anna nodded.

He looked at her closely. "Now, attend. If something happens to me before I can meet up with them, you must relate the following to Master Zar, Captain Fyr, and Captain Terreden—once the High Keep is secure, they must discern Lord Oskor's flight path, and they must launch our three best squads at Oskor's convoy: Captain Terreden's Demons, Captain Faden's Silver Swords, Captain Arrowtide's Jade Hammers. Voidbane should accompany them as heavy support. Whatever happens, Terreden and her team *must* launch tonight, at sundown, in absolute secrecy. We don't know in what strength Fel House comes, or how much support Dorómy has sent Lord Oskor. But we do know *that* he comes and when he will arrive. We have the advantage of surprise. Fel has the advantage of numbers. If we want to prevail, then we must ask the Great Sisters for luck, we must strike, and we must strike *first*. If we can kill Lord Gideon in the High Keep today, if we can kill Lord Oskor before he arrives, then we stand a good chance. Lord Oskor's sons are ambitious. If we kill him, they'll turn on each other without doubt. And when that happens, we'll have time to gather our own allies and to beg aid from Bellános on Kon. The High King will understand our need and the importance of our fight. And he'll keep his word. If we give him time, the King will send aid."

"Fel and Tevéss must've been planning this since Lord David was killed," Anna said.

Master nodded. "House Dradón must seem easy prey. Today, they'll learn that they're mistaken."

The dragon foal growled. Its white tail thrashed in the straw.

"Now," Master Khondus said formally, "repeat my message and my orders, dragon squire."

Anna nodded. "On your signal, Captain Terreden is to release Voidbane. With minimum violence, she is to imprison the House Tevéss riders and their dragons. We'll discover Lord Oskor's path and launch against him and his entourage in secret, tonight, under the cover of darkness. Voidbane as support. We'll kill Lord Oskor and send word to High King Bellános on Kon."

"Good," the Master said. "When you tell Terreden what's happened and what she must do, give her this."

Master Khondus drew a short dagger of high silver from his sleeve and handed it to Anna. The blade had been concealed in the Master's tunic, strapped flat to his inner forearm. Anna took the dagger carefully while Khondus unfastened its sheath from his arm.

The Master nodded. "Terreden's grandfather gave me this blade when I turned sixteen, after I'd completed my rites of passage. Before that, it was passed to him by his father and through the Terreden line for some thirty generations. It's served the Kingdom on many worlds. The Khondus and Terreden clans are minor houses, to be sure, but they've always been allies. When you find Sara, give her the dagger, tell her what has happened here, and repeat the plan *exactly* as I've given it to you. You understand your orders?"

"Yes, sir." Anna nodded. She glanced at Nightlove and the dragon foal. The newborn had rolled onto its back, tongue lolling between its gleaming fangs. It was still watching Anna—or seemed to watch her—upside down, eyes wide, listening to every word. She couldn't help but smile.

Master Khondus noticed Anna's gaze and nodded. "Feed them quickly. Carry out your orders. You'll name him when all this is over."

Her smile vanished.

". . . I will name him, sir? *I* will—?"

"He's your dragon," Master Khondus said simply. "I'd have to be blind myself not to see that. Stop gawking. There's work to do."

Anna stood at attention, her heart racing.

"Yes, sir! Master Khondus, sir!"

Her dragon?

She'd trained her whole life to hear those words.

The foal scrambled to its feet, sniffing at the air, tail lifting from the straw, neck craning, its white eyes wide.

Master Khondus crossed his chest with his fist and looked Anna in the eye. "Truth and honor, Anna Dyer."

Her dragon.

Anna placed her fist on her chest. Blood thumped in her ears.

"Truth and honor, Master Khondus."

Master Khondus untied his leather apron, dropped it to the straw, and handed Anna the sheath for his dagger. Then he took up his hammer, scooped d'Rent's revolver from the burnt straw, and strode from the stall like a warrior of old.

12

THE DRAGON FOAL was blind.

But it could still see.

It saw very well, in fact.

It saw through the girl's eyes.

Now, since the dragon foal had never known anything else, this situation seemed quite natural.

Whatever the girl saw, the foal saw, too.

Made perfect sense.

Perfect sense to the foal, at least.

The foal also *knew* things that the girl knew. This knowledge gave the foal a kind of awareness—a kind of understanding—that was almost unprecedented for its kind.

But, again, since the foal had never known anything different, this arrangement did not seem strange.

For example, the foal knew that the big, white dragon snoring there in the straw was its mother. The foal also knew that it had just been born. That it had been late in coming. That its fangs, its claws, and its breath were much stronger than they should have been for a dragon its age. It knew that its neck and body and wings were white and powerful.

It knew that it had beautiful, silvery-white eyes.

The girl knew these things, so the foal knew them, too.

The foal also knew other things, things it had seen inside the girl's memory.

For instance, the foal knew that the girl's father had been killed in battle three years ago. The girl had seen it, she rarely spoke of it, but it had changed her. It had hardened her heart and created a dark shadow of rage in her head. The foal knew the girl's mother and little sisters had moved away from the High Keep soon after and that the girl had not gone with them. The foal knew the girl's mother's name was Jessica, her sisters' names were Penelope and Wendi.

The foal knew other people, too. Master Khondus, a tall, broad old man with arms like iron. Master Zar, a squat dwarf of Anor, his eyes the color of purple twilight. Master Borónd, a scholar who wore fine, gold-rimmed reading spectacles. The girl respected Master Khondus more than anyone alive. The girl honored Master Zar's knowledge of arms and warcraft above all others. And the girl believed Master Borónd was the most learned man she had ever known.

The foal did not know many other faces. It knew that this

meant the girl did not have many other friends. This did not bother the girl. Since her father's death, not much did. The foal knew this, as well.

The foal knew the girl's name, too.

Anna.

And the foal knew Anna's dreams.

Soaring flights over clouds and cliffs, screaming chases over mountain and sea, heroic duels under the sun and moon . . . epic victories, all!

These dreams and more—the foal knew them.

It *saw* them.

Most importantly, the foal knew that Anna's dreams were coming true.

Battle is coming.

And, just like Anna, the foal reveled in the knowledge.

The foal wanted to serve, to fly, and to fight.

It *needed* to do these things.

And because of the magic that bound its mind to Anna's, it knew how.

The foal did not think it strange to understand these things or to see itself in this way. As far as it knew, all dragons saw the past, the present, the future, the water, the land, the sky, themselves, and everything else through their riders' eyes.

And there was no doubt in the foal's mind that that was *exactly* what Anna was: its rider.

So when Anna jogged out of the stall, taking her vision and thoughts and memories and dreams along with her, the little blind dragon did the only thing that it could do.

It followed.

13

"You MIGHT BE ready for a fight," Anna grunted as she dragged Lord Layne's charred body through the straw to the far side of the stall. "But you'll still need to wait here. We're at war. Gotta get you some gear and get you trained up first."

The foal cocked its head and then flashed Anna its fangs. They were sharp and mean.

"Beautiful." She pushed a lock of dark hair behind her ear and hitched up her apron. "You'll use 'em soon enough."

Moving as quickly as she could, Anna pulled d'Rent and the other guardsmen over to where she'd stashed Lord Layne. She was strong from her years of stable work, so the bodies were heavy but not impossible for her to move.

Nightlove had fallen asleep; she snored loudly. Anna had thought that the foal would sleep, too; it had looked a little sleepy after its meal. But when she started dragging bodies around, the foal perked up and became even more interested, watching her from its mother's side.

Or at least it *appeared* to watch her, Anna had to keep reminding herself. The blind dragon seemed fascinated by her movement, tracking her with its snout, tasting the air with its broad tongue, grunting and cooing, its silvery-white eyes wide.

"Smart one, aren't you?" Anna grunted as she worked. "Gotta find a name for you. Won't be official, 'course. Not until the High Lady says. Dragons' proper names are given by a Keep's High Lord. Or High Lady. A big deal. Big ceremony. I'll be there. Master Khondus, Master Zar, Master Borónd. All the riders and squires. Everyone. But we've gotta have something for you now, don't we?"

Anna covered the bodies with straw and wrapped their swords, daggers, and the rest of their gear in a fire blanket. She was about to hide that bundle under the straw, too, but then she reconsidered, re-opened the blanket, and took a

Tevéss dagger from the pile. The foal cooed.

Anna went to a shelf on the side wall and fetched a large glass beaker filled with the dragons' elixir. She held the beaker up to the window to be sure of its color and consistency. It was thick and viscous, a syrup made of liquid silver.

"Great stuff." She nodded. The great Queen Katherine had invented it millennia past. It would keep a dragon strong, help keep the bugs off him, make his wings soft, his scales hard, and help his flight bladders. It was also good for his gut. The foal licked its chops.

Anna poured ten measures of the elixir into a tin feeding tube and brought it to Nightlove. The big dragon didn't open her eyes as Anna slid the tube's point between her teeth. Then Anna gave one measure to the foal; it smacked its lips at the taste. Anna cleaned and stored the tube, opened a half-door in the far wall, and dragged a fat, bleating merino back into the stable. She clipped the merino's halter to an iron ring on the wall.

"Dinner's on," she said.

Neither Nightlove nor the foal seemed interested. Nightlove snored away. The foal gave the merino a passing glance, grunted, and turned its huge eyes to the buried pile of bodies, instead.

"No," Anna said firmly.

The foal went still.

"If you eat those, you'll make a mess. Someone'll see. We don't have time to clean up again. Look at this yummy thing." She patted the merino on its wooly side. "Look at all this good stuff."

The foal lifted its snout and turned away.

"Suit yourself," Anna said. "You'll be hungry soon enough. Gotta go."

The foal jerked its head up and hissed. To Anna's ears, it sounded more like distress than anger. It reared up on its haunches, eyes wide, almost as if it was worried. It hissed again, like a question, then mewled loudly.

Anna shook her head. If she was going to complete her mission and keep the foal safe—and quiet—in the stall, she was going to have to calm it down. She walked over to it. The foal promptly flopped back into the straw, rolled onto its back, and spread its wings, gazing up at her. Anna warmed her hands with her breath, knelt, and rubbed the foal's stomach and chest. Its white scales were smooth and warm to the touch, its muscles soft under supple dragon skin. As Anna massaged it, the foal's scales grew warmer. It cooed gently, its eyes slowly closing. Nightlove's snore got even louder.

"There we are," Anna said softly, after a few more moments of massage. "That's a good boy."

The foal's eyes cracked open, but just barely.

"You were brave, no doubt," Anna said soothingly. "You saved us. But you've gotta learn to reduce your aspect, make yourself a smaller mark. You need training." She let her voice go even softer, a gentle murmur. "Spread wings can be intimidating, but they make a nice target for trained soldiers. You might've scared those guardsmen a bit, but d'Rent didn't care. What would you have done if he'd hit a joint, or a tendon, or a flight bladder? Or your head?"

Anna placed her hand on the foal's jaw. It turned slowly into her touch, its huge eyes shut. Its white scales were smooth and very warm.

"You gotta learn," she said softly, lulling him to sleep. He breathed deeply. "In combat, a tight, furled shape is ideal. Small is stealth, and stealth is strong. So says Master Zar.

That's a good boy."

As it nestled further down in the straw, she looked at its right wing. D'Rent's bullet had passed clean through the leathery membrane, three fingers away from the foal's body. No blood, no real damage. The rest of the wing looked perfect.

"A very good boy."

The foal snored contentedly.

"And because you're such a good boy," she whispered, "I've got a name for you. Your name is Moondagger."

Big mistake.

The foal's eyes snapped open. It rolled over, reared up on its haunches, and spread its wings, showing her its fangs. They seemed bigger than ever.

"Oh boy," she muttered. "You like that, eh?"

Moondagger growled and did a funny little hop.

"Moondagger it is, then. My father commanded the Sun Daggers and Nightlove's your mother—makes sense, eh? Now, I've gotta go."

Moondagger hissed.

"Easy, there. Easy."

But it was too late. Moondagger was completely alert, cocking his head this way and that as if waiting for his own orders, as if sleep was the last thing on his mind. If he had a name, then he must have a mission, right?

Anna nodded. "I'll be back. You've got an important task, too, Dagger. You'll watch over Nightlove. If enemies come, you'll protect her. That's an important job. She's the best we have. Probably the best on Dávanor. That means the best in the Kingdom. You'll stay here and protect her."

Moondagger snarled, but he almost seemed convinced.

At least he settled back in the straw.

Anna took the high silver dagger that Master Khondus had given her, slipped it snugly behind her back in its sheath, and pulled her tunic over it. Then she strapped the knife she'd taken from the bundle of enemy gear against her left forearm, under her one remaining baggy tunic sleeve, just where she'd seen Master Khondus wear his own blade. She practiced drawing it several times until the knife sprang quickly to hand.

Moondagger was very interested in all this, especially the weapons. Most of Anna's formal combat training had dealt with gear used from dragon back: crossbows, bolas, carbines, net guns, lances, and the like. But Master Khondus had always made sure that his dragon squires had instruction in hand fighting too. And Mother and Father had worked with her and her sisters in basic sword- and knife-play since all of them had been old enough to hold a blade.

Of course, Anna knew that she was no match for trained soldiers. But she also had the advantage of appreciating that fact. She understood her own limits. She also understood the value of speed, stealth, and surprise. She was small. She was unthreatening. She was a mere dragon squire, nothing more than a skinny girl from a well-born family of soldiers, a girl not even past her final rites of passage. Nothing to be afraid of.

"Nothing at all," she murmured and touched the blade under her sleeve.

Moondagger stared at her, his eyes wide, as if reading her mind.

"Stay here," she said. "I'll be back soon."

Moondagger grunted.

She'd reduce her own aspect.

She'd complete her mission.

And they'd never see her coming.

14

ANNA SHUT THE stall door and set out at a jog, down the stable's central hallway, past the utility closet, up the stone staircase at the hallway's end, and out the stable's main door. From there, she followed the series of short bridges that connected the lower stables to the Dragon Steps, and from there, she took the Steps to the bottom sections of the Drádonhold's fortifications.

The Drádonhold had been built on a tall peak at the foot of the Ahkaggor Mountains, its pinnacle rising jagged and sheer from the green forests below. From a distance, on dragon back, the High Keep and its surrounding town seemed to cling to the mountain top like encrusted, silver-grey jewels, slate rooftops sparkling in the sun, the Dragon Steps winding up the mountainside like a white ribbon.

The Dragon Steps were the only way to reach the mountaintop fortress from the ground. They also provided the primary road for all traffic around the Drádonhold proper. They were a broad, rock-cut set of stairs about twenty paces wide, paved with white marble, fronted by a waist-high parapet. From the forest floor, the Steps switch-backed up the mountainside, across and through the mountain's craggy face—sometimes arched into the sky, sometimes colonnaded within the cliff side—before finally tunneling into the rock itself and opening onto the broad, fortified terrace that lay before the Keep's main gate. From there, you could either enter the main gate proper, which led to the Drádonhold's High Square and the High Gate protected there, or you could continue around the mountain to the east.

The High Keep itself had been built during the Founding, of course, after the Great Sister Aaryn had shaped Dávanor's first High Gate on the broad, natural plateau that would later become the foundation of the Keep's High Square. The usual defensive architecture had followed, carved or built up around the High Gate in the centuries between the Founding and the Plague Years. Millennia later, mostly during the Restoration, various noble clans had built mansions, stores, porticoes, squares, workshops, and homes in and around the High Keep, terracing and tunneling into the sheer cliffs, bridging chasms and clefts, spreading down and out around the fortress proper.

The lower stables, birthing stalls, and flight ramps where Anna worked were all part of a service complex cantilevered from the mountainside on the western side of the peak. Anna's destination—the dragon riders' upper barracks and stables where Sara Terreden and her men were quartered—was on the mountain's far eastern face, high on the other side of the Drádonhold itself. It would take her about a half a bell's time to get there.

It was still early, so there was little traffic on the Dragon Steps to slow her down, just a handful of lamplighters, bakers-boys, rubbish cart drivers, along with a few shepherds herding their flocks. The sky was the pale pink of pre-dawn, a few shreds of orange cloud smeared across the western horizon. A good number of messenger dragons—of all colors and no larger than geese—glided on the morning breezes above the Keep's highest towers, bringing the early missives to the citadel's offices and secretaries. On a distant battlement, a large crow watched Anna's ascent with beady eyes. A squad of guardsmen wearing House Dradón's blue and white livery marched past her, mail jingling as they tramped down the Steps to relieve the night watch at the mountain's base.

When Anna turned the Step's next switchback, a tall guardswoman wearing the blue and white of House Dradón stopped her with a whistle. The guard was leaning against the Steps' parapet, her steel-tipped spear aimed at the sky.

"Got a friend there, squire." She tapped her spear butt against the Steps' flagstones, lifting her chin and looking over Anna's shoulder.

Anna turned.

Moondagger hung there upside down from a stone balcony like a giant, white bat. The dragon foal craned his neck, looking at Anna with his huge eyes. His broad tongue tasted the air for a moment. Then he showed Anna his fangs. A shred of maroon cloth hung from the corner of his mouth, caught on one of his molars.

Anna tried to make her voice firm. "Gave you an order, Dagger."

Dagger cocked his head.

Anna stepped up, pulled the shred of Tevéss uniform from between Dagger's teeth, and put it in her pocket.

Moondagger gazed at her calmly. And he didn't budge. And it was impossible to be mad at him.

"I suppose when you're hungry, you're hungry." She stroked Dagger's face. He grunted, then gave her a gentle head-butt.

"What's wrong with his eyes?" the guardswoman asked.

"He's blind," Anna said, not looking away from her dragon.

"Doesn't act like it."

Anna nodded. "Doesn't take commands well either."

Moondagger sniffed at the morning breeze and licked his fangs.

A bearded shepherd leading a flock of sheared merinos came down the Steps, around the switchback. When he saw Moondagger, the shepherd stopped short, halted his flock, and frowned. He ticked his crook against the parapet to get the guardswoman's attention. She turned and raised an eyebrow.

"These here sheep hafta go down to the lower stables," the shepherd grunted. He spit over the parapet and nodded at Anna. "They ain't for eatin'. Just been sheared and counted proper, but they ain't for eatin', hear me? And war dragons ain't allowed to run wild, no rider on, flyin' only the Sisters know where, eatin' whatever they please. It tries to eat one of these," the shepherd cocked his head at his flock, "it'll come from her purse, count on it, sure."

"Leave the dragon to me, sir," Anna said.

But the shepherd was right, of course.

Moondagger would continue to attract attention as the High Keep woke. That's why she'd wanted him to stay with Nightlove in the first place. A blind dragon foal following a squire through the Drádonhold was hardly an ideal way to avoid notice. (And that shred of bloody Tevéss uniform dangling from his mouth hadn't helped, either.) But there was no time to wrangle Dagger back down to the stables— even if she could.

"Come on, you." Anna glanced at Dagger. She nodded her thanks to the guardswoman, gave the shepherd a cool look, and continued up the Dragon Steps.

Moondagger grunted, dropped from his perch, and swooped past Anna, landing on the stone parapet near the flock. There, he growled with feigned menace at the shepherd, nearly falling off the parapet when his right wing bumped against a stone planter, claws scrabbling on stone. The merinos bleated, jumbling away as a single wooly mass, huddling together near the far side of the Steps.

"No eat! No eat!" the shepherd shouted and jumped in front of Moondagger, waving his crook in the foal's face. Dagger recoiled with a hiss. The guardswoman stepped up and put her hand on the shepherd's shoulder.

"The squire has everything in hand, sir. Let's move you and your sheep along," she said.

The shepherd grimaced, muttering under his breath. "War beasts runnin' loose, eatin' honest servants' goods, whole cursed place fallin' to pieces." But he gave a wry grin and a whistle, turning his merinos onto the switchback from whence Anna had just come.

The guard turned to Anna. "Better get him into harness, squire. Trouble for everyone."

Anna nodded. "My thanks."

Moondagger fell backwards off the parapet, coiled in midair like a falling snake, and opened his wings with a snap. He swooped back up, landed on the parapet beside Anna, and showed her his fangs. Anna shook her head and tried to frown at him. But she failed miserably.

15

MOONDAGGER SAW ANNA cross a paved terrace and approach a large building. The sun was just up and the early sky was red, bathing the mountains with flushed morning light.

It was three years ago.

Anna was eleven years old.

But, from Moondagger's perspective, those three years past meant nothing.

For Moondagger, three years ago was *now*.

Anna opened the building's front door and walked toward a blood-stained cot. An armored man lay there. Beneath him shone a pool of dark blood.

The man on the cot was dead.

The man was Anna's father.

Armored soldiers and dragon riders gathered around the cot. Mother was there, too, standing at Father's head. Her face and armor were streaked with ash and blood. Her eyes shone with sorrow.

When Anna approached, the soldiers went silent and opened a path. Mother did not look up. Anna kept her chin high, her eyes straight ahead. Her step was slow. But she did not tremble. She did not falter. She did not cry.

She stood at the cot and looked down at her father.

Moondagger felt something open in his own heart, a deepening ache, as if a pain there was being slowly born.

He wanted to turn away, to stop the hurt.

But he could not.

Anna was strong. So he must be strong. Anna was brave. So he must be brave. Anna could see. So he must see.

Please. For a moment, let me see him.

Anna put her small hand on Father's breastplate. The steel was cold. Mother put her armored hand on top of hers.

And then there was the hole.

It was larger than Anna's fist, punched jagged into the left side of Father's chest.

A black opening.

Emptiness.

A hole that should not be.

If I reached down into it, Anna thought, *I would reach into nothing, and its steel teeth would close on my shoulder and bite . . . .*

Anna had been riding behind Father as one of Voidbane's signal hands. (And she hadn't been there because she was

Erik Dyer's daughter. She'd been there because she knew the codes and flag combinations better than any squire in the High Keep.) She and Tayne Tallerdun, Father's other signal hand, had spotted Lord Oskor and the dread Irondusk descending from above, a roaring nightmare of fang and fire. She had flashed her signals, fired her carbine, and shouted her warnings. Voidbane had reacted perfectly, banking hard, rolling, allowing Irondusk to pass beneath them with a roar and gust of thunder, his war lust shaking the air. Upside down, Anna had gotten a good shot off at the monster. But for Father, it had been too late. A little gold dragon, green House Fel war banner on its chest, had seen its chance and had dived through the defensive formation of House Dradón middle weights. Its rider had carried a simple battle lance, nothing more. And as Anna reloaded her carbine, working the mechanism as fast as she could in her small hands, she had seen the impact that had taken Father's life. It had been over before she had known what had happened. Done before it had started. Not like the poems and songs—where things made sense. Voidbane's roar had shaken the heavens.

Now, on the cot, father's armor was caked with gore

and ash. His face was pale. A cork of black blood clotted his right nostril. His left eye was open, but only its white showed. A single tear pooled in its corner.

It *was* Father.

But it did not look like him.

Anna understood then what it meant when people said that the body was just a "shell." Father's passion, wit, his easy laugh, his black rage when angered, his sense of honor, duty, and loyalty—all gone.

This thing before her? This body?

It was an empty husk.

A soldier never betrays his word. A soldier never forgets his promises.

The eyes of the riders and warriors pushed against her, the pressure of their gazes bearing down like real weight.

She wanted a moment alone. Just one moment.

Pay them no mind.

Father turned his dead face toward her.

His eyes opened. Gentle and clear and real.

Death is not defeat.

Father's mouth did not move, but Moondagger heard his words all the same.

The ache in his heart blossomed.

You have my pride and love 'til Kingdom's end, Anna. My pride and love, forever.

16

THE MOMENT ANNA stepped onto the upper barracks' terrace, she knew something was wrong.

The barracks was a fine, two-storied building made of well-cut stone. Its tall windows looked out over the terrace toward the red morning sky—but the windows' shutters were closed. Seven dragon riders, all wearing the dark maroon livery of House Tevéss, sat and stood around the barracks' front steps. They smoked their pipes and sipped their morning tea, laughing casually as if sharing some private joke, their pipe smoke barely stirred by the morning breeze.

But they were obviously blocking the barracks' front door.

Two of the seven riders wore standard scout harness-es, light leather armor over maroon House Tevéss livery. But the other five wore full battle gear. The armor's trad-itional design was modeled on the ancient panoplies of the Plague Years: the distinct, V-shaped breastplates protruding two palms away from the center of the riders' chests, their beveled surfaces designed to deflect wind, bullets, and flame. All wore short swords at their belts and several wore steel revolvers slung beneath their shoulders. Their leader was a tall, grey-haired captain who wore a thick maroon riding scarf, goggles pulled down at his throat. He leaned nonchalantly against the barracks' wall, an ancient revolver of high silver belted low on his hip. Rings of black iron adorned his earlobes. A sheathed greatsword leaned against the wall beside him. As Anna stepped onto the terrace, the captain chuckled, spat, and tapped his pipe against his hand, brushing his palms together as if he hadn't a care in the world.

Why are they here?

Moondagger landed on the parapet behind her and immediately hissed at the riders, his white tail whipping against the stone, his scales pinkish in the morning light.

The riders' laughter stopped short.

Anna shot Moondagger a hard glance.

Stealth, she thought.

Moondagger's tail went still.

"What is this?" the grey-haired captain asked, frowning.

Like the rest of the Tevéss riders, he wore sharp sideburns styled to points near the corners of his mouth. His western accent was thick. The riders looked from Moondagger to Anna, their eyes narrow.

"Forgive me, my lords." Anna bowed respectfully. "I come with an urgent message for Captain Terreden——."

"What is this animal doing out of harness, girl?" the captain cut her off. He lifted a whistle of black iron from the chain on his neck and blew it. It made no sound, but Dagger's eyes widened and he cocked his head with attention. All the riders wore whistles of similar shape.

Anna looked to the morning sky. Nothing. At least, not yet.

The rider next to the captain said to the short one beside him, "Mark its eyes. The thing is blind as a slug."

"And see the color." The short one pointed. "Must be one of Nightlove's spawn. Old girl needs some proper seed, eh?"

"Voidbane must be sick indeed if the best he can do is this sightless worm," another chimed in.

The short rider leered at Anna. His nose was strange, one of his nostrils much larger than the other, like a pig's. "Cannot fight if you cannot see, eh, sweetie?" He winked at her.

"Should not surprise," a rider said. "They will take whatever comes here, flawed or no. Look at this squire. Missing half her tunic, for the Sister's sake. Where is your sleeve, girl?"

Several of the riders grinned. The captain did not. The pig-nosed rider who'd winked at her was appraising her now, looking her over from head to foot. Anna's face flushed, but she kept her chin high and her eyes on the captain. She hadn't thought about her tunic sleeve. The one she'd used to pad Master Khondus's wound. How ridiculous she must look. She hoped they didn't notice the dagger bulge beneath her good sleeve—or the bullet hole in Dagger's wing.

"You know," the pig-nosed rider mused, "what Nightlove really needs is a proper mounting." He made a rude thrusting gesture with his hips and looked at Anna pointedly. His weird nostrils flared, and he pursed his lips.

"Mounting?" another rider sniffed. "Wait 'til Irondusk gets on her. Now *that* will be a breeding. Poor girl will never recover."

"Next foal will come out with four eyes."

"And they will *all* work!" Pig-nose snorted.

The riders guffawed, slapping their knees and pounding

each other on the back. The captain's frown deepened.

Moondagger hissed, his tail lashing the parapet. The breeze picked up a touch. For her part, Anna looked at each rider carefully, marking their faces in turn. She wasn't mad. She was calculating.

Laugh all you want, she thought.

She'd prove Dagger's worth soon enough. And to these very men.

From the east, riding the breeze, a bronze war dragon of medium weight, about twenty paces long, arced gracefully over the barracks' roof. Its scales shone like polished brass and its rigging was deep maroon, the color of House Tevéss. A maroon war banner was clipped to the underside of its chest, the three black swords of House Tevéss crossed at its center.

Anna frowned.

A banner like that would normally only be worn in combat. To any rider on Dávanor, the banner meant one thing and one thing only: war. A cold suspicion rose in her mind, but she quelled it.

The bronze dragon swung over the terrace, made a wide

turn, and landed smoothly with a muscly grunt and gust of wind beside the Tevéss riders. Its scales glimmered. Its large eyes were a luminous, pale green. Its saddle and harnesses were well-oiled and meticulously maintained. It cocked its head at the Tevéss captain, giving Anna and Moondagger no more than a passing glance.

The captain stepped to his dragon and patted him on the side.

"I asked you a question, girl," the captain said. "What is this animal doing out of harness?"

The bronze turned and stared at them. Its green eyes were cool and intelligent. Dagger returned its gaze fearlessly, a low growl forming in his throat—even though the bronze was clearly trained for combat and almost ten times his size.

"Forgive me, sir." Anna bowed. "Lord Layne commanded this foal be prepared as a target test for Lord Oskor and his Lordship's new cannon from Paráden——."

"A target for the new cannon?" The captain looked at her sharply.

Fool's error! Anna's face went hot, but she kept her eyes on the captain. Obviously, House Dradón wasn't supposed to know of the arrival of the Pretender King's guns. But how big a mistake had she made? The other riders seemed not to have noticed her slip. Quite the opposite.

"*Target practice?*" one of the riders choked, nearly spitting out his tea.

"Oh, that is rich!" another added.

"Blind worm used as a decoy!" Pig-nose laughed, his nostrils flaring. "Only here! Only *here!*"

The riders brayed. The bronze dragon sniffed, stretched its wings wide, and settled back on its haunches, green eyes flickering. Somewhere, a crow cawed.

The captain's frown deepened. "Khondus agree to this 'test,' girl?"

Anna nodded. "Master Khondus is a loyal servant of House Dradón. As am I."

"I am surprised." The captain looked at her closely.

One of the riders snickered and whispered just loud enough for Anna to hear, "Oh, how the mighty have fallen."

Someone snorted.

"Shut your holes," the captain snapped. He looked at Moondagger. "Where is Lord Layne now?" he asked.

"When I last saw him, sir, he and Captain d' Rent were in

the lower stables. I believe it was their plan to return to the High Keep."

The captain frowned. For a moment, he seemed even more suspicious. Then he shook his head and smiled at her falsely. "So be it. Give your message to me, girl. Then get you and your beast gone. I will deliver it to Terreden."

"Forgive me, sir. I was asked to give word to Captain Terreden directly. A personal matter, sir."

"And what personal matter is that, exactly?"

Moondagger growled. It was a deep, mature sound.

The Tevéss riders started at the noise, their smiles gone, hands going instinctively to their guns. The captain's bronze rose off his haunches. Dagger's eyes were mean moon-slits.

"Easy," Anna said calmly, so that they could see she had things well in hand.

Our time will come.

Dagger settled a bit, but Anna could feel his energy vibrating the air like a high, silent note.

"Calm yourselves," the captain snapped. He patted his dragon low on the neck and whispered something in its ear. Then he glanced at Moondagger, turned back to Anna, and smiled. "Give me your message, girl. I will take it to Captain Terreden. Sara and I are old friends. On my honor, you and she shall have my discretion."

"Forgive me, sir. I cannot disobey my orders. A private matter from her sister—."

"Her sister?" a rider laughed. "You been chasing the Dradón ladies again, Hendo? Need to keep your nasty mitts off the High House's womenfolk."

"For the moment, at least." The pig-nosed rider, Hendo, grinned. He stared at Anna, his nostrils flexing.

"I was unaware Terreden had a sister, girl," the captain said.

"Yes, sir." Anna nodded. "Three sisters, sir. Captain Terreden is a friend of my family. For this reason, I was sent, sir."

"What is your name, girl?" the captain asked.

"Anna Dyer."

Dead silence.

The riders stared at her. All of them. Even the war dragon looked at her for a long moment, something new in its green eyes. The riders looked from her to their captain, who seemed a little taken aback himself. Had she made another mistake? She'd have to get better at this. Moondagger glared at them, his eyes glowing with contempt. He turned his gaze to the pig-nosed Hendo and licked his fangs wickedly.

"Who is your Father, squire?" the captain asked.

Anna's face went warm.

"Erik Dyer," she said, raising her chin.

The captain nodded soberly, as if his suspicions were confirmed. The riders glanced at each other, then back at Anna.

"I knew him well," the captain said. "He commanded the Sun Daggers under the late Lord David. Your mother, she led the White Demons before Terreden."

It was not a question, but Anna answered anyway. "Yes, sir."

The captain nodded. "Your people are fine soldiers, squire. A clan of the highest honor. House Dradón's best riders, by far."

"Thank you, sir," Anna said. "And might I ask your name, sir?"

"I am Stephen Corónd, Captain and Dragon Master of House Tevéss." He spoke as if his name should mean something to Anna. It didn't.

"My honor, sir." Anna said, with a formal bow. "Your name is well-known to my family."

Captain Corónd cleared his throat. "You cannot deliver your message today, dragon squire. Terreden has taken eight of her squads along with eight of ours southwest this morning for maneuvers. They ride for the Hengén Cleft and will meet Lord Oskor as he arrives. They'll be gone at least a week— perhaps more. Your message will have to wait."

Anna nodded calmly.

But her mind raced.

Hengén Cleft. One week. It was critical intelligence, to be sure. Lord Layne had said three days. A week meant they had more time. But even so, if Terreden was gone, then who would deal with these enemy riders and their dragons? Who would release Voidbane? How would Master Khondus's plan move forward? How could they secure the Drádonhold without their dragons? And *why* was the captain telling her this? Could this intelligence be trusted? Or was the captain feeding her bad information because of her slip-up regarding the Pretender King's cannon? Most importantly, if House Dradón's dragons were already gone, then how would they be able to attack Lord Oskor's column before it arrived?

Anna glanced again at the riders' war gear, their guns, their blades, and their armor. A squad of armed riders. A trained war dragon bannered for battle. Blocking the barracks' door.

That cold suspicion that had been lurking in Anna's mind began to crawl up out of the dark. And there was no putting it back.

Moondagger hissed softly.

She *must* see inside the barracks.

"Perhaps, sir." Anna cleared her throat. "I could leave a note on her bunk? For when she returns? That might be——."

Captain Coród shook his head, still smiling. "Not a good way to communicate a private message, eh, squire? I think it best for you to wait on her return. I am sure the riders of House Dradón would not disturb your missive, but I cannot say the same for these brigands." He smiled broadly with false warmth, cocking his head at his men.

They didn't smile. Hendo stared at her nastily.

"Of course, sir." Anna nodded. "Forgive my intrusion, sir. May I be dismissed?"

"No, you may not."

Moondagger growled.

It took all Anna's willpower not to bolt for the stairs.

Captain Coród straightened formally. "Allow me to pass on my respects to your family. Your mother, she still serves here in the High Keep?"

There seemed to be more to his question than simple curiosity.

"No, sir," Anna answered. "She has resigned her post and returned with my sisters to the farm."

"I see." He nodded. "Please give her my best wishes. And the same to your sisters, of course."

"Yes, sir."

"Dismissed." He nodded.

Then, almost like it was an afterthought, he smiled with what he must have thought looked like sincerity. "And do not forget to get that animal into harness, squire."

"Yes, sir!" Anna crossed her chest with her fist, returning a fake smile of her own.

Moondagger gave the riders and the captain's war dragon a final growl, then dropped from the parapet.

Anna turned and walked across the terrace, down the steps from which she'd come. As she left, she could feel their eyes on her.

The captain said something that she couldn't hear.

Someone replied.

But it wasn't a joke.

All the laughing was over.

17

MOONDAGGER SAW HIMSELF ripping the men and their dragons to pieces. He saw lines of blood spraying bright patterns across stone and steel. He saw the men shriek, holding their hands in front of their faces, their silly weapons useless, their open mouths little caves into which he poured silver-white fire, searing their guts, scorching their flesh, cooking them whole in their funny metal suits. He saw the bronze dragon scream as he sank his fangs into its throat.

A wild delight filled Moondagger's heart.

It was a new sensation.

A violent, righteous bliss.

And it felt *wonderful*.

More than wonderful.

It was as if Moondagger had found his purpose.

To fight and war with Anna in the sky.

And as the burning men jerked and danced their crazy dance, as their dragons sang their howling death songs, Dagger's heart was filled with a savage, ecstatic joy—the kind of joy that touches those who have finally found their reason to live.

He would only have to do one thing.

Our time will come.

He would have to wait.

18

ANNA WALKED DOWN the steps, away from the terrace.

The moment she was out of the enemies' sight, she ran, leapt down the last stairs, and—instead of continuing down toward the Dragon Steps, the way she'd come up—took a hard left, crossing a short bridge, sprinting down the narrow alley that dead-ended at the service door of the upper barracks' kitchen. She tried the handle. Locked. She looked into the small window at the door's center.

Nothing. Empty and dark.

Half a bell's time before the start of breakfast and the place should've been clattering with cooks and servants and apprentices busy preparing the morning meal. But there was nothing; not even a scullery boy to be seen.

Moondagger swooped into the alley, angling sideways to fit, wing tips brushing the narrow walls. He landed at Anna's side, a bit awkwardly on account of the confined space, and nudged up against her. Anna smoothed the dragon's head absently. His scales were warm under her hand.

Master Khondus thought that *they* had the advantage of surprise, that House Dradón had the initiative.

Anna looked up the face of the terrace's retaining wall. Above her, she could just see the upper barracks' roof.

She had to get up.

She had to be sure.

Dagger inched a bit closer, gave Anna a gentle head-butt, and spread his wings.

"Soon," Anna said. She kissed the foal's wet nose. "Even the fastest learners don't take a rider, even a training squire, until the end of their second week."

Moondagger stretched his wings wide, their tips bending inward as their ends pushed against the alley's narrow walls.

She shook her head and looked to the top of the wall. "Meet me up there."

19

THE MORTAR BETWEEN the wall blocks was in good shape, but there were still a few familiar cracks Anna could use to climb. In fact, she'd climbed this particular wall often—but she was usually climbing *down* to visit the barracks' kitchen for a clandestine snack.

Moondagger was waiting for her when she scraped herself over the parapet. They were in the upper barracks' rear courtyard. The courtyard was filled with clothes drying on a dozen even lines. Most of the laundry was the blue and white livery of House Dradón, but there were a few pieces of maroon gear belonging to riders of House Tevéss as well. A light breeze stirred the empty uniforms. The morning sky was pink, the sun just set to rise.

Above and to her right, the foundation wall of the eastern stables rose up, huge and indomitable. Above that, she could see the retaining wall of Voidbane's lodge. On her left, a narrow gap between the southern side of the barracks and the retaining wall's parapet led back out to the barracks' front terrace, where she'd just left the Tevéss riders.

Anna heard a dragon roar. It was followed by an impossibly deep response. Moondagger cocked his head at the sound, his eyes wide.

Voidbane.

For some reason, hearing the giant dragon made Anna feel better. Voidbane was there. And, no matter what happened, he was a force to be reckoned with. Dagger pointed his nose at the lodge, sniffing and tasting the air.

"Your sire." Anna patted Dagger's side. "You'll meet him soon."

She walked around the courtyard's perimeter, staying out of sight behind the hanging laundry, working her way up to the barracks' back door. A neat stack of empty tubs sat there. Anna tried the door. Locked. But the shutters of the barracks' rear windows were open. Anna took one of the laundry tubs, flipped it over beneath the window, and stepped onto it. Slowly, she lifted her head so she could peek inside.

She was looking into the barracks' rear utility room. There was no one there. On the right side of the room, shelves ran floor to ceiling, filled with carefully folded blue uniforms. On the left side of the room, lines of neatly arranged brooms, mops, buckets, dusters, rags, and other cleaning supplies hung from well-ordered hooks. The wall directly across from her, opposite the window, was lined with shelves carefully stacked with clay dishes, plates, mugs, pitchers, and bowls. There was a narrow staircase in the near corner to her left that descended into the barracks' kitchen. In the far right corner, a swinging door led into the common room.

Anna pushed at the window. It swung open soundlessly. She jumped to the stone sill, slid herself over, and lowered herself inside. Moondagger thrust his head into the window, eyes wide, broad tongue tasting the air.

"Stay here," Anna whispered. "Absolute silence."

Dagger's pinkish nostrils flared, but he made no noise.

Anna opened the window all the way, so that she might leap out if necessary, then crossed to the swinging door that led to the common room. The door had a round window in its center and swung both ways to ease traffic coming up from the barracks' kitchen.

Anna put her ear to the door crack and listened.

The low murmur of quiet conversations. She couldn't make out any specific sentences or words, but the inflection and pattern was marked by that unmistakable western accent.

Anna cracked the door and peeked inside.

Soldiers wearing the maroon livery of House Tevéss filled the common room.

Dozens of them. Dozens of dragon riders—.

No.

More than dozens.

At least a hundred soldiers in all. The common room was packed with them. And not all were riders. In fact, most were ground troops. They wore round infantry helmets and heavy combat armor under maroon livery. Shields were strapped to their backs and swords hung from their belts. Several of them carried carbines over their shoulders. The Tevéss riders that she could see wore the same kind of equipment that Captain Corónd and his riders outside had worn, a combination of scout harnesses and full battle gear. There were about a dozen dragon riders in total, sitting at the head table near the room's front; the infantrymen mostly stood.

The entire group gave the impression of having been waiting for some time. The riders were checking and re-checking their blades, revolvers, and knives, murmuring and talking over the soft click of harness and gear, the scrape of stone on steel. Several ate grapes or figs from clay bowls. Water pitchers and cups sat about everywhere. The group seemed calm, but it also radiated a kind of underlying tension, the coiled energy of a war company ready for battle.

A group of infantrymen stepped away from the far corner, and that's when Anna saw the bodies. They were piled neatly on the far left side of the room. The corpses of at least two dozen House Dradón dragon riders and squires. Most of them seemed to have had their throats cut. The fronts of their blue uniforms were stained deep maroon, bloody spillage spattered neck to groin. A young dragon squire, who Anna didn't recognize, was missing an eye. His face was upside down, his mouth open, a line of blood running up his cheek. A sopping mop and bucket leaned against the corpse pile. The floor around it was dark and wet.

Anna eased the door shut. From outside the window, she could hear Moondagger breathe, low and quiet. Her mind spun. If House Tevéss had taken the upper barracks, then they surely had taken the upper stables. And that meant they controlled most of their remaining dragons, all of those that hadn't launched with Sara Terreden. *If Terreden had launched at all.* But hadn't she just heard Voidbane's roar? That hadn't sounded like battle. Perhaps the traitors hadn't reached him yet? Didn't matter. Lord Gideon's men were assembled. And they were poised for attack. *No.* Not poised for attack. They *had* attacked. In anticipation of Lord Fel's arrival, the surprise assault had already begun. *One week, my eye!* That's what CoróND and his men were doing out there. They'd *already* taken control of House Dradón's barracks and stables. And that meant that House Tevéss had taken control of House Dradón's dragons. And without dragons, they were finished.

She had to get to Master Khondus. Warn him. Tell him what had happened.

"Who the *blazes*—?!" a deep voice grunted behind her.

Anna whirled.

Behind her, a maroon-clad soldier stepped up the narrow staircase, his eyes wide with surprise.

And then the blade she'd taken from the Tevéss soldiers in

the birthing stall was in her hand—reversed along her forearm, just as she'd practiced a thousand times—and she was
charging. The soldier was only halfway up the steps, so they
were at about the same height. He was a Tevéss infantryman. He carried a large basket heaped with day-old bread,
cheese, figs, olives, and two jars of pickled eggs. Anna could
just see the man's eyes over his pile of food. He was of medium height, but his shoulders were broad. He hesitated for
a moment, almost as if he was worried about dropping his
load. Or maybe the sight of a charging fourteen-year-old girl
in a half-torn tunic seemed to pose no threat.

Anna was within striking distance in half a moment. She
feinted toward the man's eyes, rolled, and planted her dagger
in the soldier's guts with all her might—but the blade scraped
harmlessly along the breastplate beneath the soldier's uniform,
slicing the maroon livery, glancing off the infantryman's gear,
the point catching on an armored joint and lodging there. The
soldier looked to the kitchen door. Anna tried to pull her
weapon loose. Failed. She jumped back and readied herself,
casting about for a weapon. Her blade was still sticking weirdly
out of the soldier's breastplate. He took a breath to shout the

alarm. Through the open window, Moondagger leapt into the room. He landed on the staircase's railing and bit the soldier's face, his lower fangs sinking into the underside of the man's chin, upper fangs crunching through the soft bones of his nose. The man's eyes went wide, and he tried to cry out. But his teeth were clamped shut by Dagger's jaws, and the sound he made was less a scream and more a whine. Moondagger growled softly and clamped down harder. The soldier's jaw and cheeks splintered, but he still stood upright, wobbling with his armload of goodies, as if trying to hand them off to Anna lest they fall. Anna put her foot on the man's thigh, jerked her dagger from where it'd caught, obligingly took the man's basket, and stepped back. Moondagger gave the infantryman's head a single, hard thrash, breaking his neck instantly, and leapt backwards into the rear courtyard, pulling the man after him, white serpent tail whipping over the windowsill.

Anna set the food basket down and stacked its contents into a neat pile, as if it had been left by someone who might return any moment. She checked the stair, the floor, and the windowsill for blood, wiping up the few drops she found with a clean uniform. She hid the uniform in a mop bucket, slipped over the windowsill, and pulled the window shut behind her.

Outside, Moondagger had taken his prize to the far side of the rear courtyard, hidden behind the laundry lines and hanging uniforms. When Anna reached him, he'd already tidily devoured most of the Tevéss soldier, having tossed aside the man's breastplate after slashing the lateral bindings like you might open a shellfish. Dagger sat in the midst of the soldier's remaining gear, snout extended to the sky, crunching on a freshly mangled arm. A pile of red guts lay beside him, glistening in the morning sun.

Good. She nodded. He needed to eat.

Dagger chomped away with total satisfaction.

"Nice fight." She patted Dagger's neck. "But they won't all be that easy."

Dagger kept chewing, cocking his head attentively.

"Real battle is a dance, Dagger. The deadliest art. It demands strength, speed, and cunning. We'll spend years training for it. This?" She looked at the pile of guts. "This is dinner."

Moondagger stared at her and swallowed with a gulp.

"Hurry up and finish."

Moondagger took another bite and chomped away. As he did, Anna took the steel dagger she'd just tried to use and set it aside. Then she took the high silver blade that Master Khondus had given her, tested its balance, and strapped it to her forearm, concealing it under her tunic sleeve. The weapon was slender, light, and impossibly sharp; an ancient tool made for war. If she'd drawn it, she could've pushed it through the enemy's armor like a knife through water. The blade might have been meant as a token for Captain Terreden, but it was hers now. She was going to use it.

She patted Dagger's side. "Next time, we'll *both* do our proper work."

Dagger grunted softly, and pushed his white nose at her hand.

20

BUT WHAT WORK? What was the next step?

Anna looked over the courtyard's parapet, south toward the High Keep. The sun was rising huge and red, bathing the citadel's stones in bloody light. Other than the usual messenger dragons, the sky was clear, a pale purple with only a hint of cloud fading in the west. The Keep still slept peacefully, unaware that war now raged in its walls.

Somewhere a crow cawed.

Dagger came up beside her and she put her hand on his neck. If the upper barracks had fallen, then Lord Gideon already could have moved against them in the High Keep. That meant that House Tevéss might already control the citadel. And if that was true, then Master Khondus had walked into a trap.

Moondagger hissed quietly, as if hearing her thoughts. She stroked his smooth scales. He gave a low growl and flexed his talons. His white tail whipped across the courtyard's flagstones.

She thought about the strategic topography of the Drádon-hold. What was important. What was not. Where the tactical priorities of the enemy must lie. Of course, Lord Gideon would concentrate his most elite forces near the center of the High Keep. That much was obvious. He'd do this so that he could control the Keep's High Gate. If open fighting broke out in there, then Master Khondus and the forces of House Dradón would face the most experienced soldiers that House Tevéss could offer. The murders committed here in the upper barracks were key to Lord Gideon's plan, but they were also peripheral. The High Square—and the High Gate that it protected—would be the center of the action.

"Master Zar," Anna said.

Moondagger grunted.

If Tevéss wanted to take the barracks by stealth, to ruin House Dradón's ability to wage war, then the armory would be their next target. Or at least very high on their list. And they would probably try to take it quietly, too. They wouldn't strike the center until the edges were secured.

"Gotta be Master Zar." Anna nodded. "*Then* Master Khondus."

21

IF YOU COULDN'T ride on dragon back, then the quickest way to Master Zar's armory from the upper barracks was by roof.

This was something of an advantage, since Anna and the House Dradón squires controlled the Drádonhold's roof-tops. (There'd been a brief contest for the turf when Lord

Gideon and House Tevéss first had taken up residency in the High Keep, but the Tevéss squires had quickly learned that the squires of House Dradón were the territory's true masters.) Nobody knew the rooftops' secrets better.

Anna swung her legs over the courtyard's parapet. Moondagger launched into the morning sky. She slid down the parapet's side, dropped an arm's length onto the slate roof of the kitchen storeroom, then took off, running and scrambling over the tiled peaks. Dagger's white wings glowed pink in the dawn's light.

The armory itself was a quarter bell away on a rocky outcrop on the southeastern side of the Drádonhold. It wouldn't take her much longer to get there—as long as she was careful where she stepped.

"Whoa!" a young, sharp voice cried in front of her.

Moondagger hissed and landed beside Anna on a chimney top.

Below them, in the valley between roof peaks, a young dragon rider wearing dark maroon livery sat atop a small, grey dragon. Both rider and dragon looked up at them curiously but made no aggressive move.

Great Sisters take my eyes!

She'd been concentrating on the roof tiles, not scanning the horizon. Did she think that Dagger—her *blind* dragon—was going to keep the watch while she ran?

Below them, the grey dragon growled inquisitively.

The rider was a Tevéss courier, from the look of him. Or a scout. Regardless, he was an enemy that was clearly watching for something—but wait.

He wore Tevéss livery, but the rest of his gear pointed to some other allegiance. His riding harness had been dyed a light lavender. His leather armor was lavender, too; and his leather helmet was topped with a lavender plume. His riding goggles, pushed back onto his helmet, were fastened to the sides of his headgear by small, purple-headed pins. His dagger, sheathed and clipped upside-down on the leather bandolier that crossed his chest, sported a lavender pommel stone. In one gauntleted hand, he held a riding goad wrapped in purple leather. The backs of his gauntlets were marked by an inlaid sigil that Anna didn't know: a silver bull's skull over a circle of lavender. His saddle rig was finely made of Abúcian leather, well-maintained, and heavily padded. A silver bull's skull decorated the saddle's pommel. From the pommel hung a beautifully made signal horn. A steel revolver hung under his left armpit.

He might be wearing Tevéss maroon, but this was no Tevéss rider. And he couldn't be older than eighteen. His mouth was small, his eyes bright blue. Blond hair. His dragon was young, its scales a metallic grey. Its eyes were deep violet.

Moondagger quivered with anticipation.

Wait, Anna thought.

The rider's dragon was small, yes. A scout, yes. But it was at least three years old, twice Moondagger's size, and—most importantly—trained.

The pair was about ten paces in front of them, still looking up from that low spot between the rooflines, still not making a move. He was hiding here, Anna realized. Some kind of spy. But did she dare risk a fight here, in the open, for anyone to see?

The rider's hand inched stealthily toward his gun.

And then there was nothing to do but attack.

"Go!" Anna roared.

They charged.

22

MOONDAGGER SAW THE enemy. And he knew exactly what needed to be done. The enemy was bigger. The enemy was stronger. The enemy had been trained. But none of that mattered. What mattered was that battle had arrived. Real battle. The waiting was finally over.

23

A SNAP OF wing and Moondagger launched from his perch, cutting up and to the right. Anna drew her high silver blade and leapt to the left. She sprinted down the roof peak, jumped to the top of a protruding chimney, and leapt through the curling smoke straight at the rider. The grey dragon hissed with surprise, reared, and unfurled its wings. The rider had drawn his revolver, but he wasn't aiming it at her for some reason—and then it was too late. Moondagger had arced deftly up and away, returning with incredible speed as he gathered momentum with the touch of elevation. Anna slashed past the grey's wing, her dagger low and lethal. They hit their targets together, Moondagger slashing at the grey's throat, drawing blood, flashing past, snatching the grey's head in his rear claws, clamping down hard in mid-flight, spinning the dragon's head around like a corkscrew, its long neck jerking, stretching, twisting, spine popping like hot corn in a kettle. Simultaneously, Anna swatted the rider's gun aside and drove her dagger into his heart, high silver blade splitting his armor like air, a grunt as Anna twisted the blade, turning the point up, levering the tip deeper into his chest. The young man's back arched, lips and teeth frozen open. Anna clamped a hand over his mouth. For a moment, the rider looked into Anna's eyes, a puzzled expression on his face. Then he shuddered and bent lifelessly against his saddle's high cantle.

Anna stared at him. Then looked away. She'd fought in battles before. She'd seen the dead. But never like this. It had been over before she'd known what had happened. Nothing at all like the poems and songs. Never this close. Never with her own hand.

"Traitor," Anna muttered.

But the words sounded hollow in her ears. She suddenly wished her old friend—that dark rage—would come back. But it didn't.

"It's our duty," she muttered.

Dagger grunted, staring at the enemy dragon. He nudged the dead beast with his snout, then turned his eyes to her. There was blood on Dagger's neck, but it wasn't his own, bright red against his white scales. Anna blinked, wiped her silver blade on the rider's uniform, and sheathed it along her forearm.

A large, black crow landed on a nearby chimney and cocked its head at the carnage. Then it stared at her. No ruffling feathers, no cocking its head, no cawing. Just staring, its flinty black eyes flat and intelligent.

Anna looked around, scanning the horizon. The fight seemed to have gone unnoticed, which was good. At least she didn't see any other scouts. But that was no proof that they hadn't been seen.

The crow leapt from the chimney to the roof near the enemy dragon's head, its sharp beak bobbing. It peered into the dragon's violet eyes, as if assessing their taste.

"Get outta here!" Anna snarled, scooping up a shard of slate, side-arming it at the bird. She missed and the crow fluttered back to its chimney perch. It sat there for a moment, took a long look at Anna, then flapped away.

24

AFTER THIS, IT took no time to reach the roof above Master Zar's armory and they crossed without further incident. But when they arrived, two squads of House Tevéss guardsmen were waiting for them.

"All right," Anna whispered.

Maybe they weren't waiting specifically for them, but they were still in the courtyard, blocking the yard's main gate and the gate to Master Zar's armory.

Moondagger, lying belly down behind the ridge beside her, grunted what sounded like a question.

Anna nodded. "Let me take another look."

She tilted her head and peaked sideways over the roof ridge.

The armory's courtyard was a large, rectangular space, about thirty paces across and some one hundred paces long. It was open to the sky and paved with grey granite. Its long axis ran northwest to southeast, away from the High Keep. On the northwestern wall, to Anna's right, a gate of wrought iron opened into the citadel proper. This gate was shut. Five Tevéss guardsmen loitered in front of it. They were armed with spears, round shields, and short swords. Anna saw two carbines slung over guardsmen's shoulders, but no other fire-arms. On the other side of the courtyard, in the southeastern wall, a pair of bronze-bound, double-wide doors granted access to Master Zar's armory and the southeastern launch platforms. These doors were also shut. Another five Tevéss guardsmen stood outside them. In addition to the usual gear, three of the guardsmen carried carbines.

The long wall of the courtyard, the wall directly across from the warehouse on which she hid, was lined with the main forges of the High Keep. Each forge was made of well-cut stone and roofed by a shed of silver-grey slate. Their chimneys were fashioned from the same grey granite as the courtyard's pavers. In front of each forge, horned anvils of various sizes squatted on thick, iron-bound blocks. Rows of black tongs, clamps, punches, swages, pinchers, and hammers hung from iron bars tacked between the sheds' supports. Even in times of peace, the courtyard was one of the busiest areas of the High Keep, especially in the morning. But now the yard was silent.

Anna eased herself back from the roof ridge. Ten Tevéss soldiers total. Armed and armored. Five firearms. Dagger turned his white snout toward her, eyes glowing, as if he perfectly understood her thoughts.

Master Zar's armory couldn't be reached on foot except through the courtyard. In fact, the only way for her to reach the armory without passing through the courtyard would be to climb down the side of the southeastern wall of the warehouse, climb down the mountainside itself, and then enter the armory through the launch platforms. And that would take forever.

"We'll fly."

Dagger cocked his head and stretched his white wings wide. The morning sun blinked through the hole made by d'Rent's bullet. There was no other choice. There was no way to get past Lord Gideon's men. And if she didn't tell Master Zar what was going on this moment, then it would be too late. Climbing down the cliff side without tackle would hardly be less dangerous.

Dagger stared at her. The white tip of his tail quivered with excitement.

Anna scooted back away from the ridge, crawled to the eastern edge of the warehouse roof, and peered over. It was a sheer drop down the cliff side to the mist and green forests below. She nodded. They could do it. Straight out and down. Land on the southeastern launch platform. It was closest, and it was the biggest.

"Come here."

Dagger obeyed.

"Put your head down."

Dagger put his head down.

Anna took off her belt, looped it around Moondagger's neck, and latched the belt's tongue on the last buckle hole. She pulled the belt tight. There was about a palm's breadth of space between the belt and the white scales of Dagger's neck. His crest hadn't been trimmed for harness yet, so she'd have to lay on it. It would be uncomfortable, but if this plan didn't work, she'd have bigger problems than a few cuts on her chest.

"We'll launch and turn to the right." She pointed, not because he could see but out of habit. "Aim at that platform there. You dive too steep, you won't be able to pull up, and we're both dead. You dive too shallow, we'll fly over the platform, and only the Great Sisters know what'll happen to us then. Got it?"

Dagger stared at her, hissed, and spread his wings to show

her how strong they were.

"Good." She nodded, realizing that she wasn't worried at all that they'd make it. "Let's go."

Dagger scooted forward, his white tail rasping across the slate tiles. Anna stepped over his neck and smoothed down his spinal crest. She sat and leaned forward along his neck, pushing his crest flat with her chest.

"How's that?" she asked.

Dagger cocked his head slightly. Anna slid her arms beneath her belt. The backs of her arms pushed against Dagger's scales. She closed her elbows so that the belt was locked between her forearms and biceps. She pulled a couple of times against the strap. Should be all right. Beneath her elbows, Dagger's neck was whip-strong muscle wrapped in smooth white scale.

"When you launch, you've gotta lift your head a bit to keep me horizontal."

Without pause, almost like he couldn't wait, Dagger stretched his head over the roof's edge. He held himself and Anna there, perfectly still, perfectly balanced above the precipice. The drop was dizzying and deadly and—oh Great Sisters—she was strapped to a baby dragon with a *belt*.

Anna closed her elbows hard on her makeshift harness. She pressed her hips against Dagger's spine, wrapped her legs around his neck, and locked her ankles.

"Go."

A muscular grunt, a crunch of slate, and Moondagger dove out into the air.

25

OF COURSE, ANNA had ridden dragons countless times before—as a squire.

She'd already experienced the crazy weightlessness that steals your breath when you plummet earthwards like a falling meteor. She'd already tasted the thrill of a sheering, leaf-splitting roll through the lush fissures of Jorgun Gorge. She'd already felt the heartbreaking awe that wells up in your chest when a slow climb through purple twilight opens onto moonlit landscapes of endless, violet cloud.

But Anna had never ridden a dragon by herself.

And she most definitely had never ridden a dragon that could be rightfully called her own.

So when Dagger leapt from the rooftop, something *clicked*

in her mind.

It was a kind of certainty. A kind of clarity. All her fear vanished. And with it, all her rage. The past, the present, the future—all disappeared. In their place, there was nothing but a crystallized jewel of the *now*, a crazy, dizzying joy that seemed to radiate a holy light from the very center of things.

And in that frozen moment, in that eternal flash of time, Anna Dyer knew—knew with a certainty that defied all reason—that she would spend her entire life, however long or short, with Moondagger in the sky.

26

FOR THE FIRST time, Moondagger saw everything clearly.

This was how it was supposed to be.

This was how it was meant to be.

This and only this.

He and his rider.

In the sky.

Forever.

THEIR MAIDEN FLIGHT lasted all of ten breaths and ended badly.

But Anna didn't care.

And she knew Dagger didn't care, either.

Their target, the armory's southeastern launch platform, was enormous. It'd been built specifically for Voidbane about a hundred years ago and was cantilevered from the cliff side on an intricate lattice of iron trusses. All told, it was well over a hundred paces across. And that didn't include the flight ramp, which could be lowered like a drawbridge on massive chains to give the largest dragons more room for takeoff and landing.

They approached the platform smoothly, a gliding arc descending cleanly from launch point to destination. No tricks. No horseplay. Just tight, proficient flying, the wind whipping her dark hair, the morning sun warming her face, their hearts pounding in each other's chests. It took everything she had not to shriek like a triumphant demon.

But Moondagger was a newborn. And, obviously, he'd never tried to land with a rider before. *Or land at all, for that matter.* So when they neared the platform, he flared his wings a bit too late and they came in too fast, skidding, hopping, and bobbling across the platform—white serpent tail slapping crazily against the deck, rear claws furrowing wood, Anna's legs coming loose, dangling and flopping everywhere—before Dagger managed to dig in his claws, trip, and belly slide a good ten paces while Anna, still belt-locked to her dragon's neck, nearly dislocated her shoulders, the impact punching her wind out like a fist to the gut.

"Good morning, Miss Dyer." A deep voice behind her. "Looks like we've got guests, eh, Gregory?"

There was a murmur of good-natured laughter. Dagger grunted, pulled himself up, and shook himself off, nothing hurt but his pride. Anna turned, speechless, lungs on fire, and found herself standing in front of Master Zar and two dozen armorers and assistants.

They were standing and sitting around a large table set on the threshold between the armory proper and the launch platform. Most of them held their morning tea—several of them caught mid-sip, cups halfway to their mouths. Master Zar and little Gregory, his old messenger dragon, sat at the center of the group, near the middle of the table. In front of little Gregory waited a huge, steaming meat pie. Gregory sat hunched on the pie's edge, caught mid-action, his little yellow claws sunk into the pie's flaky crust, his faded blue wings stretched over his feast. He stared balefully at Anna and Moondagger with his milky eyes, as if they'd just interrupted the beginning of his special meal. Which they had, apparently.

Anna tried to say something, but she could barely breathe, so the noise she made sounded more like a sick frog than attempted speech.

"Interesting entrance, Miss Dyer." Master Zar raised a bushy, purplish eyebrow. He chomped a bite out of an apple. He had thick teeth, like a donkey's. "Your dragon's blind, your tunic's half gone, and you've lost your belt. Mind your trousers, girl."

Anna looked at the Master imploringly, pulled up her sagging pants, and tried to speak, raising her hand lamely as she tried to catch her breath.

Master Zar was Anorian, so he was about a pace and a half tall and about a pace wide. Like all dwarves of Anor, his skin was a pale purple. He actually looked less like a dwarf and more like the squat, purple trunk of an old ironwood tree. His arms were thick. His shoulders were hard, purple stones. His eyes were deeply set beneath shaggy, purple brows. He was mostly bald, and what remained of his hair he shaved to the skin. As an Anorian veteran who'd served in the Silver King's legions, he proudly carried a large, white tattoo of the Dallanar Sun at the center of his forehead, the six-pointed star nearly as large as his hand. He wore a leather armorer's apron over a sleeveless wool tunic and wool pants. Thick, iron-shod boots clad his wide feet.

"We were just about to sing for little Gregory here." Master Zar stroked the small dragon's crest. "Four hundred and four years old today. Thought Master Khondus would be joining us. He's late."

From the edge of his meat pie, Gregory glared at Anna, squeaked his displeasure, and showed her his single remaining yellow fang.

"Congratulations," Anna managed to croak. She tried to take a deep breath, but it still hurt too much.

"Shall we, lads?" Master Zar asked. "With me now."

Together, Zar and his team sang:

Long may you live, Greg'ry, live many years!

Live long till long white hair covers your ears!

And if black war, Greg'ry, takes you away,

Live long in song, Greg'ry, live long we pray!

"Dig in, little friend." Master Zar smiled.

Gregory didn't need to be told twice. He promptly buried his little blue nose, his snout, and then his entire head into the meat pie, champing and smacking.

Dagger licked his fangs.

"So." Master Zar rubbed his palm like he always did over the white Dallanar Sun on his forehead. He looked from Moondagger to Anna, one bushy purple eyebrow raised. "What's this all about?"

28

IT TOOK ANNA about a quarter bell to relate her story. She told it uninterrupted until she reached the part about Moondagger burning Floren d'Rent and his men in the lower stables, at which point one of the young assistants had cheered and was promptly told to shut his trap by Master Zar, who listened to Anna's tale in deadly earnest, stroking the white tattoo on his forehead all the while. Her final description of House Dradón's men murdered and piled in the upper barracks prompted hisses of rage.

When she finished, everyone was quiet. They looked to Master Zar. Little Gregory licked the plate's bottom clean. For a long moment, the Master said nothing.

"So." He nodded finally. "You were supposed to relay Master Khondus's plan to Captain Terreden. At Khondus's signal, Sara was supposed to lock up the House Tevéss riders and dragons. At that same signal, Khondus would make his move in the High Keep with Captain Fyr and the High Lady's Guard. They'd kill Lord Gideon, destroy the Tevéss force there, make safe Lady Abigail, ensure our control of the High Gate, and send word to King Bellános on Kon. That about right?"

"Yes, sir," Anna said.

"But Terreden and the majority of our dragons are gone on some bogus training maneuver, our remaining riders have been murdered, we don't know the status of our other dragons, but Voidbane seems all right. Eh?"

Anna nodded.

"Then we're at war," Master Zar said.

The entire company stirred, but nobody said a word. Their eyes didn't leave the Master's face.

Anna made to speak, but Zar stopped her with a raised hand.

"First." Master Zar cocked his head at Moondagger. "We need to get you and your dragon into harness. You might be our only chance to get word to our allies outside the High Keep. Most certainly, you'll be the best and fastest way we can find out what's going on in the citadel. Second, we need to secure the armory and smithy——."

"Lord Gideon has two squads outside your door——," Anna began.

"Keep quiet," Master Zar said. He stroked little Gregory's blue spine. "You'll get your orders in a moment."

Anna bowed.

"After the smithy is secured," Master Zar continued, "we'll move forward with Master Khondus's plan. We'll make for the High Gate and send word to Bellános. Tevéss's ambush is well-laid. But Lord Gideon can't replace our adepts at the

Gate until the last possible moment. Any earlier, the whole Keep would know what was happening. Once our message is through, we'll connect up with Master Khondus and see how we can best serve his plan. We act fast enough, we might be able to get ahead of this thing. Have a nice welcoming party for the great Lord Oskor when he arrives."

Master Zar's men nodded. Their eyes were dark.

"What about the Tevéss troops in the upper barracks, Zar?" a deep-voiced armorer behind Anna asked. "And what of their dragons?"

She turned and saw that it was Master Jason, one of Father's oldest friends. He was tall, broad-shouldered, and was missing two fingers from his left hand. Battle-hardened. A nasty scar, starting beneath his jaw, ran from chin to ear then disappeared around the back of his skull. He wore his steel-grey hair in a short soldier's crop.

Master Zar nodded. "Miss Dyer says the Tevéss riders wait for their own signal. We'll have to deal with their dragons, of course. But with surprise, and man to man, the advantage should still be ours. Time to out-fox the foxes."

"And if they've been quietly murdering us all morning?"

Master Jason raised an eyebrow.

Master Zar looked at his men for a moment. His eyes were fierce. "Then we'll have some catching up to do."

As one, every man in the room crossed his chest with his fist and said calmly: "Dradón!"

Master Zar returned their salute and nodded. "Time to work."

29

"We'll get Dagger set up," Master Zar told her, rubbing the white Dallanar tattoo on his forehead. "Then we'll look to your gear."

Anna nodded. The armory bustled with activity, everyone moving at once, capable and proficient. Little Gregory was curled over the Master's shoulder. His milky eyes were shut, his faded blue tail wrapped around the Anorian's thick neck, his little blue gut pleasantly distended. Every so often, he'd give a little burp.

"Weights and measures," Master Jason ordered from the far side of the armory.

"Weights and measures!" his men replied.

Iron clicked on iron as the teams readied their stations and stepped to their equipment.

"Jason and his lads," Master Zar continued, "will rig out Dagger on the scout deck, get you weighed and fitted. All you need to do now is make sure Moondagger stays calm. Can't have him injuring the fitting teams. Don't know how he'll respond to—."

"He won't spook." Anna lifted her chin and looked Master Zar in the eye.

Behind Anna, Moondagger stared at the Master. His white scales glowed in the morning sun. Little Gregory looked up, hiccupped, then settled back into his nap.

"Fine." Zar nodded. "But you'll need to be sure to keep him—."

"He won't spook," Anna interrupted him again. A few of the apprentices looked from her to the Master. "You have my word, sir. He won't spook. I *know* it."

"Look here, girl." Master Zar pulled her aside gently, speaking so that only Anna could hear. The Anorian was slightly shorter than Anna but seemed to take up three times the space. "There's no time for that. You've done a good job so far, and he could be a fine mount. But you don't 'know' anything about him. That's a fact. You don't know his strength, his endurance, or his speed. You don't know how he'll react to harness, you don't know how he's maneuvering without vision, and you don't know how he'll respond to real combat. You know that he's strong, that he's completely untrained, and that he's blind. Oh, and you know that he's got a healthy taste for blood. I appreciate your confidence. But for now, you need to cease the backtalk and exemplify some soldierly discipline. This isn't about what you know, what you don't know, or what you think you know. You're a soldier, we're at war, and I'm giving you an order. You can't obey, then you'll be relieved. These men are gonna be neck deep in blood today, some of the young ones for the first time. They're not warriors or riders like you, squire. They're technicians. And they need to see that our soldiers understand their roles and that they obey their orders. Clear?"

"Yes, sir," Anna said, her face going warm. She snapped her heels together and crossed her chest with her fist. "Thank you, sir. Apologies, sir."

"Good squire," Master Zar said mildly. He looked over

her shoulder. "You there! Take a look outside and check the enemy's position. They react to our noise, we're gonna take 'em out." Then he turned and walked away. As he left, Gregory managed to raise his little blue head long enough to give a final burp.

30

"BRING HIM OVER, Anna," Master Jason said from the scout deck, waving her over to the small dais on the far side of the armory. The dais was made of Anorian oak, but even so, it was deeply scarred by the telltale marks of dragon claws.

Anna walked to the deck and ordered Dagger onto the dais, positioning him at its exact center. Dagger obeyed her commands perfectly, grunting and tasting the air with his broad tongue. His huge white eyes never left Anna's face.

"Weight carriages," Master Jason ordered.

"Weight carriages, sir!" the armorers responded. They rolled the two iron carriages into position on either side of the dais and locked the carriages' feet onto a series of well-worn pegs at the deck's side. When positioned like this, the carriages were set directly on either side of Moondagger.

Each carriage had a slot in its frame that would accommodate a dragon's wing. Once the dragon's wing was in the slot, the scaffolds' load arms—iron bars padded with sheaths of leather and sheep's wool—would be set on top of it. The load arms were cabled and geared to a stack of iron weights at the rear of each carriage. The purpose of the carriages was to assess the strength of a dragon's wings and shoulders and to help determine a dragon's potential weight load.

"How's he doing there, Anna?" Master Jason asked quietly. Then, louder: "Carriages secured and locked."

"Carriages secure and locked, sir!"

Dagger stared at Anna, tense but calm, pinkish nostrils flaring at the new noises, but otherwise perfectly still. Anna realized that Dagger wasn't acting this way out of nervousness; it was as if he knew exactly what was expected of him.

"Solid, sir," Anna answered.

"Very good." Master Jason nodded. Then, in a much softer voice, he added, "We're going to need him back on his haunches so that we can get his wings into position. I know you've seen this a hundred times, but this'll be your first time fitting your own mount, and he's untrained. I also don't understand what's going on with his eyes. If we can't get him fitted, if he balks at the weights, or the harness, or the noise, I won't risk my crews, understand? We'll pull him out and that'll be that. If I see even a hint of fire, Great Sisters forbid, we'll douse him immediately, and he won't like it." He lifted his eyebrows to the snarl of water pipes and spigots hanging from the vaulted ceiling above the scout deck.

"Yes, sir," Anna said.

"Very good." Master Jason nodded. Then, louder, so that the weight crews could hear, "Back and spread for weights." He turned to Anna. "At your ready, dragon rider."

Anna had been waiting to hear those five words her entire life. She stroked Dagger's white snout one last time, stepped back, and said in a soft, commanding tone, "Dagger, back and spread." As she said this, she squatted slightly and spread her own arms, as if they were Dagger's wings.

Of course, she had no idea what exactly was going to happen and, for a brief moment, had a horrible vision of herself squatting with her arms flapping stupidly in front of the armory's weight crews while Dagger stared at her with blank indifference.

But Moondagger responded as if he was born to it. He squatted back on his haunches, tail straight behind him, and spread his white wings wide. They slid perfectly into the carriages' wing slots. Anna kept her arms outspread. Dagger copied her exactly. His silvery eyes never left her face.

"Smart." One of Master Jason's younger assistants grinned as he fit the weight arm down over Dagger's left wing. A soft click of iron on iron.

"There's the hole from the traitor's bullet, just like she said." An assistant lifted his chin at Dagger's wing as he fit the weight arm on the other carriage. Clicks of iron as the carriages' mechanisms engaged.

"First weights," Master Jason commanded.

"First weights, sir!" his team replied.

"He'll need to lower his wings at the shoulder. The carriage slots will keep them extended properly."

"Of course, sir," Anna said.

She slowly lowered her arms and said, "Down."

Dagger mimicked her movement.

"First weights, on," Master Jason ordered.

"First weights on, sir!" the crew responded, locking and

clacking the first iron plates into position at the rear of the carriages.

"All right." Master Jason nodded.

Anna took a deep breath and raised her arms to shoulder height. Dagger followed her action, raising his wings. As Anna had guessed, there was hardly any resistance from the first set of weights. Dagger's shoulders were already as large as those of a full-grown scout, probably larger.

Master Jason's crew repeated the process four times. On the fifth set of weights, Dagger strained to lift the carriages' iron but did so in the end. On the sixth set of weights, the last set available on the scout carriages, he couldn't do it.

"Easy," Anna whispered. She lowered her arms until they were at her sides. Dagger lowered his wings, copying her. "Well done." She stroked Dagger's white snout and kissed him between the eyes.

"Weights off," Master Jason commanded.

"Weights off, sir!" the team replied as they unshackled the weights and rotated the padded arms away from Dagger's wings. He still sat between the two carriages, but his wings were now free of the mechanisms.

"Impressive," Master Jason said. "Easily passes the weight class of a big scout. Can't see any reason we can't fit him with light harness now. If his bladders are all right, then he should be fine. He'll be a strong one, Anna. Interested to see what he can do in a month or so. Couple of years should really be something. Give him a decade, I wouldn't be surprised if he outclassed Voidbane. Like father like daughter, eh?"

"Thank you, sir," Anna said, trying to keep the insane pride out of her voice.

"How's he navigating without sight? Master Khondus have any ideas? Master Boрónd?"

"I don't know," she said truthfully. "He flies as if he could see. As if he knows things."

"Boрónd'll figure it out."

Anna nodded.

"Let's measure his bladders across the board."

"Yes, sir."

"Retire carriages," Master Jason ordered.

"Retiring carriages, sir!"

The team rolled the weight carriages away from the platform

and set them in their spots against the station's walls.

"Bladder cords," Master Jason ordered.

"Bladder cords, sir!"

"We'll want his deepest breath, Miss Dyer."

"Yes, sir," Anna said.

Four assistants stepped to either side of Moondagger while Anna took position at Dagger's front. In the same crouched stance that she'd used before, she took a deep breath and rolled her shoulders back so that her chest stuck out, holding her breath like that for a moment. Then she let her breath out. Dagger followed her example, took a huge breath, rolled his massive shoulders back, and let his breath out.

"Good," Master Jason murmured. "One more time and hold."

Anna took another deep breath, just as she had before, holding her breath, raising her chin. Again, Dagger mimicked her. But this time, as Dagger held his breath, his upper chest continued to swell as his flight bladders took in additional air from the gill-shaped intakes under either side of his jaw. After half a moment, there was additional swelling along his flanks, his lower spine, and his groin as his flight bladders filled.

"Hold," Master Jason said.

Anna held her breath. Dagger did the same.

"Cords," Master Jason said.

The four assistants stepped to Dagger and swung their bladder cords around his chest, flanks, lower spine, and groin. They called out the measurements in turn.

"Twelve palms, four fingers!"

"Nine palms, four fingers!"

"Seven palms, two fingers!"

"Six palms, one finger. And . . . six palms, even!"

An assistant took down the measurements on a board then ran to a far door that led beneath the armory to storage.

"Let's get him stretched out and balanced," Master Jason said.

"Yes, sir."

"How much you weigh, Anna?"

"Seven stone, almost exactly, sir."

"When you weigh last?"

"Three days ago, sir."

"All right." Master Jason nodded. "Balancers, seven stone."

"Balancers! Seven stone!"

Two big armorers went to the wall for a saddle weight, retrieved a seven stone strap, and carried it back to the dais, holding the strap between them. Four other assistants stepped up onto the platform. The first two stood near Dagger's chest, where the saddle weight would be placed, the second two stood at Dagger's tail with a wooden crate of tail weights. Dagger kept his eyes on Anna, completely ignoring the assistants' activity.

"Extend," Anna commanded, bending forward and lengthening the word, craning her neck so that Dagger could understand what she wanted.

Moondagger got it immediately. He pushed his head forward and stretched his white tail straight back. His form was near perfect, like he'd already been trained. Anna stepped up and touched two fingers to his throat, raising his head slightly.

"Good." She nodded.

Master Jason said softly, "Let's get his wings open."

Anna stepped back, crouched, and spread her arms. Dagger unfurled his wings, spreading them wide, neck craning forward, balancing on his hind legs. His rear claws gouged into the dais's wood.

"Saddle weight," Master Jason ordered.

"Saddle weight!" the crew repeated.

The two assistants at Dagger's neck smoothed down his spinal crest. The moment they had done so, the two big armorers with the saddle strap gently lowered the seven stone belt across the base of Dagger's neck. As Dagger took the weight, his rear claws flexed, digging into the platform's wood, and his tail went up—but only slightly. The moment his tail rose, the two assistants at his rear placed a weighted strap over the tail's tip. They'd estimated the weight correctly. Dagger leveled out immediately and was able to relax his claws.

"One and one half stone!" an assistant at Dagger's tail called.

"One and one half stone," Master Jason repeated, shaking his head. "Really quite fine. Near perfect form, too." He turned and looked at Anna. "Well done."

"Thank you, sir." Anna smiled.

The assistant who'd taken Dagger's bladder measurements had returned from storage, bringing four other crew members with him. Between them, they carried the components of a leather scout rig. At the same moment, Master Zar and little Gregory came back with a simple suit of scout armor, pads, harness, undergear, and riding tackle, all slung together on a storage hanger.

"How'd he do?" Master Zar asked Master Jason, glancing at Moondagger.

"Flawless," Master Jason replied.

"Good." Master Zar nodded, looking Dagger over with an appraising eye. Little Gregory cooed from his place on Master Zar's shoulder and nuzzled the Master's ear.

"Those Tevéss idiots in the yard still blocking our door?"

Master Jason nodded.

"Any reaction to the noise in here?"

"No," Master Jason said.

"Their mistake." Zar shrugged. "Let's get her saddled and armed." He unslung a wool bag from the storage hanger and tossed it to Anna. "Get those clothes off. Here's your undergear. Use that closet there. Think I got your size about right. Be quick about it."

"Yes, sir!" Anna nodded. She patted Dagger on the side and

jogged to the closet. There, she stripped, rolled her clothes into a ball, and stuffed them into the wool bag. She stepped into the undergear, adjusting its straps at all the proper joints. Like all such gear used in House Dradón's armory, this set was made of white Eulorian silk and fit well. Tight at her wrists, ankles, and neck, but a bit looser at the joints. A number of loops, frogs, and clasps would fasten the under-gear directly to the padding she'd wear beneath her leather armor. She spun her arms in a few circles and twisted this way and that to be sure there was no bunching or pull. All felt in order, so she left the closet, jogged back to Dagger, and stood directly in front of the dais.

"Trim work," Master Jason ordered.

"Trim work!" the team replied.

"Let's get him flat for a moment, Anna," Master Jason said.

Anna nodded, stepped up to Dagger, and said, "Down. And steady."

Moondagger lowered his head to the edge of the dais. Master Zar stepped onto the deck with his trimming knife and clippers, smoothly lifted the crest from Dagger's back, and cut the thin fin tissue between the splines in front of the dragon's shoulders where his saddle would rest. As was typical for scouts, the Master would trim Dagger's crest from his shoulders to about a quarter of the way up his neck. As Master Zar snipped the splines away, he murmured soothingly and dabbed a waxy touch of silver sealing balm onto each spline after it had been cut. Moondagger behaved perfectly throughout, as if he didn't feel it.

Master Zar stepped down and shook his head. "Like he's already been trained."

Master Jason made an affirmative grunt. Anna tried, with zero success, to keep the giant smile off her face. Master Zar lifted a bushy purple eyebrow and rubbed the Dallanar Sun on his forehead.

"He makes it to ten years, Anna, nothing in the Kingdom will stop him," Zar said. "Nothing on Dávanor, that's for sure."

"Thank you, sir." She nodded, dizzy with pride. Master Zar's compliments did not come quickly. Or often.

Dagger snorted.

"Pad and saddle," Master Jason ordered.

"Pad and saddle, sir!" his team responded.

The armorers moved forward as a unit, placing the pad over Dagger's neck and back where his crest had been trimmed. The leather saddle followed. It was a typical scout rig, small and light. It had no horn, and its fork and gullet had a deep, concave profile that tapered smoothly into its leather belly pad. This pad would allow a rider to lay flat along a dragon's neck and would keep both soldier and mount comfortable. The saddle's stirrups and fenders were also mounted farther back than was normal, the assumption being that the scout rider would spend most of her time prone.

As the team buckled and clipped the saddle in place, an assistant stepped up to Anna, measured the length of her arms, then called out the length to another assistant who fixed a grip belt on Dagger's neck at the appropriate distance away from the saddle. The grip belt carried two leather-bound handles set inside molded leather wind screens, one along each side of Dagger's neck. This was the typical position for a scout rider's hands. Like all scout rigs, there were no reins. Instead, speed, direction, and elevation were communicated by voice and by pressure applied to the dragon's neck through the grip belt and through the rider's knees. Obviously, the rig was set for speed, not combat. A series of ten bronze clips—three along the inside of each thigh, one at the outside of each hip, one above the crotch, and one at the tailbone—would lock her leather riding harness to the saddle, while two buckled thigh belts would provide the primary points of attachment. Hooks and clasps jingled as the team finished up.

"Arm rider," Master Jason ordered.

"Arm rider!" the second team of assistants answered.

As the first team continued to work on Moondagger's gear, the second team armed Anna. She handed the silver dagger Master Khondus had given her to Master Jason for safe keeping while they worked. They started with light padding over her undergear, then fit the leather plates of her scout armor over that. When her armor was secured, they fit her riding harness over it and buckled it into key points of her gear.

Master Jason handed back Khondus's high silver dagger. Master Zar handed her a light helmet of Abúcian leather, a pair of riding gauntlets, a steel revolver, a bandolier of shells, a riding scarf, and a set of goggles.

"No Dradón marks on this gear, Anna," Master Zar said, looking over her armor. "Don't know what you'll run into. Might be an advantage *not* to look like a House Dradón rider."

Anna nodded, lifting her chin so that an armorer could buckle the collar of her neck guard.

"Want you to have this, too," Master Zar said. He handed her a brass telescope. Three pale moonstone buttons were set along the telescope's long axis. The oculus was ringed with lapis lazuli.

"Thank you, sir," Anna said.

"Comes from Kon," the Master said gruffly. "Lord Garen gave it to me two years ago. Has some interesting properties. You'll see."

Anna saluted him, sheathed the telescope in the leather loop at her side, and pulled on her riding gauntlets, locking their straps down tight. She holstered the revolver at the small of her back, swung the bandolier over her head, and slid the high silver dagger into its inverted scabbard across her chest. She tucked her helmet beneath her arm, took a deep breath, and turned to face the launch platform.

The morning sun and the endless sky beckoned. Behind her,

as if on cue, Moondagger rose on his haunches, spread his white wings wide, lifted his head to the vaults, and roared.

In unison, the armory crews saluted them.

Anna returned their salute, crossing her chest with her fist.

"Arming master," Master Zar asked formally. "Is the rider ready for orders?"

"Sir." Master Jason nodded, fist crossing his chest. "The rider is ready."

31

MOONDAGGER SAW A massive, black dragon.

Anna was playing on him.

She was five years old.

The dragon was impossibly huge. He had enormous black horns, a gigantic black tail, and wings like the black sails of a mighty ship. His eyes were deep, orange slits, the burning color of a volcano's heart.

Anna was tiny. Just a child. And yet she still managed to climb up the front of the dragon's nose, using his giant, hooked fangs to hold onto, climbing until she sat between his nostrils, a tiny speck of a girl planted squarely on the broad shelf of the black dragon's massive snout.

She settled herself there, crossed her legs, then bounced up and down a couple of times.

"Wake up!" Anna shouted.

The fiery eyes of the dragon stayed closed. He gave a contented sigh.

"Wake up, sleepy!" She patted the scales beside her. "I wanna talk to you!"

"Gentle," Father said from across the stable. "He's resting." Father checked the flight log at the small desk, goggles up on his forehead, gauntlets folded and stuffed up into the bandolier at his chest. "He wants to take a nap."

Anna paused. "I wanna *talk* to you," she whispered. "I wanna *tell* you something."

The dragon barely cocked his head. Anna put her little hands down to keep her balance.

"See!" she cried. "He *wants* to play!"

She patted the big dragon fondly. Her tiny hand was smaller than his smallest scale. She scooted toward the front of his snout and stroked his delicate facial scales, the fine silvery hairs on his black nostrils.

"He's a good boy," Anna stated.

"That he is." Father walked to her and patted the dragon's massive jaw. The dragon rumbled contentedly, the bass vibrato unbelievably deep.

"He's old," Anna pointed out.

Father nodded. "To you and me. But dragons live their time differently. By his own life, he's just become a young man."

"He's a good young man," she said.

Father smiled. "Indeed."

"I want to ride him."

"You ride him all the time."

"I want to ride him like *you* ride him."

"If I step down, or if I'm killed, then Lord David will choose his next rider. Maybe it'll be you. Then, when you step down, or if you're killed, the next High Lord will choose another rider. And so on."

"You won't be killed."

"Death isn't defeat." He pulled her ear and winked.

"You *always* say that." She squirmed away.

"It's true. My father died in the service of Lady Tamara, Lord David's mother. He wasn't afraid to die. Your mother and I fight for Lord David. We're not afraid to die."

"I'm not afraid either."

"'Cause you're so smart." He kissed the top of her head.

He smelled like clean leather and straw and fresh air. "There're things more important than life."

"Honor, love, and family." She nodded.

"Exactly."

"You won't die," Anna said confidently. She leaned over and kissed the massive dragon on the nostril. It was kinda wet, but she didn't care.

"Listen here, young man," she told him. "You don't let him die. Hear me? *That's* your job. You keep him safe. *You* protect *him*."

The dragon's massive orange eye peeled open, huge and eternal, a glowering pit of unquenchable heat. Moondagger saw his own eyes reflected in it, two pale lozenges surrounded by timeless fire.

And in that moment, Moondagger understood his ultimate duty.

It was not just to fight.

It was to protect.

32

"My orders?" Anna asked. Holding her leather helmet beneath her arm, she pushed a lock of dark hair behind her ear.

Master Zar nodded. "You'll launch immediately for the upper stables. There, you'll release Voidbane."

The armory crews stirred and murmured. From Master Zar's shoulder, little Gregory squeaked his approval.

Master Jason raised an eyebrow. "Think that's best? Bane's been uneven for years, ever since we lost Erik." He tilted his head at Anna.

"Don't know." Master Zar shrugged. He rubbed his palm over the Dallanar crest on his forehead. "But I do know this. If it comes to blows, Voidbane will shred Irondusk without half a thought. He's twice as smart, twice as fast, and he'll be hungry for a rematch. We give Bane the opportunity, Irondusk won't stand a chance. Voidbane *loved* Erik. Given the opportunity, he won't need an excuse to destroy Fel's dragons. Truth be told, the real problem will be getting him to stop."

Master Jason nodded.

"Fel knows that, too," Master Zar continued. "No way

these traitors didn't consider Voidbane in their plans. They won't be able to touch him, but they'll still need to keep him out of the action. They know he's all we need to turn the tide of any battle. Probably what those dragon riders were doing at the upper barracks in the first place. Anna's gonna cut in there, evade whatever guards they've got in place, and set Voidbane loose. Simple as that. Besides, the big guy has known Anna since she was a baby. She's the only rider for the job, especially considering his temperament of late."

"And us?" Master Jason asked.

"We're gonna follow Master Khondus's plan. We're gonna kill those traitors in the courtyard, meet up with Khondus and Captain Fyr at the High Gate, and get a message through to Bellános on Kon. Once that's done, we'll keep taking out the rubbish 'til the Drádonhold's been scrubbed clean."

"Will Bellános come?" Master Jason asked.

"How can he not?" Master Zar replied. "His thrice cursed brother arms House Fel against us. And why? So that he can take control of our stables and our dragons. Bellános knows all this. We get him a message, he'll keep his promise. He'll come."

"And if we can't get him a message?"

"It means Fel controls both Dávanor's High Gates. It means we're cut off. It means that we stand alone against Lord Fel, Lord Tevéss, and the Pretender King."

33

HER HAND ON Moondagger's neck, Anna put her foot into her stirrup and lifted herself up into the saddle. There, she clipped her harness into the saddle's safety clasps and belted up her thighs. Dagger shifted beneath her. His neck was a coiled spring of muscle beneath smooth white scales. She lay forward along the saddle's belly pad and double-checked the distance between her saddle and her grips. She twisted side to side and pulled hard against the restraining clips and belts. Everything felt in order, so she secured her helmet, checked her equipment one more time, and pulled her flight goggles down over her eyes. Master Jason and Master Zar stood together on the far side of the launch platform. She nodded at them. Good to go. Master Jason returned her nod. Master Zar gave her a formal salute, his huge purple fist across his broad chest. Little Gregory glared at her with his milky eyes and gave a little squeak.

"Platform clear!" Master Jason ordered.

"Platform clear, sir!" his team replied.

"Rider ready!"

"Rider ready, sir," Anna replied.

"Launch!" Master Jason commanded.

"Launch!" the team cried.

"Launch," Anna whispered.

A muscly grunt, a scrape of claw, and they leapt together into the sky.

34

THEY ARCED INTO the air and dropped away from the platform, diving along the walls, the carved cliffs, and the jagged rocks of the mountainside. Dagger's white tail was a perfect line, his form impeccable, his neck strong and warm beneath her chest, his response to her grips and knees immaculate. A cliff tree flashed past them with a snap of twig. They banked hard and started their long circle around the eastern side of the Drádonhold.

Anna's goggles were clear, and she kept a sharp lookout for enemy sentries and riders. She saw none. Messenger dragons still flurried across the sky as the Drádonhold woke to the day, but it was eerie, as if the citadel had chosen this particular morning to slumber late, unaware of the coiled violence now seething within its walls.

They raced along the eastern side of the mountain. When they'd gone far enough, she lifted Dagger's nose and began the slow, careful climb to Voidbane's lodge.

"Let's go even higher," Anna said. "Come in from up top."

They'd approach the lodge from above. If the enemy saw them, they'd have the advantage of elevation and could drop away, fast. Dagger pumped his wings and banked upwards, angling against the cliff side, climbing steadily. After several moments, they landed on a narrow cliff ledge above the Drádonhold.

Anna sat up in her saddle, looked down at the High Keep.

Voidbane's lodge was directly below them. It was a massive stone building nearly a hundred paces long and half again as tall. Because of the mountain's topography, it sat at one of the highest points of the Drádonhold, connected to the upper stables and barracks by a series of narrow stairs and rock-cut bridges. The lodge's foundation had been carved directly into the mountain top, its wall courses cut from the cliff side.

Its huge, gabled roof was tiled with the same silver-grey slate as the rest of the Keep's buildings.

She pulled her goggles from her face, set them on the brow of her helmet, and frowned. Dagger grunted. There was no one there.

She couldn't see the front of the lodge, but the enormous side yard was empty and the big southern and eastern windows were open. Voidbane's launch door was open, too. It was as if he was already out. She could see into the stable proper.

Empty.

But how could that be?

"Makes no sense."

She took the telescope from the leather loop at her side, extended it, and pointed it at the lodge. Everything became huge and clear.

But still nothing.

No movement. No Dradón soldiers. No Tevéss soldiers. No dragons. No Voidbane. Nothing.

She moved the sight of the telescope over and around the lodge. As she adjusted her grip, her finger pressed one of the telescope's moonstone buttons. A loud, wet gasp sounded in her ear. She jumped and jerked the telescope from her eye. Dagger growled. As soon as her eye no longer touched the telescope's brass oculus, the sound ceased. She checked around, saw that she was clear, and pressed her eye once again to the telescope. There was no sound. She pressed the moonstone button again. The sound returned.

It was a huge, rattling breath, moist and deeply labored.

The sound of a massive dragon.

A massive dragon that couldn't breathe.

Anna collapsed the telescope with a snap.

"Go!" She pressed herself to Dagger's neck as he launched from the ledge, diving straight at the lodge, straight through the stable's rear window, unfurling his wings the moment he was inside, landing perfectly in the golden straw.

Voidbane was there, lying on his side.

But he didn't move.

"No!" Anna cried.

She unclipped and leapt from her saddle.

He was an enormous dragon, over sixty paces long. His scales were black as night. His black tail was long and thickly crested, his huge head marked by massive obsidian horns. The tip of one horn had been broken three years ago and had yet to heal. The other was nearly as long as Anna was tall. His huge eyes were shut. He didn't stir, not even with their landing.

Anna saw no wounds or punctures or blood. But there was an unhealthy smear of dark, bone-colored foam on his mouth. The scales around his lips were crusty, grey, and dead-looking. The straw in front of his snout was sticky with slime. One of his feeding tubes had been discarded in the straw beside his head.

She ran through the straw, lifted the tube, put her nose in it, and recoiled. The stench was strange and sweetish, cloying.

Voidbane gave a massive, wheezing gasp. His sides shuddered. She put her hand on his side. His scales were barely warm, not clammy, but holding none of their usual heat. He didn't stir at her touch. She noticed a dead messenger dragon hastily buried in the straw beside him. Its neck had been broken. She bent down and searched its harness. Nothing. But beneath the tiny dragon's body, she found an ancient message tube of engraved high silver, whatever message it had carried long gone. Without thinking, she tucked it into a pocket inside her armor.

Dagger crawled up, sniffing, extending his nose toward Voidbane's snout. The big dragon growled at his approach. The sound was impossibly deep—but was cut short by another weird, wracking spasm in the dragon's side. Dagger retreated with a low whine.

Anna stepped to Moondagger, swung into her saddle, and clipped on.

"Go!" she cried.

Master Borónd.

As fast as you can, Dagger. As fast as you'll ever fly.

Moondagger seemed to hear her thoughts and leapt for the open window as if shot from a catapult.

35

THEY LANDED ON the southern balcony of Master Borónd's library with a scrape of stone, the gust of their arrival stirring the well-ordered rows of plants and herbs that lined the porch's sun-kissed ledges. A large crow sat there, pecking the dirt of a potted Dayádian clover.

Anna unhooked, leapt from her saddle, and ran through the

covered portico toward the glass doors of Master Boród's library.

"Nice to see you again, girl." A short dragon rider in maroon livery stepped in front of her. He held a bloody straight razor in one hand. "So very nice."

Hendo. The pig-nosed villain she'd first met on the upper barracks' terrace. His eyes glimmered wickedly, catching the morning sunlight at a freakish angle. His weird nostrils dilated. Anna stopped and calmly backed away, out into the sun. Hendo followed, pursing his lips.

"What are you doing here, girl?" Hendo asked, wiping his mouth with the back of the hand that held the razor. Its edge flashed. Both his hands were red with blood. A curved dagger was tucked into the front of his riding belt. His maroon livery was blood-stained, too.

Moondagger growled. Hendo seemed not to notice it.

Anna raised her hands. "I'm here to see Master Boród, sir—."

"Got yourself into proper harness, eh?" he said, looking her over, coming toward her, paying Dagger no mind. "Got your little worm ready for his riding? That is good. That is *very* good."

He reached for the iron whistle that hung from his neck.

Anna turned, made as if to run toward Dagger, and Hendo took the bait, coming up behind her, reaching for her shoulder. The moment he touched her, Anna screamed as if in terror, feigned collapse, grabbed his wrist, twisted it, and rolled the little man hard over her shoulder, sending him straight toward her dragon. Dagger took the handoff perfectly, bit Hendo's ankle as it flipped toward him, and tossed the rider nonchalantly over the balcony's parapet into the yawning chasm. Strangely, the man didn't scream as he plummeted to the toothy rocks below. Anna clapped Dagger on the jaw, ran through the portico, and opened the library's glass doors.

Inside, two Tevéss soldiers stood on either side of Master Borónd. They were leaning over him, whispering something. The Master was bound to his reading chair, ropes at his ankles, wrists, and waist. Several of his fingers had been broken. Blood pooled the floor beneath his chair from some wound she couldn't see. On the writing desk, his delicate, wire-framed reading spectacles had been smashed under a broken pot. An iron cauldron rested on a tripod at the center of his desk, suspended over a cooking lamp. The cauldron was surrounded by an assortment of glass vials and beakers, many of them empty or spilled. A pile of books smoldered in the far corner. The volumes were large and priceless, the stink of burning velum like a haunch of merino left too long over fire. Several of his bookshelves had been broken off the walls. More broken pots lay shattered at Anna's feet. Master Borónd moaned. The Tevéss infantryman with his back to Anna hissed, and slapped the Master across the face. Neither had noticed her arrival. Or Hendo's departure.

Anna drew her revolver from the small of her back, took a calm breath, and whistled. The Tevéss soldiers looked up, and she shot them both between the eyes—one, then the other—heads cracking back, bodies crumpling to the floor. Master Borónd glanced up, recognized her, and looked down, his head wagging.

". . . Anna," he whispered, not looking at her.

She ran to him and knelt beside the chair. His slender nose looked wrong and when he spoke, she could see that one of his front teeth had been broken. There were five precise cuts on his forehead, beginning right below his blondish-grey hair, each longer than the last. The cuts were fresh. A line of blood ran past his eye. They'd shaved one half of his beard and moustache away. He wouldn't look at her, but instead stared at the smoldering pile of books, as if ashamed of his appearance. His bottom lip quivered. Anna holstered her weapon, drew her dagger, and cut the ropes away from his ankles, wrists, and waist, the high silver blade parting the ropes like air.

"They're killing everyone," Anna said gently, putting her hand on his shoulder, re-sheathing her blade. "They've poisoned Voidbane. He needs—."

". . . I know," Master Boród whispered. He held his destroyed hands in his lap.

Something in his voice stopped her.

He still wouldn't meet her gaze.

She looked at the cooking cauldron on the desk. The litter of strange ingredients around it. She stepped to the desk, put her nose into the pot, and recoiled at the familiar strange and sweetish smell.

". . . they made me . . . " Master Boród said, staring at the smoking books. "They brought Lady Abigail. They brought her here. She didn't know what they were doing. She stood right there, and Gideon pointed a gun at the back of her head. She couldn't see it. She's so small. He showed me what would happen if I refused. I couldn't . . . . They made me take it to him . . . . They made me. Because Voidbane knew me . . . . They knew he'd take it from me . . . ."

Traitor!

Outside on the balcony, Moondagger roared. The glass doors shook. Anna's mind raged. And just like that, her old friend—her dark rage—was back, hungrier than ever. Her head spun. She glanced outside at Dagger, caught his eye, and took a breath. Quelled it. What was Borónd supposed to have done? Let them kill the High Lady?

"Is there a remedy?" she asked calmly, taking another deep breath. "Can we give him something? Quickly now. He still lives."

Master Borónd nodded. ". . . yes. Above the medicine cupboard in the closet there, above the top shelf on the left, behind the rack of Jagaean tonics. A small, silver box tucked below the far rafter . . . ."

Anna ran, grabbed a stool, and found the box. It was intricately fashioned of strange, silvery wood, its top carved with a design of interlaced vines and plants.

It was locked.

"The key?" she asked.

"Around my neck." He bowed his head.

She found a silver chain and lifted it over her head. There were several other keys on it.

"Which one?"

"The smallest."

She took it. Opened the box. At its center was a small, crystal vial held in a sculpted hand of high silver. The vial shone with pale, white radiance.

". . . if anything can help, that is it." Master Boród swallowed. "From Kon, five years past . . . a gift from young Garen Dallanar."

Anna took some writing paper from a drawer, wrapped the vial, and placed it inside her breastplate.

". . . it will work, Anna," Master Boród said.

"Thank you," she said steadily, turning for the balcony. "Now rest——."

"Fel will be here two days after next . . . three days. Through Jorgun Gorge. I heard them speak of it—."

"Not Hengén Cleft?" Anna turned, her eyebrows shooting up.

"No. Through the Gorge. I'm sure of it. Why would they lie? Three days. Fastest route from the Felshold. Through the Gorge."

If it was true, then it meant that Captain Corónd, the Tevéss dragon master she'd met at the upper barracks, had deliberately fed her false information about Lord Fel's arrival, knowing that she'd pass it on, exactly as she'd suspected. Outside on the balcony, Moondagger growled impatiently.

"I'll send aid when I'm able," Anna said.

Master Borónd nodded and slumped in his chair. She ran to the balcony, mounted, clipped on, and launched.

36

MOONDAGGER SAW WHAT happened next backwards, as if the scene played out from the end to its beginning. First, he saw three enemy dragons tearing Anna to pieces. Then he saw them dive at her, their talons flexed and deadly. He saw their riders' eyes glint in the morning sun, just before they launched. He saw the enemy riders scanning the mountains, weapons ready, alert and on the watch. And then things stopped—and moved forward again. And three enemy dragons were falling silently toward them. He could not see them anymore, but somehow he perfectly understood their presence and position, as if he saw the entire encounter from a distance.

And then he saw Anna's Father astride Voidbane in front of him, radiant and glowing with silvery-white light. Father held a long, silver war lance in his hand. Voidbane roared, the thunderous sound quaking Dagger's mind. Father aimed the lance at Moondagger's heart.

"Protect her," he whispered.

Moondagger knew how. So he did.

37

ANNA AND DAGGER launched from the balcony of Master Boród's library. She kept good watch, carefully avoiding the easiest paths, skirting entire areas in their attempt to preserve speed and stealth, circling up the mountainside as they raced east to Voidbane's Lodge.

The enemies' assault was soundless—at least Anna hadn't heard anything. It was Dagger who saved them from the initial attack, his preternatural reflexes somehow anticipating the aggressors' strike moments before they hit.

"Let's go ahead and head back around—," she started.

But Dagger collapsed his wings, rolled, and dropped straight down the cliff side, a near vertical dive, the intensity of the speed stopping her heart, her breath catching in her chest.

An angry cry rang out above her. Anna glanced over her shoulder and saw three Tevéss riders—one on a red scout dragon that had crashed into the mountainside just where she'd ordered Dagger to turn. The red's rider was uninjured, but his dragon's shoulder was damaged. The red clung there to the rocks, immobilized and out of the action, but his rider's comrades were circling back, rolling, and diving after them. One rode a small green scout, the other on a lightweight gold in full battle gear. The gold dragon wore a maroon battle standard across its chest, the three crossed swords of House Tevéss emblazoned black at its center. The rider who'd crashed drew his sidearm and aimed at her.

Anna looked away, pressed her chest to her saddle, and squeezed her grips.

"Go!" she cried.

Dagger went, pulling his white wings tighter to his sides, the expelled air from his bladders hissing like steam from a forge. The mountainside shot past them, a blur of smooth grey stone. Three shots rang out. A chip of rock blasted past her face. Dagger furled his wings with a snap, pulled them up, took a massive breath, his intakes pulling huge amounts of air into his flight bladders. The Tevéss riders blasted past them, taken totally off-guard.

"Ha!" Anna roared. "After those traitor dogs!"

And then *they* were the hunters.

The little green banked, cut right, leveled, and started climbing back toward the Keep. The gold cut left, but still dropped, drawing them away from his smaller, faster comrade, both riders looking over their shoulders, assessing Anna's position, a flurry of hand signals flashing between them.

"The gold can wait," Anna snarled, turning Dagger up toward the little green.

Dagger banked up and right, pushing forward at speed,

closing on the green immediately. Anna took a split moment to assess the armament of her opponent. The Tevéss rider was pressed flat against her own saddle's belly pad, her long blond hair streaming back from the hole at the top of her leather helmet. A scout—virtually unarmed. The scout dodged right. Dagger followed and closed. She dodged left. Dagger followed—closer still. She rolled and dropped, dodging insanely near the cliff side. But Dagger tracked her perfectly, dropping onto the green's hips, his talons sinking into the base of the dragon's green tail, pulling them up like a spear hawk plucking a fish from a stream. The green screamed, head down, wings flapping uselessly. The Tevéss scout reached for her sidearm. Dagger took a massive breath, his talons still sunk into the enemy's tail, and blasted dragon and rider with a searing column of silvery-white fire, flesh and scale melting to formless char. He banked away and released them, hurling the burnt corpses into the cliff crags, his triumphant roar shaking the mountainside.

"The next one!" Anna thundered.

War lust blossomed hot in their minds, and Dagger was already rolling, already diving, his agility extraordinary, plummeting back the way they'd come. But the Tevéss rider and his gold were there already, fearlessly coming straight at them, knowing they had three times Dagger's weight. The Tevéss battle banner snapped against the gold's scaled chest. The rider crouched in his war saddle, his form perfect, his war lance aimed flawlessly at Dagger's head. Dagger dove, cut high, rolled away to protect Anna, the enemy's lance hissing harmlessly beneath him, grazing his scales, no blood drawn and—*snap!*—Dagger talon-snatched the rider from his saddle. Clasps and buckles shattered and belts tore as Dagger yanked the rider off his mount, smashed him flat against the rocks, and leapt back into the sky, launching straight at the gold with a savage roar. The gold dragon arced, turned, and charged them head on, its own roar savage with grief and rage, golden wings wide, talons flexing with blood thirst.

"No, Dagger!" Anna cried. "Don't grapple!"

But it was too late.

The dragons collided with a roar, spun, fangs flashing ferociously, a flurry of wings and blinding sun, Dagger weaving and snapping as agile as a knife fighter, Anna holding herself tight to his neck with all her strength.

But the power of the gold's weight and training was immediately evident. It lashed its tail around Dagger's, furled its wings, and jerked them downwards to the hungry rocks, heedless of its own life, knowing only that its rider was dead and that its enemy lived. Dagger sunk his teeth into the gold's throat—once, twice, clamping down, thrashing his head back and forth—but the move was a desperate one, without skill and to no effect. Still they dropped, plummeting now, Dagger trying to detach but to no avail, the gold's talons sunk into Dagger's tail, blood spraying, the gold's strength unbreakable, the dragons' wings colliding and battering against each other, their roars savage and final, whipping past the trees of the mountainside. Anna's back smashed against an outlying tree trunk, crushing her chest into Dagger's neck. The gold peered over Dagger's shoulder, drawing in its own breath, preparing to burn them both alive as they fell. Then Dagger went limp and lifeless, as though he'd been shot through the skull. His neck bent back toward Anna, his throat naked and exposed.

"No!" Anna cried uncomprehendingly.

The gold roared triumph, unfurled his wings, took a

massive breath, its lungs and bladders near bursting with deadly heat.

But Dagger's collapse had been a feint.

His head flashed up at exactly the right moment, faster than a striking snake, jaws wide, biting into the enemy's mouth as it dropped, snapping the gold's jaws shut with incredible force. Molten dragon fire spewed sideways through its eyes and the corners of its mouth, melting skull and scale, its grip slacking immediately. Dagger pulled up, hard and away, barely clearing the ground, as the Tevéss war dragon plowed into the rocks, its head a smoking ruin.

"We need that banner!" Anna shouted. She turned her grips hard into Dagger's neck, doing the same with her knees.

Dagger turned smoothly and landed next to the gold's broken body. Anna unclipped, leapt from her saddle, and unhooked the maroon Tevéss battle standard from the gold dragon's chest.

It was torn, bloody, and burned.

But it was enough.

It was open war. And now she had the proof in her hands.

They launched for Voidbane.

38

THEY REACHED HIS lodge without further incident, but when they landed, the big dragon wasn't breathing.

Anna unclipped from her saddle, ran, and knelt in the straw at Voidbane's side. She placed both her hands against the scales of his massive jaw. They were cold. Dagger approached, too, nudging the massive dragon's black snout with his own.

Voidbane gave a long, trembling shudder.

"Thank the Sisters!" Anna cried and reached inside her breastplate.

But it was damp there. The paper in which she'd wrapped the vial was moist.

Crushed.

The crystal vial had broken in the fight.

"No! *Ah!*" She pulled her hand from inside her armor. A splinter of jagged crystal stuck in her fingertip. Blood welled around it. The red seemed to crawl up the side of the shard.

At the stable's eastern window, a large crow landed with a ruffle of black feathers. It peered into the stable, black eyes glittering.

Anna pulled the splinter from her finger and smeared the residue of Master Borónd's silvery cordial against Voidbane's snout. Where she touched him, the dead, greyish scales went glossy black almost immediately. The big dragon opened his massive jaws, his pale tongue touching at the spot where she'd applied the cordial's balm, searching for it, knowing, somehow, that it could save him.

Moondagger whined.

But there wasn't enough.

Whatever ancient magics the vial had contained, whatever timeless lore had been spun into the silvery liquid, more was required.

"Great Sisters, no!" Anna cried. She reached into her damp undergear, smeared the faint wetness she found there on Voidbane's pale scales and lips. Again, the scales went black. But it wasn't enough. It just wasn't enough.

Voidbane's side shuddered, and he groaned. The sound was impossibly huge but still so weak.

It was the sound of death.

And then something opened in her mind and Anna heard Voidbane's bellowing rage shake the mountains the moment

Father had been hit, the dragon's sorrow and fury shuddering everything within her. Voidbane knew what she'd known then. He'd *felt* what she'd felt. Father was dead. *My rider is dead.* She'd screamed with the big dragon until her voice was raw, screaming, knowing she was failing her duty, not caring, reloading her carbine—*Maybe the wound isn't mortal? Maybe we can get him back?*—firing at any enemy she saw, screaming at Voidbane over and over, "Get him home! Get him home!" The blood, the gouts of blood running and streaming along Father's armor, coursing dark rivulets from the black hole in his chest. The big dragon turning desperately, slow in his bulk, trying as hard as he could for speed. But it wasn't enough. Not enough.

She shook her head. Voidbane's massive eyes peeled open, as if seeking her out. Once burning orange, his eyes were a cloudy, pale pink, like the milky eyes of a feeble old man, pupils glazed and unseeing. The big dragon shuddered. His great side shook.

"No," Anna mumbled, cast around, looking—for what?

She didn't know. There was nothing she could do. And her head was spinning. The old, black rage was there, and there was nothing she could do to stop it. In her mind's eye, she saw the lance hit Father's side. The spray of blood from his mouth.

He's supposed to live forever.

And then the fury was *everywhere*, spinning through her entire self. The unspeakable anger. Maniacal, driven, and ravenous. A hissing worm of black acid scalding her mind— *becoming* her. The crow cawed.

Moondagger nudged Voidbane's snout, trying to wake him, the little dragon's efforts becoming more and more determined. Voidbane's eyes seemed to refocus for a moment. He cocked his massive head, just slightly, toward Moondagger. Dagger pushed his snout against Voidbane's cheek, hard, mashing his scales against those of his sire's, cooing and growling, trying to revive him. Voidbane's side hitched and he tried to breathe, but something stopped him, and he went suddenly still, his mouth half open. His eyelid sagged, his pupil rolled, its glow fading, fading . . . gone. Over a hundred years old, the best dragon on Dávanor, Father's mount, lost in an instant.

It could not be.

Dagger rammed his head against Voidbane's head. Again. Then again and again, trying to rouse him, cooing plaintively, growling, butting his head against the massive black jaw, casting around, silvery eyes wide, white tail thrashing the straw. He hit Voidbane's jaw again and again with his head, a strange whine coming from his throat. Again and again.

Anna stared. Swallowed. Tried to breathe. It was hard. She reached out and put her hand on Dagger's side. That felt better, but it was still difficult. She was having a hard time swallowing. Dagger rammed his head against Voidbane's jaw, harder and harder and *harder*, trying to wake him. Anna blinked. Tried to swallow, the tears threatening to come, but she bit her tongue and held them back, touched her own head against the cold wall of scales, Voidbane's cheek.

"No," she growled at herself. "No. Think, curse you. Push and *think*!"

Then Dagger roared, long and deep. She turned, wrapped her arms around her dragon's neck, and took a deep breath. Then another. Managed to swallow. Shook her head. Took another breath.

Push it back.

She ran to the far side of the lodge, where Voidbane's flight and feeding records were kept. There, she folded down the small desk from the wall, ripped a shred of blank paper from the back of Voidbane's log, and opened the ink pot in its wooden holder. With a poorly-trimmed quill, she wrote the following:

To Lord Bellános Dallanar, Duke of Kon and High King of Remain —
Dávanor is now besieged from within by Murderous Traitors
bent upon the Complete Ruin of our High House. We call,
most urgently, for your Arms and Aid. Loyal Soldiers and very
Good Dragons die here for Your Sake, their Sworn Oaths upheld
in accordance with our good High Laws. In the Great Sisters'
names — help us.

Anna Dyer, Dragon Squire
House Dradón

She took the high silver tube from the inner pocket of her breastplate, the one that she'd found on the dead messenger dragon. She rolled the letter, slid it inside, then tucked the tube back in her pocket. She knew that Master Khondus would have his own message and his own plan to get word to Kon.

"But Master Khondus could be dead," she said suddenly.

She looked at Voidbane.

She had to admit that.

Moondagger whined.

They could *all* be dead. Anna shut her eyes.

Dagger hissed and whined.

"Listen to me," she said, eyes still shut.

Dagger went quiet.

She opened her eyes, looked at him. "I swear to you, on your life and mine, we *will* have justice here. And *we* will bring it."

The crow cawed, even louder. Anna looked at it, reached for her pistol, then stopped herself.

She had more urgent targets.

The crow seemed to sense her intent and leapt away with a lonely caw.

Then, somewhere far below in the High Keep, a single gunshot rang out.

Dagger's head jerked up.

Another gunshot. A distant report.

Dagger growled. Anna cocked her head.

Another shot. Very distant. But unmistakable.

Gunfire.

In the High Keep.

Two more shots, widely spaced. Then a short volley, a spattering.

Then a distant battle cry and a long flurry of gunfire.

A deep explosion. Cannon.

Then a long, high cry followed by an eruption of gunfire and the crash of metal on metal.

It was happening.

39

SHE RAN TO the stable's flight door and looked out. From her vantage, she couldn't see down into the High Square, but the crashing din of all-out battle was unmistakable. Above the Square, at least two squads of dragons circled, the maroon battle standards of House Tevéss fluttering against their chests. Anna counted. Two heavyweights—a big red and a huge purple—at least six middleweights—all blues and greens—and more than ten lightweights of various colors. High above the combat, Captain Corónd soared on his bronze, a long maroon pennant streaming from the top of his war saddle. A young signal hand rode behind him, flashing coded flags from his perch. A red flag flashed twice and the two heavyweights swung into the High Square, dragon fire spraying from their mouths, shrieks of horror and pain rising like a hellish storm.

Anna frowned. Whatever the tactical situation inside the Square, with no air support, House Dradón had no chance.

It'll be an all-out slaughter.

Moondagger nudged her, his eyes wide.

"I know," she murmured, looking skyward.

They might be able to get up there, to engage Corónd and his bronze, but even if they could kill him—which she doubted—what then? Fight two dozen enemy dragons?

A flight of middleweight silvers blasted over Voidbane's lodge, over her head, House Dradón banners streaming blue from their tackle. The lead rider sounded his battle horn, the note high and clear. The Tevéss dragons answered, turning to meet the threat. But the Dradón riders didn't engage. Rather, they swooped in, banked, fired a carbine volley into the Tevéss formation, knocked a middleweight green from the sky, and arced away from the Square, diving over the

Keep's southern fortifications. Coród didn't take the bait. Instead, he signaled another strafing run to the Tevéss heavyweights. The big dragons executed the maneuver to horrible effect, the nightmare screams rising again. But then the House Dradon middleweights were back, silver flashing in the sun, skirting the enemy formation, firing with perfect coordination, this time targeting the massive purple. Their marksmanship was deadly, and Anna saw the purple's rider sag in his saddle while another half dozen rounds found their marks in the heavyweight's side and neck. The giant beast angled off and sagged in the air. Its right wing smashed into the Square's bell tower, and it spiraled out of control, crashing head first into the far colonnade. The Dradón middleweights dodged away, gone again over the southern fortifications. This time, however, it was too much for Coród. A flurry of flag signals from his bronze and three Tevéss middleweights and five of the Tevéss lightweights broke formation and launched after the Dradón flight, knifing over the southern wall. The moment they did so, a thunderous barrage of cannon fire roared and the flight of Dradón silvers was back, untouched, climbing directly for Coród. The Tevéss dragons dove to meet them and full aerial combat was joined.

Anna pulled out her telescope, pointed it at Corónd, then turned it to the lead Dradón rider.

"It's not Terreden," Anna said. She didn't know who the lead Dradón rider was. And it didn't matter. She leapt to her saddle, clipped on, and they launched for the High Square.

40

THEY LANDED A moment later on a rooftop near the Square's eastern edge and quickly hid behind a roofline. Carefully, she looked over the ridge.

Inside the High Square, a brutal melee raged around the High Gate. The Gate itself was a huge, pointed arch of high silver, five times the height of a man, seeming to rise from the foundations of the Square itself. Around the Gate, combat seethed, a smashing mass of blue and maroon uniforms. The elaborate pattern of the Square's flagstones was slick with ash and gore. Five House Dradón adepts, their blue robes stained with blood, lay dead around the Gate, surrounded by four grim squads of Tevéss heavy infantry. One side of the Square was a blackened carnage of burnt bodies, stone and flesh melted and smoldering.

Anna didn't see any of House Tevéss's adepts. That meant that the High Gate might still be open. It might still be theirs. For the moment——.

A shout and a roar and there was Master Khondus on the far side of the Square, his hammer swinging. Blood flowed from two bullet wounds in his back. Master Zar was at his side, his face a purple mask of rage, using a strange flame weapon against the enemy, blasting the Tevéss ranks with ropey gouts of silvery fire. Jenifer Fyr, Captain of Lady Abigail's High Guard, was there, too, twin revolvers blazing, Dradón guardsmen rallying around her with grim determination. Master Khondus, Zar, Fyr and their men were pushing hard toward the High Gate. But they still had to cross more than half the Square. Anna touched the silver message tube she'd placed in her armor's pocket. The note that she'd written might not be the most well-written message that the High King had ever received, but it might be all they had.

Then, in the corner of her eye, Anna saw little Gregory.

The old messenger dragon was crawling across the flagstones, making his way toward the High Gate, pulling himself over bodies and through the combat. He still wore his leather carrier harness and it looked like his message tube was intact—but his left wing had been broken, a splintered tube of bloody bone spiking at the sky. His right leg was gone too, crushed to a pulp of blood and faded blue scale. The end of his tail had been hacked off. But he was still moving, still trying, crawling toward the Gate with a slow, wobbling little crawl. His little neck strained forward. His old milky eyes were wide. His mouth was open, his tongue hung past his one, yellow tooth. A trail of blood smeared the flagstones in his wake.

A thunderous explosion and the eastern wall of the Square erupted in an inferno of silvery flames. A cascade of rubble fell inwards and a heavily armored formation of Tevéss soldiers charged into the Square, maroon banners streaming above them.

There were at least a hundred of them.

"Tevéss!" they roared as they charged into the plaza. "Lord Gideon!" They crashed into the blue forces of House Dradón that barely managed to turn to meet the new threat.

Behind the charging Tevéss warriors, in the dark of the walls' breach, Anna saw the massive, silvery maw of an ancient great cannon withdraw into the shadows, its huge bore shaped as a snake's mouth, vile fangs stretching 'round the smoking hole. Another Tevéss squad came through, a dozen big men. This squad was different from the others. They wore ancient plate mail of black iron and carried huge, iron-bound shields. There was something at the squad's center. A flash of deeper maroon. Anna looked closer. A group of five young women, hooded in burgundy robes. The centers of their foreheads were marked by silver Dallanar Suns. Around their necks, they wore silver amulets representing the five tokens of the Great Sisters: the tear, the sword, the book, the scales, and the cornucopia.

They were Lord Gideon's adepts. Tevéss meant to take the High Gate now, this moment. Dagger growled, his claws scraping stone.

"For Dradón! For Dávanor!" Master Khondus roared, recognizing the danger.

"For the Remain!" Master Zar bellowed. "For Lady Abigail!"

Captain Fyr screamed for blood, and her guardsmen attacked with fury. The men of House Dradón roared and pushed back hard against the Tevéss reinforcements. Master Khondus drew his pistol and fired twice at the sister adepts—but they were too well-protected, his bullets glancing off the heavy armor of their guardians, the ancient mail sparking with deflected force. Master Zar unloaded again with his strange flame weapon, its weird, silvery fire splashing and sizzling over the front line of the Tevéss soldiers, screams of horror and pain flooding their ranks. Then Master Khondus bellowed and launched himself full force into the center of the enemy's line, swinging his hammer in huge, bloody arcs, crushing limbs, bodies, and skulls, his pistol held in his off-hand, waiting for a target. The Tevéss front parted like a wave before him, and House Dradón rallied behind, the roar of battle rising.

But they couldn't hold, Anna realized.

Even with Master Khondus's ferocious charge, even with the dreadful damage caused by Master Zar's bizarre weapon, the blue livery of House Dradón was being slowly squeezed between the maroon Tevéss forces already in the High Square and their reinforcements from the breached wall. Five Dradón messenger dragons banked hard, dropping toward the Gate, the pointed arch glowing silvery-white at their approach—but a roar of perfectly coordinated Tevéss gunfire blasted them to smoking pieces, the remains of the dragons' small bodies tumbling and cartwheeling across the flagstones.

Little Gregory was only about ten paces from the High Gate now. He was stopping to rest more often than he moved. His broken left wing pointed at a freakish angle into the air. And when he did move, Anna noticed, he moved much more slowly. His blue scales, already pale, had taken on an unhealthy, whitish tint.

The little dragon was bleeding to death, Anna realized.

He wouldn't make it.

A few House Dradón squads still struggled near the Gate, but the battle's focus had wholly shifted toward the breach in the eastern wall.

And the tide was already turning.

Master Khondus, Master Zar, Captain Fyr, and her men were being slowly pushed back by the Tevéss advance, step by hard-fought step back toward the High Gate.

When the House Tevéss adepts reached the Square's center, they would take the Gate. When that happened there would be no way to send word to anyone, no way to communicate with the rest of the Realm. No one to send them aid.

Anna pulled the Tevéss war banner from her saddle bag, swung off Dagger's back, and clipped the banner's brass rondels to her rig's flag hooks so that the maroon standard hung across Dagger's neck and chest. She tugged it twice to make sure it was secure, then remounted and clipped on.

"Go!" she cried and Dagger launched, knifing hard along the western side of the Square, the maroon banner cracking and snapping, walls blurring beneath them, white wings taut and fast.

They landed right behind little Gregory with a crunch of stone and claw. Two squads of Tevéss infantrymen turned as one, perfectly disciplined, leveled their weapons at them, but did not fire.

"You idiots!" Anna sneered, doing her best to mimic their western accent. She pointed at Gregory disdainfully. Automatically, the Tevéss soldiers followed her extended finger. She unhooked and jumped from her saddle, pulling her goggles off her face to glare at them. "This worm has been making its way through our dead for the last ten moments and none of you fools have the presence of mind to crush its skull and take its communication? Great Sisters curse you fools! Who is in 'command' here?"

A huge, blond sergeant, wearing a thick, maroon headband instead of a helmet, saluted her somewhat skeptically and nodded. "I am." His eyes were pale grey. He searched her uniform for some rank, some sign of authority. His western accent was very thick.

"What is your name?" she demanded. A bullet buzzed past her ear. She didn't bat an eye.

"Lodáz," he replied. His pale grey eyes searched her face.

Anna nodded, bent, and picked up little Gregory as gently as she could without betraying that she cared. His body was barely warm. His head drooped as she lifted him from the flagstones.

"Lord Gideon wants the messages these dragons carry." She lifted Gregory slightly, showing them the message tube tucked into the leather cache at the little dragon's chest. "You were told to control that Gate and to *intercept* all missives. What do you fools think this fight is all about?" She lifted her chin at the carnage around them, pushing the western accent as hard as she could to get it right. "If you blast all their messengers to shreds, we will have to waste our time searching the mess for the intelligence Lord Gideon demands. What do you have net guns for? Think, man, *think!*"

The big sergeant looked at her uncertainly.

In her arms, little Gregory trembled and gave a faint squeak.

The sergeant began, "We were told——."

"*Now!*" Anna cried, hurling herself sideways, her arms shielding Gregory's shattered body as she rolled behind an armored corpse.

Moondagger was ready. He blasted the enemy's center—neck stretched forward, eyes clamped shut, silver-white fury roaring from his mouth—and the Tevéss line melted. Several soldiers tried to roll away, but Dagger tracked them, burning them to slag, hissing blood and metal spattering the flagstones. Some preternatural instinct shrieked in Anna's mind. She jerked her head back. A crossbow bolt hissed past her eyes. A Tevéss crossbowman crouched there, ratcheting his weapon, not ten paces to her right. Hugging little Gregory to her chest, Anna drew her revolver, fired, and blew a hole in his throat. The man fell, and Anna turned to the Gate, holding little Gregory before her. A pair of roaring, lightweight dragons, blue and brown, crashed together into the Square's far colonnade locked in savage melee, flames hissing, claws and fangs streaming blood. Behind her, a horrible scream as someone died. She kept moving. The big Tevéss sergeant, Lodáz, had dropped flat in an attempt to evade Moondagger's fire, but he'd been too slow. She stepped over his fried body. As she did, the High Gate began to glow with silvery-white radiance. The Gate was responding to Gregory, of course— the primordial songs woven into the ancient message tube at his chest firing the Gate's timeless magics.

Anna ran forward. As she got closer, the huge arch burst to life with a surge of silent, silver flame. An intermixed roar of triumph and fury rose through the High Square. At her back, Dagger continued to cover her, to engage the enemy, his white snout bobbing and weaving, short jets of silver-white fire punctuating longer, roaring blasts, huge eyes wide, tail flashing like a white snake, whipping this way and that over the bloody cobblestones as he turned to face any threat. He had taken light fire—a black crossbow bolt protruded from his saddle, a trio of bullet holes marked his right wing, and there was a short cut running along his ribcage—but he was otherwise unharmed. Still, he looked tired.

"Hurry!" someone cried above the din. It sounded like Master Khondus. Then, louder: "Hold, lads! For all our sakes! *Hold*!"

On impulse, Anna took the message tube from her pocket and pushed it into position beside the one Gregory already carried. She placed Gregory on the ground, about a pace in front of the Gate. The air framed by the silver arch went hazy, filling with silvery mist. Careful not to touch either the Gate or the glimmering space that it framed, Anna scooched Gregory forward with her toe. The old dragon wobbled forward, his head and neck craning toward his goal. First his snout, then his eyes, then his whole head vanished into the silver sheen. Anna could just see the empty flagstones on the other side of the Gate's haze, where Gregory's head should have been. It was as if Gregory crawled into nothingness. His shattered wing vanished, then his smashed leg, then his lopped-off tail, and then he was gone entirely. The Gate's silvery mist thinned and dissipated.

A ragged roar of triumph went up, quickly lost amid the crash of combat. Anna sprinted to Moondagger, dodged a thrown spear, and emptied her revolver at a Tevéss rifleman who pointed his carbine at Dagger from behind a column. She pulled out the bolt sunk in Dagger's saddle, swung up, and latched on. She scanned the sky. Dradón and Tevéss dragons still battled, but the combat had devolved into a series of brutal duels, the dragons of House Dradón hopelessly outnumbered. She could see neither Captain Corónd nor his bronze. She looked to the High Square. Maroon everywhere, pushing hard against a thin blue line.

She could help.

Dagger growled, tired but ready for more action.

"Fly, Anna!" Master Khondus shouted hoarsely, waving his arm. "Fly!"

She couldn't see his face, but his voice was clear.

"Fly home! Tell your mother! The minor houses! You must bring aid —."

His arm dropped and vanished.

"Go!" Anna cried.

Dagger leapt to the air, cut hard to the left, then hard to the right, bullets hissing past them. The thrust of his wings was astonishing, and her heart skipped as they cannoned out of the Square, skimming the battlements, staying clear of the fighting dragons. The sound of battle quickly dropped away.

She looked over her shoulder.

The last thing she saw was a small, churning clump of blue fighting its way toward the Square's western door, surrounded by a dark maroon sea.

41

THEY RACED OVER the southern bluff, the High Keep's walls falling behind them, cliffs and mountainside dropping away as they cruised into the open air. Far below them, the green farms and forests of House Dradón spread far and wide, the horizon a huge, hazy arc where verdant land kissed the cloudless sky. Dagger flapped twice, the thrust of his shoulders good, but waning. Then he took a deep breath, held it, and stretched his wings wide, flight bladders swelling, riding the air like a silent falcon, the only noise the rush of their own wind. They glided past the southern-most watch tower. There should've been a pair of Dradón guardsmen stationed there. But the tower was empty and House Dradón's banner hung limp in the listless air.

42

It took them less than half a bell's time to reach her family's farm, and they arrived without incident.

The farmhouse itself was a wide, low-beamed building, roofed with silver-grey slate. It was fronted with a broad courtyard enclosed by a wall of dark stone. The court-yard proper linked the two barns on the eastern side of the compound to the workers' quarters on the west. An over-sized House Dradón banner, freshly laundered and pressed, hung from an iron pole fastened to the right of the court-yard's gate.

At the center of the courtyard, two farm hands were crossing the cobblestones. They wore clean work clothes and carried pitchforks. Anna knew them both by their gaits. Dagger banked hard, his shadow growing, then shrinking, as he dropped to the courtyard's center. He landed behind the hands with a muscly grunt.

"Ho there, rider!" the shorter of the two hands, Master Jon, shouted in surprise. Seeing the Tevéss war banner still fixed to Dagger's chest, he dropped immediately into a pike-man's stance, pitchfork held at the ready. He squinted up at

Anna, eyes narrow against the sun.

The taller of the two, Master Fredrik, laughed and slapped his buddy on the back, shielding his eyes. "Ha! Miss Anna! Good day!"

"Great Sisters!" Master Jon grinned. "Good morning, Miss Anna! Didn't recognize you, miss! Your mount wears a Tevéss war banner?"

"And see there!" Master Fredrick cried, pointing at the cut on Dagger's ribcage. "He's wounded!"

"Good day, gentlemen." Anna nodded quickly, tired. She unclipped, swung a leg over her saddle, and dropped to the cobblestones, her knees wobbling a bit. She clapped Dagger on the chest and pulled her goggles from her face. Dagger shook his head, growled, and spread his white wings wide, settling back on his haunches. His broad tongue tasted the farm's air. He was tired, too.

"Good to see you both." Anna nodded. "Time's short. Is Mother near?"

"Right here, dragon rider." A strong voice behind her.

Anna turned.

Mother stood in the front doorway, her face hidden by the

shadow of the door's gable. She was tall, broad-shouldered, and wore a simple, grey work dress under a leather apron. She was wiping her hands with a white towel, one hand then the other, cleaning each finger with a twisting motion. A steel cleaver and a wooden spoon were tucked neatly into the flat leather belt at her stomach. Anna's youngest sister, Wendi, who'd just turned five, stood halfway behind Mother's dress. She was looking out into the courtyard, her eyes alert and curious, taking it all in—especially Moondagger.

Anna went to them.

"That dragon can't see," Wendi said matter-of-factly.

Dagger's tail swiped at the cobblestones. He snorted and gave a huge yawn. His scales shone brilliant white in the sun.

"That's right," Anna said. "But we fly and fight just the same. Mother, something's happened. Let's go inside."

"How's that work?" Wendi asked.

"What's going on?" Mother asked, frowning. She looked from Dagger to Anna's armor and gear.

"He looks strong," Wendi said. "What's his name? I want to ride him. When can I ride him?"

"Moondagger," Anna said a little too sharply. "Not today."

She pulled off her gauntlets, folded them in half, and shoved them up into her bandolier. "I'm here under orders."

"Oh." Wendi nodded and bowed her head. "Orders. Sorry. I see. Moondagger. Sorry."

Anna shook her head. Why was she snapping at Wendi? The kid hadn't seen her in months. Anna picked Wendi up from the threshold and kissed the top of her head. Her hair was warm and clean and smelled like home.

Mother looked past Anna, assessing Dagger's wounds and the Tevéss war banner at his chest with a practiced eye. Her hair was dark, just a touch lighter than Anna's; she wore it in a tight, functional bun. Her mouth flattened to a grim line. Wendi giggled and leaned away as Anna kissed her, pushing at Anna's face with her tiny hands.

"Come inside, then." Mother nodded, smoothing a lock of hair behind her ear. "You have time for food?"

Anna nodded, setting Wendi on the ground. "I'll need something for my mount, too. Right away." She turned to Mother and hugged her.

"Gathered as much." Mother hugged her back, cleared her throat, and clapped her on the armored shoulders, pushing her back and turning into the house. "Come on——."

"What's this ugly-butt baby *dragon* doin' out here?!" Penelope shouted from the far side of the courtyard, jogging up behind Dagger, her smile enormous. "And who's this gangly-bones rider? Don't they know how to rig you people out up there? Jon, Fred? C'mon! You gonna stand by and let this white worm *poop* on your freshly cleaned yard? Great Sisters save us, lads! Where's your *pride*?!"

The farm hands smiled, but it was forced. They'd heard Mother's tone and they knew something was wrong. Penelope looked at them with a quizzical expression as she crossed the courtyard. She was twelve years old and tall for her age, almost as tall as Anna. She had Mother's hair, Mother's eyes, and Father's square chin. She wore a leather work apron over a long-sleeved work shirt, leather breeches, and a pair of shin-high boots. Her shirt's sleeves were stained bright blue with the family's signature dye. Her boots were toed with caps of black iron and caked with fresh merino dung. Her eyes flashed as she jogged across the cobblestones straight up to Moondagger—then stopped short.

"This dragon's wounded," she said, shooting a hard look at

Anna's gear and Mother's expression, taking everything in at once, her eyes flashing. "Jon, send for Master Kellen immediately. Move, man! Have him bring his full kit."

"Yes, Miss Penny." Master Jon bowed and immediately took off toward Master Kellen's study.

"What's happened?" Penny ran up to Anna.

"Come on." Anna turned into the farmhouse.

Mother patted Anna on her back as she passed and said over her shoulder, "Fred, send Dógun out to get a sheep and some fresh water for this mount. Then, bring some hot water and fresh linens here for Master Kellen. He'll tend this dragon where he stands. From what I gather, he won't be here long."

43

"PENNY, GET MY maps," Mother said when Anna had finished her story. Her voice was cool, but her eyes smoldered. "We'll adjourn to the library."

They were in the freehold's kitchen. Penny was looking at Anna, her face pale. Wendi was still wiping angrily at her eyes with her little hands; she'd cried when she'd heard about

Voidbane. Anna had eaten quickly as she'd told her tale, shoving it down as she spoke. As always, the kitchen was bustling with activity, a dozen young women going to and fro, working on the freehold's evening meal—and trying hard not to eavesdrop. Copper kettles, pots, pans, utensils, and rows of drying herbs hung from the ceiling. Four stone ovens lined the far wall, the centermost glowing with a low fire.

"This moment, ladies," Mother said.

The three sisters nodded, stood from the kitchen's work table, and walked from the kitchen, down the central hallway, toward the family library.

"Cass." Mother stopped one of the kitchen staff as they left. "Finish supper. Then tell everyone that we'll meet in the courtyard two bells before sunset. Every single man, woman, and child on this freehold. Clear?"

"Yes, ma'am!" Cass bowed, glanced at Anna's gear, and quickly moved to obey.

"Wait." Mother smoothed a lock of dark hair behind her ear. "I also want you to send Rocky with a message to Captain Fomór. Have him come this moment. And I want messenger dragons sent to every minor house within three days flight of the

Drádonhold. They're to send courier riders to us immediately."

"Yes, ma'am!" Cass bowed.

"Have Jon and Fred unlock the weapons. We're at war."

44

WITH THE EXCEPTION of the windows on the southern and eastern walls, the Dyer family library was set floor to ceiling with beautifully made bookshelves. The shelves themselves were packed with carefully ordered tomes, envelopes, files, and scroll cases. The organization of the collection was by subject, and Anna knew it well. Like all the Dyer children, a large portion of her early years had been spent right here with her first tutors. In the southern corner of the room, an ancient writing desk of Anorian oak sat before a pair of large windows that looked south into the courtyard. A brass globe, showing Dávanor's counties and geography, stood on the desk's corner beside a simple clay pot filled with pens and quills. A pair of large books bound in red leather rested at the desk's center, several pages marked with clean strips of white cotton. The library's eastern windows looked out over the orchards and the forests beyond. A well-polished reading table ran down the room's center.

"Penny, the maps," Mother said.

Penelope nodded, rolled a sliding ladder along the far wall, and scaled a set of shelves. Mother lifted Wendi onto a reading chair so that she could see the table top, lit a pair of brass safety lanterns, and set them on the table.

"Mother," Anna started, "Master Khondus said—."

"Quiet for a moment," Mother said. "Let me think."

Anna closed her mouth. Mother had fought in nearly as many battles as Father. Under her leadership, House Dradón's White Demons had become a legendary squad, renowned for their ferocity and cunning. Penelope came back carrying a leather tube. It was sealed with a bronze cap embossed with the Dallanar Sun, a six-pointed star with a single tear at its center. Mother removed the cap and handed it to Wendi. She took it and rubbed the convex impressions with her tiny finger. Mother thumbed through the maps and pulled forth a large sheet of rolled velum. She smoothed it flat across the desk, placed one lamp on each of its far corners, and hung another lamp on an iron hook suspended over the table.

"Master Khondus's initial plan is correct." Mother looked from the map to Anna. "Even with a message through to Bellános, House Dradón must strike. We must attack Lord Fel and we must attack *now*. We don't know what's happening in the High Keep, but it doesn't matter. If we kill Fel, his sons will tear each other to pieces. The oldest, Halek, is ill and of no consequence. But Malachi and Philip detest each other. Any confusion we can sow in the enemy's ranks is an advantage. Especially if our message made it through to Kon. We need to give Bellános the time he needs to come to our aid. If he sends Michael, this will be over before it's started."

"Who's Bellános?" Wendi asked, pronouncing each syllable of the name with special care, looking at the map.

"The High King," Penelope answered. "The true King of Remain. He wars now against his brother, Dorómy."

"Bellános will help us." Wendi nodded.

"Here's Jorgun Gorge." Mother traced her finger over the snaky canyon that slithered its way through the Green Mountains. "The best and fastest way through. Lord Oskor will come through here." She tapped the map with her fingernail.

"So said Master Boród." Anna nodded. "But the Tevéss Captain, Coród? He said Hengén Cleft. He must've been lying."

"To throw you off, in the hope that you'd pass that bad information to your superiors." Mother nodded. "Coród was always a vain, pompous fool. Regardless, the Cleft makes no sense. It's nearly five times the distance. Penny, pull my map of the Gorge out of there."

"Yes, ma'am," Penelope said.

"The real question," Mother mused, still looking at the map, "is *where*? Where in the Gorge can we hit him? We must strike from above, around midday, the sun above and behind us. That's clear. But is there a particular turn or a bend that we might use to our advantage? Hakon's Hook, of course. But it's obvious. It'll be watched and guarded, without doubt. But if not there, where?"

"Here you are, Mother." Penelope handed her a slightly smaller map. The map showed the topography of the Gorge in detail.

"Good. Help me spread this out. There we are. Now, attend."

She ticked her fingernail against the western mouth of the Gorge.

"For a foot soldier, passage through the Gorge is about a two week march—maybe three, if they're moving heavy arms and artillery. For dragons—alone and unencumbered—call it two or three days. When we'd go through, we'd always stop here or here," she pointed at two wide spots equidistant from the Gorge's middle. "Sometimes both, to rest the dragons. Those close quarters can be pretty hard on war mounts, especially at the western side of the Gorge here, lots of weird crooks and twists. And, if there's been good rain for the last couple years, like what we've had, then the cliff trees in here, and especially through here, will be completely overgrown. Some of these narrowest points will be completely choked off, all the way up to the tree line—in order to pass you'd need to either clear the thing out or actually climb your mounts straight over and through the thickest stands. A big dragon like Irondusk won't like that. If what Khondus said is true, if they've been planning this for some time, Fel probably logged the pass this last year—."

"What does that have to do with choosing a position?" Anna interrupted.

"It affects your cover. You won't just be able to hide in the deep of the cliff trees and drop on him from wherever you like."

"How can we know that it's been cleaned out?" Anna asked. "That's a huge project. How can we be sure—?"

Mother raised her hand. "Of course we don't know for sure. But that's not the point, is it? The point is to anticipate the possible tactical prescience of the enemy, to grant the enemy tacticians the respect that they deserve, and to craft and execute a proper battle plan based on what we know of the battlefield's topography and the enemy's mind. Lord Fel is a villain, without doubt. He's also cunning and extremely intelligent. His sons—especially Malachi—and most of his top advisors are equally skilled. Irondusk is not the kind of dragon to tolerate the starts and stops and delays and the unscheduled crawlings of an impassable forest. And he's too big to climb over the mountains proper. So if Lord Fel comes with Irondusk, if this attack has been in preparation for some time, then we can be virtually certain that Fel's engineers have cleared the Gorge of any obstructions that would waste Irondusk's energy. And that includes useful cover from which we can launch. Clear?"

"Yes, ma'am," Anna said, slightly embarrassed.

"Good." Mother looked her in the eye. "You need to be armed and out of here in one bell. Less, if possible." She turned back to the map. "We'll need a good spot, a spot that puts you south and east of him with a nice, high launch point, near a bend so you can mitigate their superior numbers a bit."

"What's 'mitigate?'" Wendi asked.

"It means 'make it smaller,'" Penelope said, staring at the map. Wendi nodded.

"Like I said," Mother continued, "Hakon's Hook would be a good spot, here." She pointed to a big switchback turn, near the eastern side of the Gorge. "Famous battle site. And it's closer to us, so you could get set up properly, maybe even by tomorrow morning, if your dragon can make it through the night. The downside, as I mentioned, is that everyone knows it. Fel's scouts and guards will be all over the place, here and here specifically, at the beginning and the end of the Hook, so you'll need to be crafty. Obviously, if one of his riders sees you, it's over. Stealth is everything. You'll need to hide well if you want your chance. That means we'll need to get you into position without being seen well in advance—*well* in advance. And you'll need to stay hidden until moments before you strike. One thing in our favor, though. Fel thinks that he's the one doing the surprising, right?"

Anna nodded.

"What're your thoughts for the engagement?"

"For—?" Anna began.

"For the attack itself." Mother looked up at her. "Do you have something specific in mind?"

"Well . . . ." Anna started.

She suddenly realized the full nature of what they were planning.

"Anna." Mother put her hand on top of hers. "It has to be you. There's nobody else. We don't keep war dragons out here. I can't ride Dagger; I'm too big. And there's no time to gather support from the minor houses, the closest of which is a day away. Fel comes. If we want to try for him—which we must—then it must be now, and it must be in the Gorge.

Anywhere in the open is suicide. From what you've told us, Moondagger is up for it. You've been training for this your whole life. Is it an ideal plan? No. But it has to be you. And it has to be now."

Anna looked at Dagger through the southern windows. He lay on his side, licking his chops while a farm hand cleaned up the gory remains of his dinner. Master Kellen sat on a short stool at Dagger's side, stitching up the cut on the dragon's ribs.

"I understand." Anna nodded.

"So what are your thoughts?"

"Well . . . his fire is strong."

"No." Mother shook her head. "Dragon fire in a near vertical dive? A dive high and fast enough to keep Fel's marksmen off you? Think about it. Half of Dagger's flame will end up in your face. And neither of you will be able to see, breathe, or fight, to say nothing of potential injury. You can't risk a carbine, either. You might get one or two shots off, but even if you hit him, he'll be well-armored and after your first shot his formation will close up and his scouts and lightweights will launch for you before you can attack again. Make no mistake, Anna: Fel has some *mean* lightweight squads. Every bit as fast as the White Demons, maybe even a bit tougher. If they get their claws into you, you and Dagger won't last half a moment."

Mother paused and gazed at the map.

"It has to be a lance." She nodded. "You drop from above, somewhere in here or here," she tapped the map, "angle into proper form, strike, done. More importantly, if you miss, Dagger might be able to snag him as you pass, drop him to the rocks. The Gorge is steep and narrow here. With Irondusk's wingspan, they'll be pretty high up, at least two hundred paces above the river bed. You unseat Lord Fel in Jorgun Gorge," she tapped her finger against the map, "he won't survive."

Mother looked at her. Her eyes were hard. Anna realized quite suddenly that this woman with whom she now spoke was not her Mother. Rather, she was Jessica Dyer, former Captain of House Dradón's White Demons, one of the most ruthless dragon knights of Dávanor. And she was ordering Anna into battle.

Anna cleared her throat. "Lance it is, then."

45

THEY LEFT THE library, walked back through the kitchen, and crossed the courtyard. Moondagger napped in the heat, enjoying the bright sun after his meal, warming himself on the hot flagstones. His eyes were shut. He barely seemed to notice them as they passed. It was nice, Anna realized, to see him like that for a moment. The calm before the storm.

The fastest way to the armory was through the dyeing barn. They crossed to it and entered by way of the small hatch nested in the barn's sliding door. When they were inside, the smell of the dye vats and the bustle of activity pushed a wave of nostalgia through Anna's mind. The place hustled with movement, two dozen workers stirring, straining, and working the vats, transforming the white wool cloth and yarn of the surrounding countryside into the sky blue of House Dradón. For Anna, the smell, the place, and the work always filled her with pride. While her clan had grown crops and merinos for generations, it was their ancient proficiency in that most perfect of colors that had made the family fortune.

They walked past the vats, wringers, and dye barrels, through the barn, out the back door, and toward the armory, which was set in a back room at the rear of the stable. The stable itself was a long, two-storied building made of dark stone, roofed with silver-grey slate, and fronted by a long feeding pen enclosed by a split rail fence. Anna knew that Mother still kept several dozen messenger dragons—Rocky being the oldest and the fattest—in addition to a dozen other lightweight mounts. Those dragons were for trade, transport, and travel, however. None were trained for war.

When they stepped into the stable, the sharp smell of straw and dragons filled Anna's nostrils. Mother grabbed an iron safety lantern off its hook, lit it from the lantern that Penelope carried, and walked toward the armory door at the stable's rear. Above them, the family's messenger dragons hung from their perches—a host of reds, blues, purples, yellows, oranges, and greens—a kaleidoscope of scales and hues, cooing and hissing and snapping, peering down at them with eyes every color of the rainbow, gleaming bright in the rafters' dark. The family's lightweight dragons were there, too, most of them sleeping in the golden straw, snoring fitfully, pink tongues lolling through fangs. Of course, had they been strangers, Anna knew they never would've been able to set foot inside the stable at all. Messenger dragons could be extremely dangerous in a swarm and, given a chance, could reduce an intruder to bone and entrails in half a moment. There was a reason that the armory was located in the stables.

Mother took an iron key ring from her apron, separated a silver key from the others, and unlocked the armory's latch. She slid the door open, well-oiled wheels running silent on their tracks.

"Get the lanterns, Penny," Mother said.

"Yes, ma'am." Penny turned, lit the lanterns on either side of the door, then walked deeper into the armory, lighting other lanterns as she went.

The Dyer clan's armory was part functional weapon house, part family shrine. Both of its functions would be served today. It was forty paces wide and twenty paces deep. Along the short wall to their right, five well-made cabinets carried knives, daggers, poniards, stilettos, falchions, bolas, nets, revolvers, and other small arms. The cabinets' wood and hardware shone with careful polish. On the other wall, to their left, a series of racks and brackets held swords, lances, pikes, carbines, and long rifles running horizontally across the wall, a pattern of well-maintained battle gear.

Directly across from the doorway through which they'd entered, evenly spaced along the armory's long wall, eleven suits of family armor waited in silent vigil. Father's armor stood at their exact center, mounted on a wooden stand placed on axis with the door. A scarred House Dradón battle banner, its blue cloth burned and torn, was draped over its right side, as if the armor wore the flag as a cloak. There was a hole punched through the left side of the armor's chest. The armor hadn't been cleaned after Father had been removed from it. Mother hadn't allowed it. Instead, the ash and dried blood that caked the gear had become a permanent part of the display, a sacred relic.

Directly behind Father's armor hung a large, elaborate tapestry of Eulorian silk. In some ways, the tapestry was the most important object in the armory. It was hundreds of years old and its imagery was always acknowledged before battle with sacred words that went back to the first centuries of the Kingdom's Founding.

At the center of the tapestry, there was a large Dallanar Sun. It was a stylized, silver star with six radiating points and a single inverted tear at its center. It was the High Seal, Acasius's Star, the Dallanar family sigil, the imperial crest to which House Dradón and House Dyer had sworn allegiance since time immemorial.

At the end of each of the Sun's points, woven into the tapestry, there was a large tondo. At the center of each tondo was a life-sized portrait bust. It was to these portraits that the sacred words were always spoken.

The tondo at the top of the Sun was the largest of the six and held a portrait of the Remain's First King, Acasius Dallanar. As always, he was shown full-faced, pensive, and brooding, his eyes downcast and prophetic. He held his token—a silver chalice—in a disembodied hand at his proper right. The next tondo, below and to Acasius's right, held a portrait of the First Great Sister, Erressa the Lost. Her eyes were dark, beautiful, and wise. Her delicate face was shown in perfect profile as she gazed away from the sigil's center into her token at her right—a silver tear. The Second Great Sister, Alea the True, was next. Alea's was a cheerless face, her portrait set at three-quarter profile so you could see the famous scar on her left cheek. Her deep, blue eyes looked sadly to her proper right where her token—a silver sword—filled the rest of her tondo. Aaryn the Chronicler, the Third Great Sister, was at the bottom of the crest. She was shown full-faced, like her brother Acasius above her, and her eyes were filled with mischievous joy. She held her token—a silver book—in a disembodied hand, and she seemed to be reciting from it, her mouth just slightly open. Next came the Fourth Great Sister, Kora the Just. Her face was shown in three-quarter profile. Her features were narrow and sharply boned, but her eyes were soft and kind. With a floating hand, she held her token—a set of silver scales—shown in perfect equilibrium, as if held thus by her gaze. Finally, coming full circle to Acasius's left, was the Fifth Sister, Margo the Gentle. She was a happy, round-faced girl with shining eyes and a gentle, dimpled smile. She was shown in perfect profile, her token beside her face—a silver cornucopia. Her eyes glittered with hidden satisfaction and, perhaps, some secret sorrow.

Anna stopped with Mother and Wendi in front of Father's armor as Penelope finished lighting the room. When Penny was done, she joined them and placed her lantern below Father's destroyed breastplate. The lantern's glow hit the armor's intricate chasing, the steel spirals and arcs flickering delicate patterns across the armory's walls and ceiling. The black hole punched through the armor's left breast seemed to yawn larger than ever.

If I reached down into it, Anna thought, *I would reach into nothing, and its steel teeth would close on my shoulder and bite . . . .*

Mother stepped up, placed her hand on the breastplate, right above the hole. She bowed her head, closed her eyes, and whispered the ancient words.

"Great Sisters, exemplars of history and time, let us look to our past's best as we forge our future. Let us learn from our mistakes, let us honor our families and our lands, and let us do what is right—always. Great Sister Erressa, patron of quests, grant us the will to begin this war with determination and resolve. Great Sister Alea, patron of swords, grant us the strength to make this war with ferocity and zeal. Great Sister Aaryn, patron of wisdom, grant us the knowledge to wage this war with foresight and reason. Great Sister Kora, patron of justice, grant us the courage to win this war with principle and honor. Great Sister Margo, patron of plenty, grant us the grace to end this war with speed—and to foster a lasting peace."

Mother stepped away from the armor. She looked into the empty helmet.

"A soldier never betrays her word," she whispered.

"A soldier never forgets her promises," Anna, Penelope, and Wendi answered together.

Mother turned and looked at Anna. "I'll make a space beside him." She gestured to Father's armor. "But I don't want to fill it, you understand me?"

"Yes, ma'am," Anna answered.

"Execute your orders and come straight back here. Not to the Keep, not to Khondus, not to Zar. Nowhere else. Home. Straight home. Clear?"

Anna nodded.

46

MOTHER PICKED A light lance from the wall rack and handed it to Anna. She tested its weight and balance. It was about three paces long, noticeably shorter than the medium or heavy lances on the wall, but much easier to use. The steel vamplate, which would cover and protect her hand, was shaped as a dragon mouth, the lance proper extending between its open fangs.

"How's that feel?" Mother asked.

"Good." Anna nodded. She tucked the lance under her right arm, her hand and side firmly fitted behind the lance's swelling, and crouched as if on dragon back. "Maybe a little heavy at the back."

"When we fit the point, that'll even out. We can always add a counterweight. Can you use it?"

Anna nodded.

"Good," Mother said. "Your saddle isn't set for combat, but that doesn't matter. We don't have a war saddle that'd fit Dagger anyway. When he's bigger, you can come back and use some of Voidbane's early rigs as he grows. He'll fill them out. He has his father's form. But for now, you're stuck with a scout rig. I don't think that'll make much of a difference with the kind of maneuver that we're planning. This is no tournament, and you won't have to aim for long, just enough for you to execute your orders. No need for a specialty harness, either." She paused. "The moment you dismount Fel, drop everything and fly like the wind."

"Yes, ma'am."

"Let's find a proper lance point."

They walked together to the right-hand wall. Penelope and Wendi had gone quiet. Mother unlocked and opened a long, sliding drawer. Two dozen steel lance points, each carefully polished and laid out on a pad of sky blue velvet, rested inside. Most were standard war points—sharp, long, and variously decorated with geometric, plant, or animal motifs. Several were tournament tips, shaped like fists, maces, or flattened rams' heads.

"Only a couple here made for a light lance, I'm afraid. Here on this side. Which strikes you?"

Anna looked at the half dozen smaller points to which Mother gestured. The head of each was about three palms long, their sockets about the same length, wickedly sharpened.

"I can't see," Wendi said, standing on her toes in front of the drawer, nose between her finger tips. Penelope picked her up and slung her on her hip. Wendi looked into the drawer.

"What's the difference?" Wendi asked.

"No real difference," Mother said. "Just tradition. A rider always chooses her gear. She's especially careful about this piece. If all goes well, it's the only thing she'll leave behind."

Anna took a point from the felt, hefted its balance. It was three and a half palms long, razor keen, with a point sharper than a dragon's fang. Simple, clean steel with no ornament.

"This one." She nodded.

"That was his." Mother cleared her throat. "When he was a squire."

47

THEY WALKED OUT into the courtyard's sun together. Anna held the lance at her side along with a leather satchel of food and supplies. Everyone was quiet. When they approached Moondagger, he yawned and stretched like a cat, flaring his white wings, his huge eyes wide. He looked a little tender but otherwise seemed fine.

Mother handed Anna a short map tube that contained the detailed chart of Jorgun Gorge.

"Pick your spot well. And when you strike, strike without fear."

Anna nodded and turned to Moondagger, but Mother stopped her and turned her around, holding her shoulders.

"When you launch, Anna, you must be *fearless*. Crazy fearless. Your commitment must be absolute. No doubts, no worry, no fear. His gear is the best in the Realm. But it will make no difference. He rides a giant monster. But it will make no difference. He's protected by a hundred riders. But it will make no difference. All that matters is this." She put her palm on Anna's armor, over her heart. "There are things that are more important than life. There is honor, there is love, and there is family. When you strike, strike *hard*—and strike for us."

Penelope and Wendi were on either side of her, their hands on her armor. Mother cleared her throat, clapped her brusquely on the shoulder pads, and stepped back.

"Truth and honor, Anna Dyer." Mother crossed her chest with her fist.

"Truth and honor," Penelope and Wendi said together. Wendi's tiny fist was so small. She blinked in the sun, looking up into Anna's face. Anna placed her fist on her chest. Then she turned away, sheathed her lance, mounted, and settled into her saddle. Dagger growled, strong beneath her. Tired but eager to fly. She patted his neck, clipped on, and took a deep breath.

She turned and saw them from dragon back, their fists still across their hearts. She looked at each of their faces for a moment. Then she saluted one last time and launched with a grunt and a gust of wind.

She was already over the courtyard's wall when she heard a tiny, high cry.

It was Wendi.

"Win, Anna!" Her little voice rang out, clear and real and true. "Win!"

48

THEY FLEW FOR the rest of the afternoon, well into the evening, staying away from the roads, the riverways, and the villages, taking particular care to avoid common roosts and look-outs. Anna was sore, and Dagger was tired, but she knew they had to put some time between themselves and the Drádonhold. If House Tevéss controlled it now—and she had to assume that they did—then Lord Gideon would begin regular patrols almost immediately.

Ahead, the Green Mountains loomed, a line of craggy peaks covered by rich forests, the mountaintops finally free of winter's snow. Below her, the farms and freeholds of the Drádonhold passed in silence, becoming even more scattered as she left the immediate vicinity of the High Keep, the cultivated lands finally giving way to lush, unbroken forests. Jorgun Gorge lay just under a day's ride distant. She could make its mouth by midnight and Hakon's Hook by morning, if she so wished and they flew through the night. But they'd arrive exhausted. And she didn't know what they'd encounter. Or when they'd attack.

"Let's get some rest," she said.

A shred of cloud raced beneath them and the smoke from the chimney of a tidy, isolated farm beckoned. When she landed, her gear and manner commanded immediate obedience from the farmer, his wife, and their children. She paid for lodging, food, water, and a fat merino for Dagger. Sated, they crawled into the farmer's well-made barn. There, she removed her saddle, rubbed Dagger down thoroughly, and curled up with him in the straw. She slept, snuggled against his warm chest. You couldn't tell where dragon ended and girl began. They did not dream.

49

THE NEXT DAY started well enough. She breakfasted with the farmer and his family, fed Moondagger, and saddled him, noting that he'd probably outgrow his current gear in a matter of days.

"Getting big." She patted his muscly side.

Dagger grunted.

She mounted up, clipped on, and launched for the mountains.

50

IT TOOK THEM six bells to reach the mouth of Jorgun Gorge. They didn't rush. There was a small village at its front, right where the mountains opened and descended into the gentle foothills, but Anna avoided it, opting instead to fly over and around the far mountainside, to the north. She'd take a long break there for their lunch and then push over the mountains' peaks, into the ridges and plateaus to the north of the Gorge by late afternoon. By this approach, they'd reach Hakon's Hook in the early evening with good elevation and from an unsuspected direction. If she saw the enemy, she could flee and find another site from which to attack. If she didn't, then she'd cross back across the Gorge, pick her launch point, and hide. The route would take a bit more time, but it would be safer, and it would be worth it.

51

SUNSET. THEY'D CLIMBED over the mountains without incident and now glided above the forested ridges due north of the Gorge, above Hakon's Hook. The sky was mostly clear, deepening to lavender in the west, the sun low on the horizon, its bloody light painting the trees and mountain rock deeper shades of red.

Then—to her left, on the southern side of the Gorge, about a hundred paces distant—something caught her eye. She landed Dagger and pulled out her telescope, training it across the chasm.

It looked like . . . an *easel*.

Yes. It was an easel. Like for painting and drawing. It was set up on top of the ridge on the southern side of the Gorge. A large piece of white drawing paper waved from its clips. It was the white of the paper that had caught her eye.

But where is the artist?

Anna scanned the surround and the Gorge itself. Then she double checked with her telescope. Nobody. At least as far as she could see. She pulled Dagger back into the tree line and waited, on the alert. Half a bell's time passed. The artist did not return.

"Let's go take a look."

They launched, crossed the Gorge, and landed next to the easel. It was finely made of light-colored wood. The paper fixed to it was blank. A leather scroll case, dyed dark green and stamped with the two-headed golden dragon of House Fel, lay open on the ground beside it. There was some parchment rolled up inside.

Anna walked Dagger a few paces up the ridge to check its southern side, just to be safe. As she ascended, she saw that the ridge was really just a low crest of rock that dropped immediately away to the south onto a narrow, wooded plateau—and there were bodies there. Bodies everywhere. A giant pile of bodies. And dragons, too. The bodies wore the sky blue livery of House Dradón.

Dagger snorted and growled.

Directly below her, leaning against the ridge, Anna saw Captain Sara Terreden. She was dead. Two small bullet holes marred her back. Her dragon, a silver middle-weight named Lightdancer, lay beside her. There was a single bullet hole in the back of his skull. Bone and blood everywhere. Flies everywhere. The buzzing stench was horrific. She put her hand over her mouth and gagged at the stink. Sara's eyes were shut peacefully, her beautiful face painted red by the setting sun. Too many bodies. One heaped mass of bodies. Dragons, mostly lightweights, pale and bloodless, their eyes blank in death. Blood everywhere. Too much to see. Anna shook her head. She put her hand on Dagger's neck and shut her eyes. She didn't want to see anymore. But she must. She opened her eyes and tried to pay attention, saw the remains of some campfires scattered along the plateau. The smell was so bad. They must've camped here for the night. Before they started the "exercises" that Captain Corónd had described. There were a few Tevéss riders, too, she realized. But not many. It looked like someone had tried to burn the heap of bodies, but for some reason they hadn't been able to get the fire to take. A large crow sat on the pile's top. It wasn't eating. Rather, it stared at Anna, head cocked, black eyes glittering like crafty, black marbles.

And just like that, her old rage was back, as if it'd never left, drooling and hungry from the dark. But it was different this time. Dagger growled and jerked his head. *Murdered. Murdered as they slept.* It was cold. An icy knot in Anna's chest, as if her heart had clad itself in frozen iron. No hot anger, this. Instead, it was a ruthless, calculating rage. The rage of cold vengeance.

The crow cawed.

She backed Dagger off the ridge, unhooked, slid off, and walked to the easel. She stooped at it, pulling the sheaf of paper from the green leather tube. The first sketch was a drawing of Sara Terreden. It was well done. The fly that the artist had drawn on her cheek seemed to crawl on real, living flesh. Great attention had been paid to the graceful contour of her chin.

The crow cawed, louder.

The other drawings were the same. Carefully rendered drawings of the dead dragons and the dead riders of House Dradón. There were over a dozen of them, drawn from many positions and angles. Anna didn't examine them all but rather paged through them, letting the pages fall to the ground as she went.

The last one was different, however. It was a drawing of a living person: a sad young man. He was no older than twenty. Handsome. Clean shaven. His dark hair worn in a short, soldier's crop. His eyes were particularly striking. Dark, fixed, and extremely intelligent—the eyes of an aristocrat—but unhappy, as if the purpose of the drawing was to capture his regret. The angle of the portrait made it look like it had been drawn from a mirror. Directly beneath the image, there were two letters:

$$\mathcal{M.F.}$$

Anna looked at the green scroll case and the golden, double-headed dragon that adorned it. She knew that Lord Fel's second born son was named Malachi. She looked around, suddenly self-conscious of her position, pulled out her telescope, and scanned the mountains, the Gorge, and the horizon. Below her, on the pile of bodies, the crow cawed. Its head bobbed gallingly. It cawed again, mocking her. It began to peck wetly at the cheek of a dead Dradón rider, the ticking sound moist and repulsive.

Anna double checked her surroundings, stepped up the rocky crest, drew her revolver, and carefully aimed at the crow. As if sensing her intent, it leapt into the air. She fired once, clipped its right wing, but it was already at the far edge of the plateau and dropped away to safety.

Even a couple of steps closer to the bodies made the stench much worse, she realized; the light breeze blowing from the Gorge didn't help. She shook her head, put her hand over her mouth, and almost retched. The stench was overpowering.

But this could be the spot.

She slid down the ridge, hand over her mouth, and walked through the carnage. About twenty paces to the west, the ridge dropped away and the plateau opened sheer, directly onto the Gorge. Dagger followed her, stopping to sniff at Sara Terreden's face. He nudged her pale cheek with his snout.

Anna glanced over the plateau's edge. She was looking down into a sharp, forested bend of Hakon's Hook. And she was looking from the south.

The angle and position for attack couldn't be better. The mysterious artist had chosen his spot well.

If Fel came through the Gorge here, if he came four bells before or after noon, then the sun would be directly in his face. And if his column was of any length, then its front wouldn't be able to see its back. The position was several hundred paces above the Gorge's floor, screened by light woods and a low ridgeline. Better yet, she had the perfect camouflage within which she could hide from Lord Fel's scouts: a reeking pile of betrayal and death.

Anna nodded. It would work.

She walked back, climbed the low ridge, and hid the easel, the leather tube, and the drawings in the brush. Then she climbed back down, dragged a dozen riders' bodies closer to the plateau's edge so that she could lie with them and still see into the Gorge. Finally, she smeared herself with cold gore from a deep puddle of blood that had not yet dried. She retched at the smell, but she was getting used to it.

"Come here," she commanded. Dagger obeyed.

She wiped some blood on Dagger's face and neck, careful to avoid the stitched wound on his right side.

"Lie down." She pointed at the cliff edge. "Stay perfectly still."

From there they'd watch. From there they'd strike.

52

THEY WERE VISITED three times that evening by scouts from House Fel, but none of them stayed long. The corpse stench was too strong. Night came cool and cloudless, the stars soaring overhead in the black, the moon rising massive and silver to make its soundless way across the sky. Dagger sighed beside her, his silvery eyes wide in the moonlight, his white scales comforting and warm. But they did not sleep.

53

LATE MORNING OF the next day. A Fel scout squadron in dark green livery came in from the west and landed on the ridge line with a crunch of claw. Neither Anna nor Dagger moved, their eyes mere slits. The scouts looked around for a moment, hands and riding scarves over their mouths, their dragons hissing, then launched eastward, along the Gorge, checking every crag, corner, tree, and shadow. It was three bells after dawn.

Dagger growled.

Lord Fel comes.

No sooner had she had the thought than a vanguard appeared in the Gorge, gliding around the far bend of the Hook, some two dozen middleweights of various colors, dark green pennants streaming from spears and mounts.

They were well below her, far to her northwest, the sun in their faces. Carefully, she eased her telescope from her side to examine them more carefully.

Meticulous formation. Perfect gear. The dragons' motion clean, strong, and well-rested, the green of the Gorge lush around their glimmering war gear. A pair of lightweight reds flew at the very front of the vanguard. Their riders wore leather scouting gear and tackle. The majority of the column behind them wore full battle panoply. The sun gleamed off plate and helm. After the vanguard came three flights of mixed heavy and middleweights, at least forty drag-ons, green war banners streaming from their chests. Their riders' lances and carbines and helmets shone like mirrors. The column was like a floating river of men and dragons, bristling with spear and steel, soaring silently through the mountain pass.

And then the great Irondusk came around the bend.

Anna trained her telescope on him.

He was massive. Well over fifty paces long. His scales rust-red, like burning bronze, his wings casting a mighty shadow over the streambed below. At least a dozen lightweights flew beneath him, wary for any movement on the ground. On his huge back, Lord Oskor Fel sat in an elaborate commander's war saddle. His posture was perfect, his dark green livery fluttering in the wind. Three pennants of dark green streamed behind him, each marked by the golden, two-headed dragon of House Fel. His helmet was of high silver, a golden plume coursing from its top. A sword was sheathed before his saddle. Opposite the sword was a round shield of high silver. He wore a revolver slung beneath his left arm. An ancient, high silver carbine was scabbarded behind his shield, within easy reach. Directly behind him, on his saddle's signal deck, a pair of young signal hands flashed test flags to a flight of lightweights that followed in Irondusk's wake.

Anna lowered her telescope and shot a quick look at the surrounding peaks, crags, and trees.

No other sign of the enemy.

It is time.

Dagger hissed, his tail thrashing.

Moving carefully, she stowed her telescope and slid her lance from its scabbard. She took the point from its sheath in her saddle bag, kissed it, and screwed its socket down over the lance's end. It was razor sharp. She smoothly mounted Moondagger, clipped on, and patted his side.

Her hands were warm. She felt no fear. She pushed her forehead into the back of Dagger's neck, feeling the coiled muscle beneath his warm white scales. He grunted and arched his head against hers. She kissed him on the top of his head, and he growled impatiently.

Anna looked over the plateau's edge. Lord Fel was almost in position. She pulled her goggles down over her eyes.

And then he was exactly where she wanted him. It was happening so fast. But there was no time to think or question or doubt. It was this moment or never.

They launched.

54

SILENCE. THE TOTAL silence of the first moments of free fall.

Then the wind came as they gathered speed, hissing in her ears. Lance tucked tight to her side, snug in her saddle, feet locked firmly in her stirrups, her target below her, utterly unaware, Moondagger's power warm beneath her chest.

Time slowed.

Dagger's wings were furled to his sides, his form perfect as they dropped from the sun. Her lance was steady and weightless in her hands. Her breath was even. Her vision absolutely clear. No reaction from the enemy. None at all. It was as if the convoy flew in slow motion, the occasional flap of dragon wings slow, ponderous, and completely silent, the streaming green pennants frozen in time. She was halfway down the Gorge now.

And still they didn't see her.

55

MOONDAGGER SAW THEM dive, at last.

But he saw it as if he watched from outside himself, as if he watched at a great distance.

They were a spear of pure, silent energy, plummeting from the sun. A glowing meteor, white-hot, unstoppable, a silver star falling against the verdant green of the canyon's towering walls, united in purpose, strength, and will.

One mind. One being. One force.

Brilliant. Shining. Speed.

56

AT THAT MOMENT, Anna realized that they'd succeed.

It was done. And they would do it.

They were still dropping at Irondusk with unbelievable velocity. And still, there was no reaction from Lord Fel, from his dragon, or from the rest of his entourage. The wind cut Anna's face, hissing like a hurricane. Dagger's form was so clean, their position and angle against the sun so perfect, that none of the enemy riders could see them. And because of their speed, even those who might have noticed them at a distance were too far away to defend their master.

Mere moments now.

57

AND THEN, FROM somewhere deep inside him, Moondagger saw a fierce cry beginning to form, a tangible thing, a shimmering, silver shape of pure energy.

Hold it.

But no. It was wrong to hold it in. Wrong to hide it. Wrong to hold it back.

58

So she unleashed it, all of it. And the cry peeled from her throat and she was roaring.

No words.

Nothing that made sense.

The clean, primal shriek of a knife raptor falling on its prey.

Long and high and utterly pure.

And she was not alone.

Moondagger roared with her, his throat bellowing fury and justice and rage, their voices blending in a savage harmony as they plummeted toward death and triumph.

A warning horn sounded from somewhere, a low moaning through the canyon.

At last Lord Fel looked up. Saw them dropping toward him. Pulled at Irondusk's reins. Too late. They were too close. Irondusk veered slowly away from the green cliffs, toward the center of the chasm. Fel's eyes widened with certain knowledge.

"For the Kingdom!" Anna roared.

Her voice was huge. And in the strange slow time of her attack, she looked into Fel's eyes and saw in them a timeless acknowledgment as old as war itself.

"For the Remain!" she screamed at him.

Impact!

Her lance hit her target perfectly, on his breastplate, just to the left of center.

But it didn't penetrate.

Instead it slid away, tearing his dark green livery to reveal the shimmering shine of indestructible high silver.

No!

But they were already past him. Then Dagger hooked Fel with his rear claws—the force incredible, speed barely checked, clasps and buckles ripping, springing, blasting loose—the snap of bone, a grunt from the enemy as Dagger tore him from his saddle. Irondusk roared his rage. But the big dragon was too slow to do anything but roll his giant black eyes and watch his rider dangle behind the flashing knife of their passing, the white hot blade that had speared his master from the sun.

"Finish him!" Anna cried.

Already Lord Fel's weight was pulling them down.

Dagger banked hard against the Gorge's forested walls,

leaves and branches whipping past, bringing his snout skyward, against the flow of the enemy convoy.

Now!

Dagger released Lord Fel from his claws, rising immediately against the Gorge's wind.

A strange silence as the man arced into the sky, the fluttering gold plume of his helmet the only real movement, a small, golden bird against the immense green of the Gorge as he plummeted to his doom, a silent, bloody burst popping from his helmet as he smashed bonelessly to the river bed's hungry rocks.

"A thousand deaths to traitors!" Anna roared, her fist in the air.

She dropped her lance to the Gorge.

Dagger banked just as a pair of gunshots rang out.

Bullets whickered over her head.

They were racing below the convoy now, flying west back around the bend from which Fel had come, fast below the enemy. But now the Fel gunners had them in their sights, and they were wasting no time.

"Go!" Anna pushed her chest hard into Dagger's neck.

He leapt forward in the air, gaining speed with each thrust of wing.

Anna glanced over her shoulder.

The enemy convoy was wheeling now, turning as a unit, understanding, at last, the unusual nature of the attack, smaller scout dragons peeling off fast and mean, dozens of them arcing around into new trajectories, a low roar rising up from the Tevéss riders and dragons, followed by sharp, professional commands, the rip-snap of signal flags.

Dagger dipped a wing. A bullet hissed over Anna's head like an angry wasp. Irondusk had purposefully crash landed into the trunk of a massive, recently felled tree, turned, roared, and now launched himself directly at them. He was too far away, of course, but there was no question as to his murderous intent. The massive pulse of his wings shuddered the thrashing trees in his wake. The Gorge's walls were tidal seas of violent green. A volley of bullets snapped through the leaves around her, cracking and thunking into branches and tree trunks. Moondagger flapped with all his strength. Through her legs, Anna could feel his heart pounding, steady and strong.

There were at least thirty enemy scout dragons diving at them now. They had superior altitude, dropping at them like well-aimed stones. Dagger tried to gain more speed and elevation. The first bola spun above them, its low humming like a weird bird. Another volley of gun fire. A bullet tore the tip off Dagger's right nostril and hot blood sprayed, spattering her face. Another bullet punched through his neck, below Anna's knee. Blood bubbled but did not flow. Instead of slowing him down, the wounds seemed to give Dagger new strength. He tried to dive, to roll, to gain speed, flapping harder, and then harder still, as he tried to save them. The next bola hit Dagger's right wing, the splinter of hollow bone as the weighted cords spun, cinched the wing joint against itself, the force of Dagger's own muscle ripping his shoulder ball from its socket. He tried to keep them aloft with one wing. Insane careening and spinning as they hurtled toward the Gorge's tree-clumped cliffs. Leaves whipped Anna's face, scratched her goggles, cut her cheeks. And then they crashed nose-first into a jagged tree stump, into the eggshell crunch of bone and darkness.

59

MOONDAGGER SAW A factory. A factory filled with little girls and silver machines. It reminded him of the factory where Anna's family made the sacred dye of their war cloth. But it was different. They did not make color here. They made something else.

The silver machines hissed and moaned and rumbled as they opened and closed. Silver-white steam shot from silver vents. Great silver cogs turned eternally on silver tubes—opened and closed, opened and closed, opened and closed—the machines' noise a low, perpetual clumping. The pipes, the gears, the floors, the walls, the machines themselves, all shone with a soft, silver glow.

The machines looked powerful. And they were. But they were fragile, too, Moondagger understood.

Dozens of little girls worked the silver machines. They wore silver booties on their tiny feet. They stepped with little steps. They were several years younger than Anna, Moondagger saw, about Wendi's age. They wore silver gloves on their little hands, silver nets over their hair, and silver masks over their mouths. The masks protected the work.

The work must be protected. The promise must be kept.

A girl placed something into a machine. She pulled a silver lever. The machine whispered and clumped shut. When it hissed open, a glowing, silver tear sat in the machine's center. The tear was hot and perfectly smooth, about the size of a small apple. The girl took the tear from the machine and turned to Moondagger, holding it up to him with both hands, a silent offering. The glowing tear steamed with power.

Dagger stared into it. And for a moment, he imagined something dark turned inside——.

Then she dropped it and the tear shattered like a broken mirror. A black, segmented thing jittered amidst the glowing shards, its black feathers crystalline, obsidian casings splitting and ticking against the silver floor as the dark thing quivered and shook, finally sliding its way to a silver drain, dropping into darkness.

Somewhere below, a massive door thundered open and a terrible sound echoed up from the deep. The sound of a hundred rotten hooves pounding on rusty iron. The sound of the men that worked the *other* machines, the machines deep below. The tear's creature had set them free.

The silver doors crashed open and a gang of filthy men shamble-swarmed into the factory. Their uniforms were oily shrouds. Black slime dripped from their robes and sleeves. Their hands were crusty raptor talons, ancient and cruel. But the worst was their faces: like fleshy, black eggs. Their mouths were gummy slits. They did not have eyes. The egg faces reflected no light.

An egg-faced man grabbed the girl in front of Dagger, drove a shard of black iron into her chest, and dropped her to the silver floor, his weapon coated with molten silver. Dagger tried to roar, to protect, to do his duty, but he could not move. He could turn his head, but the rest of his body was frozen, as if shackled by invisible chains.

All around him, the egg-faced men killed. In pairs and in groups, they held the little workers down, ripped the silver masks from their faces, and cut into their throats, their legs, their arms. But there was no blood. The girls did not bleed. Instead, brilliant, liquid silver poured from their wounds, flowed silver, while the egg-faced men hacked and stabbed and howled. There was another sound, also. A constant, weeping cry as the voices of the little workers blended together to become a single, tremulous wail.

More tears shattered. More black things scuttled chitinous and feathered into the darkness below. More iron hooves pounded up from the dark. More egg-faced men, their smooth, plump egg heads bobbing and nodding as they crashed through the silver doors, toothless mouths gaping, black tongues flitting at edges of lipless mouths.

But the egg-faced men did not touch Moondagger. Indeed, while the massacre raged, every so often an egg-faced man would stop in front of him, bow deferentially, and pass him by.

The work must be protected. The promise must be kept.

Another tear shattered to the floor. But this time, instead of a skittering, dark creature, a large crow shook its feathers, leapt from the shards, and landed on the silver machine near Moondagger's head. When they saw the crow, the egg-faced men looked up from their killing and followed it, their heads tracking the crow as a single group, as if their eyeless faces could see. They pushed around Moondagger, gathering and shuffling around the silver machine where the crow had landed, shambling and murmuring. They were tall. Their oily clothes stank of fire and charred bone. They did not touch Moondagger but gathered close, encircling him until they enclosed him entirely, their eyeless egg faces black and nodding, their slit mouths muttering.

The crow cocked its head at Moondagger.

"You may choose," it cawed in its weird crow voice, a voice blended from a hundred mouths.

Choose what?

"Who lives, of course." The crow cocked its head, its dark eyes beady and intelligent. "And, who dies."

An egg-faced man threw something to the floor at Dagger's feet.

It was a body, mangled and crushed, a bloody mess, tattered and stringy, as if gnawed by beasts and left to rot in some culvert. The sky blue livery it wore was shredded and gore-stained, the leather armor blown wide. Moondagger could see the silver floor through the holes that were its wounds.

Dagger roared, flared his wings, suddenly free, and took a massive breath, blasting the circle of egg-faced men with a thundering funnel of silver-white fire. They melted away, black fog coiling into night—but then returned, exactly as they had been before—ropes of dark vapor twisting into being.

An egg-faced man toed the body over.

It was Anna. It was her. His rider. Her face was bloodless and horrible, her mouth open, lips peeled back, gums red, a silent nightmare's gape. But the worst was her eyes. Her eye sockets were burnt-out holes, the skin around them scorched and black.

Dagger snarled blind fury. He would kill them all!

Every last one.

He roared, blasting silver-white fire, turning his head slowly, making sure he got them all.

And this time, they did not flee.

Oh, no.

This time, they *burned*.

He took another breath and blasted them again.

Oh, how they burned!

Howling weirdly, their oily robes caught fire, blazing up like dried kindling, their weird egg faces pulp hissing atop jittering columns of raging white flame. Then they went still. The white fire still raged through their bodies, they still howled their toothless howl, but they did not move. They just stood there, straight—and burned.

The black egg heads began to split and crack. There were other things, *darker* things, inside. And now these things clawed through splintering black shells. A wicked flash of scale and feather, the dark edges of black swords.

"And so you have chosen," the crow cawed, its strange voice ringing from a hundred different throats.

Moondagger lunged at the crow, biting, but his fangs snapped down on wisps of black smoke.

And then there was nothing but a deeper sinking, a slow fade into nothing.

60

ANNA ROSE TO pain. Dizzying, bone-deep pain and darkness.

The air was cold and smelled of damp and ancient stone. She lay on a slab of rock. Her head, her back, her knees—her whole body—ached horribly. Especially her head. Gingerly, she waved a hand in front of her face. She couldn't see it. The darkness was absolute.

"Dagger," she whispered into the black.

Her head throbbed.

She'd been dreaming. A terrifying, bizarre nightmare. And although the memory of it was already fading, its effect lingered, as if some larval thing from the dream world had clawed through in search of a deeper nesting place, a hollow near the center of her chest where it could hide and grow.

She blinked at the darkness. White ghost shapes flitted across her vision. The rock slab where she lay was cold and hard against her back, covered by a layer of cool dust. She tried to open her eyes wider, but there was no light.

She was in some dungeon, some prison somewhere. The blackness was total.

But no.

That wasn't true.

On the far wall, she could just make out a faint seam of moonlight. A small window, she guessed, shuttered against the night. She took a deep breath, but a knifing pain stabbed through her ribs and stopped her. She groaned.

She didn't know where she was exactly, or how long she'd been there, or how she'd arrived. But she did know this: Moondagger's presence in her mind was missing.

She closed her eyes. When she did, she saw them crashing

into the trees, heard the crunch of bone, the rip of muscle and tendon.

Dagger.

Anna reached out with her mind, not sure what she was doing, but trying all the same, feeling for his presence.

Nothing. It was like reaching into a gaping, black hole.

Anna sat up. When she lifted her legs, a chain clinked and she felt the weight of dead iron shackled 'round her right ankle. She was barefoot. Her armor and weapons were gone, of course. She was wearing only her riding undergear and a few shreds of her armor's padding. Powdery dust caked her feet and palms.

Chained and imprisoned. And Moondagger was almost certainly dead.

"But we got you all the same, didn't we?" Anna whispered, the realization dawning. Her mouth was tender as she spoke. From the sound of it, her cell was very small. Her lips were swollen and raw. There was something wrong with one of her front teeth. Chipped, her tongue discovered. Anna smiled in the darkness, her bottom lip splitting open with the grin. The pain felt good, in a way.

"Because we got you," she breathed carefully.

"Yes," a man's low voice purred near her in the darkness. "You did, indeed."

Anna stifled a surprised gasp and turned it into a deep breath instead, calming and readying herself.

"Who's there?" she asked simply.

"You've nothing to fear from me, dragon knight," the voice murmured. "But, forgive me. You're not afraid. How could you be? What on this world—what on any world—could scare the dauntless, indomitable Anna Dyer?"

Anna didn't answer.

There was a rustle of cloth as the man stood. Footsteps crossed the cell's dusty floor. A shape blocked the crack of light in the wall. The soft click of a window's latch. Then a shutter swung open, bringing with it a flood of moonlight. Anna squinted against the sudden brightness. The moon made a perfect, blue-white square on the cell's flagstones. Motes of ancient dust churned in its glow.

"I'll leave my lantern hooded, if you don't mind," the man said. "I've always preferred moonlight to fire. 'As the world sleeps,' so the ancient poet says, 'mother moon shines her silver light into dreams and onto dreamers.'"

"What do you want?" Anna asked.

"I'm a friend," the man said in a clear, articulate manner. "Or, perhaps more honestly, someone who would be your friend. As the poet says, 'Our days are like the last beams of the moon, a turn away from——.'"

Anna sighed.

"Don't care for ancient literature?" the man asked. "No songs or poems of old? You strike me as one who might savor the Kingdom's early ballads. No soaring flights? Heroic duels? Epic victories?"

"Leave me be," Anna sighed. Her voice sounded strange in her own ears. Older.

"I am Malachi Fel," the man said.

Anna tensed and nodded. Made sense. Lord Oskor's heir. Come to avenge his father. Her ankle chain clinked in the dust.

"Please," Lord Malachi continued. "Don't be alarmed, dragon rider. You've nothing to fear."

She said nothing. She wasn't afraid.

"I'm not here to harm you, Anna. I'm here to thank you. And I'm here to ask for your help. A small favor, nothing more."

She didn't respond.

"I understand." The dark shape nodded at her silence. "But it's true. You're a hero, Anna. Both to your people and, in a sense, to mine. You deserve all of our thanks—."

"Let me sleep, traitor," Anna said, leaning her head against the wall. "I'm tired."

"Of course. I ask only a moment. Will you hear me?"

She shrugged.

"When you killed my Father, you changed things, Anna. My older brother, Halek, cannot assume title. I am next in line. I thus find myself in a new position, a position from which I hope to do good. In essence, your courage has made me High Lord of House Fel. And in a week's time, if you are willing, your courage will make me High Lord of Dávanor."

"I'd rather die," she said plainly, wincing at the pain in her side. She touched her ribs. At least two were broken.

"Truly, your spirit is as fierce as they say."

"Yeah?" Anna chuckled. "Why not unchain me then? See how 'fierce' my spirit can be?"

"I don't think so."

"Bravo." She sighed. "It's not every High Lord who dares face a bound, wounded squire in the middle of the night, chained unarmed to a rock."

The man laughed. It was a surprisingly comforting sound.

The cell was still dark, but the square of moonlight lit the cell with a blue-white glow, and Anna's eyes had finally adjusted. Lord Malachi leaned against the far wall, across from the window. He was a young man, Anna saw. No older than twenty. Clean shaven, wearing his dark hair in a short soldier's crop. He was a bit disheveled, but well-groomed. His face was completely covered in grey dust, except for two circles around his eyes that had been protected by his riding goggles. His eyes were striking. Dark, steady, and keenly intelligent—the eyes of a young man accustomed to the pain and joy of command. The young man whose face she had seen in the drawing above the Gorge.

She inspected him. The general impression he made was that of a seasoned, professional courier who'd just spent several long days on dragon back. He wore a light riding harness of dark green Abúcian leather, dark green riding pants, and dark green riding boots, all well-worn and well-maintained.

He was unarmed except for a short, undecorated dagger sheathed and clipped upside down on the bandolier across his chest. A pair of unassuming dragon gauntlets was folded and tucked into his bandolier, as an experienced flier might carry them. A hooded lantern of black iron sat in the dust at his feet. Beside the lantern, leaning point-down against the stone wall, there was an iron poker, like the poker you might use to stoke a fire, but shorter and thicker. Its handle was wrapped in black leather.

Anna cleared her throat. "What do you want?"

"As I said, I'm here to thank you. And to ask for your help. I've much to offer."

"Offer, then, for the Sisters' sake." Anna sighed. "Or let me rest. Or kill me. Or release me. I don't care. You and your traitor clan can rot for all I care. I've done my duty."

"Indeed." He inclined his head. "And what of your family? Your friends? What of Master Zar? Master Khondus?"

"They're alive?" She opened her eyes.

He nodded. "Fyr and Borónd, too. And your family. All here in the High Keep. Safe and sound."

"My dragon?"

The question hung there. Her chest twisted with the chance, with the possibility—however impossible.

Lord Malachi looked at her for a long moment, something strange in his eyes. Then he shook his head. "I'm sorry. He was dead when they recovered you. Killed on impact. A brave mount. Worthy of song."

She groaned and the sorrow squeezed her heart with dark claws. She tried to take a breath, but her throat caught. She tried again, doing everything she could to focus herself into calm. And then she realized that something *else* was missing, too: her old friend—her rage. She wished it would come back. But it didn't. She was just tired. And it had never been her friend at all, she realized. It had been the opposite. A silly, spoiled child taunting her to play with a razor. She'd played. And now Moondagger was dead.

Death is not defeat.

Empty words.

"Thank you for telling me." She swallowed. But she was dizzy and her head was starting to ache, a low pounding. "Where's my family? Where are the Drádonhold's captains?"

"In the infirmary. Their injuries were grave, but they live.

My physicians attend them. Your family is unharmed, for the most part."

"What happened?" She carefully rubbed her hands together for warmth. "If you want something, let me see them."

"Of course. But allow me to give you this, first." Lord Malachi reached behind his back and withdrew Master Khondus's dagger. He unsheathed it. In the moonlight, the high silver glowed with ghostly, ancient power.

"An impressive weapon." He held the blade up to the window, turned the dagger to the moon, white shards of light reflecting against the cell's walls. "Timeless, indestructible, priceless. It will be yours again, if you have the courage to take it."

Lord Malachi smiled. His teeth were clean and straight. A good-looking young man, Anna realized.

"I have more to offer. You will hear me?"

"Speak," she said.

"First, when you've recovered, I offer you a commission in my scout corps here on Dávanor. Second, if in that post you show the same talent and courage you've so far evidenced, I'll appoint you to Dávanor's cavalry. You will serve me and our world's forces in the High King's war. Third, upon our victory, which should be quite soon——."

Anna closed her eyes. "You misjudge the tactical situation, I think."

"The High King's advantage is insurmountable." Malachi shrugged. "In any case, upon our victory, you'll return here to the High Keep and take command of the remaining House Dradón dragons. Fourth, and finally, I will double your family lands and bestow a handsome reward upon you and your clan. I know your people aren't poor, Anna. But my riders and my soldiers are well paid. My top commanders even more so. In sum, your friends will be healed, this high blade will be yours, you'll serve as a flight officer in our world's forces and, upon your homecoming, you'll receive land, title, and coin."

"And in return?" Anna asked. "You want what?"

A large crow fluttered outside the window and landed on the sill. For a moment, its wings blocked out the square of moonlight, casting black shadows into the cell. It turned, stepping slowly, cocking its head. Its eyes were glittering jewels. It settled and looked down over the distant lands below. There was something wrong with its right wing. The blue moonlight glimmered black on its glossy feathers.

"In return," Lord Malachi continued, smoothing an eyebrow, "a small service, nothing more."

Anna opened her hands, waiting.

"Word of your deeds has spread, Anna. In the last days, the news has traveled most of Dávanor. The messenger dragons have been busy. On one hand—to my allies and to the allies of my house—you're a dangerous foe whose bravery is both respected and feared." He smiled at Anna's frown. "It's true. Even those who loved my father cannot deny your courage or daring. On the other hand—to my enemies—you're a hero and a symbol. Lord David had many friends. As does your family. Those friends are loyal to House Dradón and to Lady Abigail. While I hold the High Lady in protective custody here in the High Keep, violence has already broken out between factions across many of our duchy's counties. As we speak, our world runs to the very edge of war. I need your help, Anna—,"

"Forgive me, my Lord," she cut him off softly. "We're not at the 'edge of war.' We're at war. A war that your house—

that your father—started. We should've destroyed you trai- tors three years ago. But Lord David was merciful, if not just, Great Sisters forgive him. And this war—this war which now rages, this war which *you* began—is the result."

"Perhaps." He pursed his lips. "But we have now a chance for peace."

"No." She sighed tiredly. "There is no 'we,' my Lord. And there is no 'peace.' I serve Lady Abigail Dradón, the High Lady of Dávanor. By extension, I serve her rightful liege, High Lord Bellános Dallanar, the Silver King, the true Lord of Remain. You are Malachi Fel. You are the son of a murderer and a traitor, the lord of a murderous and traitorous house. I'll do nothing for you, your family, or for the Pretender King before whom you grovel. You are the enemy of my house, the enemy of the Kingdom's ruling family, the enemy of the Realm's High Laws, and the enemy of the Kingdom itself. I'd gladly die a hundred times before lifting a finger in service of your thrice- cursed clan."

In the window, the crow cocked its head and ruffled its feathers.

"Please, Anna." Malachi raised his hand. There was a note

of real concern in his voice, and for a moment, Anna thought she saw the young man's shoulders sag. "More hangs in the balance than you can know. Many lives, from both our high houses, from across the duchy, are at risk. Will you put your hatred for my family above your love of Dávanor? Will you not hear me?"

"If we're at risk, then it's a risk you created. As Master Boród says: 'If you dislike the crop, examine the seed.'"

"Maybe so." He paused. "There is no doubt that my father was ambitious and cruel. But I am *not* my father, Anna. I inherited this conflict. I did not create it. You inherited this conflict. You did not create it, either. And now we have a chance to put all to rights and start anew for the good of our peoples, our Houses, and our world."

"You're a *usurper*, my Lord. Can I be more plain?"

"I would be your friend, Anna. A friend to both you and your family."

"At the cost of my word and honor? At the cost of my dragon's faith?" Anna looked him in the eye. "Never."

Malachi stroked his jaw, then continued, as if he hadn't heard her. "In exchange for land, title, and coin, this is what I want:

tomorrow morning, in the High Square, before the High Gate, in front of the inhabitants of the High Keep, you will kneel and swear a public oath of loyalty to me as the High Lord of House Fel."

Anna sighed. Her body ached. Her head was beginning to pound again.

Malachi continued: "Then, in one week's time, I shall take Lady Abigail to wife. After that ceremony, you'll once again swear public oath of loyalty to me as the High Lord of Dávanor. Between your own courage and reputation and the courage and reputation of your parents, your words will carry weight. Our enemies will be given pause. Those uncertain of their position will join us, for the sake of good order."

"I won't do it." Anna rubbed at her temples. "I'll never do it."

Malachi sighed. He looked at her for a long moment. Then he tucked Master Khondus's blade behind his back, reached down, and took the short, iron poker from its place against the wall. The crow stirred on its perch, turned, and peered into the cell, black eyes glittering.

"You *will* swear," Malachi said softly. He held the poker away from him, as if it repulsed him. "You'll swear or, by the Sisters, you'll serve me in another way."

"Trying to prove your bravery again?"

Malachi bowed his head. "I'll not harm you now, Anna. But tomorrow morning, if you don't swear, you'll force me to make an example of you and your family. There's no other way. Your people will suffer. It will not be quick, you understand."

Anna's stomach knotted, but her gaze didn't falter.

"You," Malachi said, holding the poker in the square of moonlight, moving it in and out of the crow's shadow, "you will lose your eyes. But only after you've seen your family and friends destroyed. You'll then spend the remainder of your life in this cell, sightless and alone, to be brought forth when my enemies require a reminder of my authority." He looked at her unhappily. "So you see, Anna, you *will* serve me. One way or another. Would you serve with glory, honor, and wealth? Or with torture, horror, and death?"

Anna lifted her chin. "To live and die as a loyal soldier of a great Lady and a great House is glory and honor enough.

A soldier never forgets her word. My family knows it. My dragon knew it. I know it. Death is not defeat."

"Fine words." Malachi nodded. "But what of your family? What of *their* deaths? Your mother? Your sisters? Your friends? Must they be made to suffer, also? My advisors will insist upon it. And they'll be right."

Anna swallowed. "If I betray my word, then I betray my dragon's memory, my clan, and my High House. My people understand this better than anybody. So take my blood and take your vengeance, my Lord. My oath you'll *never* have."

"'Vengeance?'" Malachi's eyebrows shot up. He shook his head. "Oh no, Anna. Not 'vengeance.' I loved my father, to be sure. As much as any highborn son can love his lord and master. But the horrors you suffer tomorrow aren't retributive. Quite the contrary." His voice went quiet, like he was talking to himself. "Better to think of it as a kind of performance, a kind of theatre. You'd be closer to the truth."

Anna frowned.

He looked at her. "A show of cruelty can make a powerful memory in an audience, Anna. The memory becomes a scar, and the scar becomes a lesson. When I hurt your friends and family, I won't enjoy it. But I'll do it so that my people can see what happens to those who defy my authority. Likewise, when I take your eyes," he glanced disdainfully at the iron poker he held, "I won't enjoy it. But I'll do it so that my people can see that my power is the one thing—the one thing above *all* others—that they must fear. The entire display is a simple, calculated path to a simple, calculated end. And that end is 'peace.'"

Anna looked away. On the window sill, the crow cocked its head.

"For a handful of viewers," Lord Malachi continued, "your blinding will make you a martyr, of course. But for the vast majority, your mutilation simply will be feared. *Feared.* Nothing more. That fear will become a tool, a tool with which I can fashion order and peace for our world. Of course, tomorrow's spectacle will be terrible. But isn't one terrible day preferable to a thousand? Isn't it better for one young soldier to endure such a fate than for an entire world to suffer? Either way, you misunderstand me. It's not 'vengeance,' Anna. It is duty. The duty of statecraft."

She said nothing. She could feel Malachi's gaze on the side of her face.

"Consider carefully. My offer will stand as given until dawn. It's not your life alone that you hazard. Think on your friends. Think on your family. Think on your world."

She started to speak, but he raised his hand to stop her.

"I know a hero must shut her eyes, Anna. That she must 'believe,' in order to act, to fight, and to win. But you've already acted, Anna. You've already fought. And you've already won. You've already done everything that you could do. Open your eyes. Our world doesn't need a hero now. It needs a leader. It needs a savior."

He paused, looked at her closely, and cocked his head. "You've called me a traitor. Perhaps that's true. Much depends on point of view. But think on this: What do you call a warrior who lets beloved innocents die for nothing?"

She shook her head. The crow gazed at her, its dark eyes gleaming.

Malachi took up his lantern, made to go, but then abruptly stepped toward her and touched her cheek. His touch was warm, almost tender. He held his hand there for a moment.

She didn't flinch at his touch.

He sighed. "I ask you, truly: is there any difference between the death of your father and the death of mine?"

She looked up into his eyes, realizing with dawning horror that she wanted to lean into his hand, to take comfort in the safety and kindness and reason that he offered, to save herself, to save her friends, to save her family—.

Are you mad?

She pulled away, put her head against the wall, and shut her eyes.

"Until tomorrow, then." He paused. "My beautiful, blind dragon."

He stepped away, tapped on the cell door. The lock clanked, the door opened, and he walked out. The door shut behind him.

The crow cocked its head and turned away, hunkering down for the night.

Anna's head throbbed. She felt slightly sick.

"I must be strong," she whispered. "For Dagger. For Mother. For everyone. I must be strong."

But her whole body shook. And it wasn't just from the cold.

She took a deep breath and looked at the square of blue moonlight on the cell's floor. But it wasn't a square anymore. It was a weird, crooked trapezoid, crow's shadow hunched in the corner, bent by the motion of the moon.

61

MORNING CAME FAST, the early light pinking a cloudless sky. The crow still sat at the window, its only movement the slow shift of weight from one foot to the other, an occasional ruffle of feathers.

Anna hadn't slept. At least she didn't remember sleeping. But she must have. She was stiff, her hands were freezing, and her head ached worse than ever. There was a clammy hollowness in her stomach and chest, as if something vital had been removed.

She missed Dagger. She missed him terribly. If she could just put her hands on him again, feel his smooth power under his warm scales, touch her forehead to his, look into his eyes one more time.

She shook her head. At least she hadn't dreamed. And yet even the most horrific nightmare would've been a kindness compared to what she would face today.

Is that true?

She didn't know. She did know that today would be the last day that she'd see her people alive. That today would be hell itself.

"I must be strong," she said to the crow.

The crow turned, stepping carefully, and stared at her with attentive eyes. It cocked its head, as if asking a question.

Did she have to be strong?

Did she have to be tortured? Did she have to watch her friends and loved ones destroyed in front of a crowd?

She couldn't stop imagining the sounds, the screams, knowing that they died for her plan, for her failure.

But you didn't fail.

She had to keep reminding herself of that.

So why couldn't she banish Lord Malachi's offer from her mind? Was there even a decision to be made?

No.

For the hundredth time.

Because she'd made her choice a long time ago. When she was nine years old. When she'd put her tiny fist on her heart and made a promise to Lord David, to her Father, to her Mother, to House Dradón in front of the High Gate along with all the other dragon squires of her cohort.

That was when she'd chosen.

And that decision is the only one that matters.

"A soldier never betrays her word," she whispered. "A soldier never forgets her promises."

That was truth.

Because if everyone forgot their promises in the face of war and horror and murder, then what remained?

"Nothing," Anna told the crow. "Nothing at all."

The crow cocked its head.

Those words sound fine, she could imagine it saying.

Oh yes, they sound fine.

But they didn't help.

And they won't save their lives.

Her hands shook.

The pit of her stomach clenched with cold knives.

Were "fine words" really worth betraying Moondagger's faith and memory? Were "fine words" really worth the *lives* of her friends and family? Or was there more there? Was there something real, something *true* behind the words?

The crow stared back at her, black eyes glittering, its head bobbing silently, as if nodding with ancient answers— answers that it would not share.

62

THE DOOR CLANKED.

Anna looked up.

Lord Malachi walked into the cell.

A crowd of murmuring soldiers and courtiers waited behind him in the dungeon's hallway, most of them dressed in the dark green of House Fel.

Lord Malachi himself wore an emerald green tunic under a breastplate of dark riding armor, dark leather pants, and dark riding boots. A short sword hung from his hip, a high silver revolver slung under his left armpit, all the gear well cared for and well-used.

And that was the point, Anna realized. This was Lord Malachi in costume. His "warrior's costume." Indeed, the only mark of office the young lord displayed was a simple signet ring emblazoned with House Fel's crest, the two-headed dragon. "He's a fighter," his costume said. "He's all business. He's a leader worth following." But when she looked closer, Anna saw something else. His eyes were alert but ringed by dark circles. He was exhausted. He was upset. And he was nervous.

"I see neither of us slept well," Malachi said, as if reading her mind. He tried to smile, but it came across as a frown. His eyes were haunted, and for a strange moment, Anna found herself pitying the new lord of the House of Fel.

Outside in the hallway, someone snickered at some jest.

"Quiet," Malachi ordered softly.

All sound ceased.

"Forgive me, Anna." He stepped to her and knelt at the edge of the rock slab. "Have you decided?"

"Yes," Anna said. "I agree with what you said last night."

His face brightened.

She shook her head. "I agree, my Lord, that you and I could have been friends, had the circumstances been different."

"What does that mean?" he asked so that only she could hear.

She paused, then lifted her chin. "It means that the circumstances are *not* different. It means we're at war. It means that I must refuse your offer, my Lord. It means that my word is not for sale."

He closed his eyes for a moment. Then he looked at her and nodded. "I understand. I'm sorry."

She returned his gaze. Her voice was utterly composed. "We've each made our vows, my Lord. The only difference is the people to whom they were sworn. In that, there can be no apologies—especially between soldiers who honor their duty."

"This doesn't feel like duty."

"Sometimes," she heard herself say, "that's what duty feels like."

He cocked his head for a long moment, his eyes thoughtful. Then he nodded, turned, and walked out the cell door.

"Take her."

63

HER WRISTS WERE locked behind her back in iron manacles. Those manacles, in turn, were locked to an iron bar that ran to a chain between her ankles. The position and length of the bar forced her back into an unnatural arch, making it hard to breathe and to walk. She could take small, awkward steps, but it was challenging. She was barefoot, and she kept stubbing her toes against the cracks in the stone floor. She tried to keep pace with the soldiers around her, but sometimes they would just pick her up and carry her for a stretch. They were not unkind. A huge sergeant with fresh burns on the left side of his face even stopped the procession to adjust the iron bar at her back so that her posture was a little more natural. When he was done, he lifted a clay cup to her lips.

"Drink," he said soberly. His horrible burns didn't allow his mouth to open fully. It seemed to pain him to speak. "Drink."

Anna didn't hesitate. Cool, clean water.

"My thanks," she said wetly, emptying most of the cup. She couldn't remember tasting anything so good.

The sergeant nodded and gently dabbed her chin with the back of his glove. His eyes were pale grey, his left eye totally bloodshot, its corner sealed by freshly scorched flesh. He did not wear the dark green of House Fel, but rather the maroon of House Tevéss.

"Let's go," he said. They moved out.

They made their way out of the High Keep's dungeons, up toward the High Square and the High Gate, up stone staircases, through corridors and passages, across bridges, and under colonnades. The men of House Fel were everywhere. Absolutely everywhere. Dark green banners, adorned with Fel's two-headed golden dragon, hung from every gate. Soldiers in dark green livery stood at every intersection. Green clad riders and their dragons perched on every lookout.

House Dradón had fallen.

That much was clear.

But how badly have we been defeated?

What had happened after she'd flown from the High Square? If word had spread to the loyal minor houses, then they'd come with more than half of Dávanor behind them. Yes, it would be bloody, but these traitors would receive the justice they deserved. But at what cost?

You can still change your mind.

The thought came to her unbidden. She cringed at it.

And there was something else, too. Something strange. Every so often, she would see herself at a distance, as if time skipped moments, as if she looked down at their little procession from some high vantage, as if she was not in her own body. The crowd of soldiers around her, the low mutter of their voices, the click of armor and buckle, the tread of boot on stone—all had taken on a dream-like quality, blurry at the edges, sharper at the middle, her own mind centered and luminous above it all. She could no longer feel the manacles at her wrists or ankles. She could hear her chains, the jingling scrape of iron against stone, but their weight was gone.

And then, quite suddenly, she realized that she didn't resent the men who now led her to torture and death. How could she? They were her enemies. And she was theirs. Yet they were the same. Something had been twisted, somehow. They were alike, but yet they fought. An image from her nightmare, from the strange, silver factory, flashed before her, a cold talon on her heart.

The work must be protected. The promise must be kept.

She stopped walking abruptly and almost fell on her face. The burned sergeant caught her just in time, bringing the entire crowd clattering to a halt.

When the sergeant had righted her, she asked in her most commanding voice: "Give me your name, soldier."

"Lodáz," he replied, an automatic response to her order.

Anna started with recognition. The big Tevéss sergeant from the High Gate. She'd thought him dead, killed by Dagger's flames. His left eye could not see, she realized. Destroyed by dragon fire. She regained her composure.

"Thank you for the water, Sergeant Lodáz," she said.

"You are welcome, dragon rider." The big man nodded professionally. There was no malice in his voice. None at all.

"Come," Anna said. "Lord Fel waits."

64

THEY WALKED UP a set of dark steps toward an arch of light. She could hear the crowd out there, thousands of voices, but hushed in that way you hear before the beginning of a play, the low murmur of a hundred soft conversations. Her procession stepped into the open, and the murmuring stopped, as if cut by a knife.

She looked up. Squinted against the sunlight. It was blinding but also warm, almost luxurious, against her skin. She closed her eyes and turned her face into its heat, the light red against the inside of her eyelids. She took a deep breath.

Felt the crowd watching her. Heard their shuffling silence. Saw herself from far away. A fourteen-year-old girl in torn white silk surrounded by a dozen men in green and black and maroon; a white light at the center of darkness.

And she could save them all.

Gentle pressure against the iron bar at her back. She opened her eyes and the sounds and the scene came in.

From every wall of the High Square dark green banners hung barely moving in the faint morning breeze. Green-clad soldiers were everywhere, on the Square's walls, on the ramparts, on the tower tops. And then there was the crowd. A silent, motley mass of all sorts—men, women, children, merchants, servants, and nobility from House Fel, House Tevéss, and House Dradón—filling the four sides of the High Square, a kaleidoscope of peasants' wool, court finery, and every-thing in between, packed onto the wooden benches used for pageants and celebrations.

On the Square's northern side stood a large contingent of House Tevéss soldiers and nobles, all in dark maroon. Lord Gideon Tevéss stood in front of them, surrounded by his high guard. He was tall, slightly fat, with a reddish face, thinning, grey-blonde hair, and a thick, grey beard. He wore velvet leggings and a velvet doublet of rich burgundy. A dress dagger, pommeled with a maroon stone, swung from his belt on an ornamental chain. Both his ears were clasped in elaborate gold casings. A rich amulet decorated with maroon jewels hung from his neck, shining in the sunlight. He looked at her curiously.

Behind Lord Gideon—in the stands, in the surrounding buildings, on every balcony, in every window—people watched, their faces an amalgam of interest, scorn, and sympathy. And above them all, high on the ramparts' tallest peaks, a dozen of House Fel's and House Tevéss's largest dragons waited. Captain Corónd was there on his bronze, its pale green eyes curious and alert. And there was the great Irondusk, looming at the Square's highest point, his rust-colored claws sunk into the wood of a massive perch. His saddle was empty. His black eyes smoldered with unfettered hatred. His growl was a steady rumble of low thunder. He had not forgotten his rider's killer.

The High Gate stood at the center of the High Square. It was a pointed arch, five times the height of a man and crafted of the eternal high silver. Its luminous surfaces reflected arcs of sunlight across walls, faces, banners, and dragons. Five Fel adepts, wearing the dark green robes of their High House, tended the Gate. Four of the adepts were hooded. These knelt at each of the Gate's legs on dark green cushions. Their eyes were shut, their palms flat against the Gate's surface, their lips moving silently with the Gate's sacred descant. Their leader—the head adept, a young woman no older than Anna herself—stood at the Gate's center. Her dark green hood was thrown back from her head, and her arms were crossed protectively across her chest. Her mouth barely moved as she whispered the mystical counterpoint to her sisters' ancient song.

It was truly over, Anna realized. With the High Gate controlled by House Fel, they were truly alone.

No one can save you.

Lord Malachi stood in front of the High Gate. He looked at her, but his eyes were strangely blank. Behind him and to his left, on their knees, Master Khondus, Master Zar, Master Borónd, Mother, Penelope, Wendi, and a couple dozen wounded House Dradón riders and soldiers waited in two ragged blue lines, their arms chained behind their backs.

When Anna entered, many of the Dradón soldiers looked up to her, their faces shining with hope and dread, as if they knew she could save them.

Master Khondus didn't look up. And he could not, Anna saw. They'd cut the iron head off the stable hammer and had hung it around his neck, the weight pulling his head toward the flagstones. His long, grey hair had been shaved to the nub, his scalp lacerated and bloody. His right eye was swollen shut, his nose broken. A fresh line of blood ran from one of his ears. Blood pooled on the flagstones in front of him. His good eye stared glassily at the ground, watering and unseeing. He nodded like a dotard, a spider thread of red spittle running from broken lips.

Master Zar knelt at Master Khondus's right. His stout Anorian frame leaned against that of his friend, barely able to stay upright. Both his eyes were black, swollen shut. His lavender skin had gone pale and sickly. A dirty bandage was wrapped loosely around his forehead. The front of the bandage was stained deep red. Anna cringed. A weird, torn patch of purplish skin had been pinned to Master Zar's chest—its shriveled surface marked with a white Dallanar Sun.

Beside Zar, Master Borónd looked at the ground, his destroyed hands held before him, his head bowed. Mother knelt beside him. She was unharmed, thank the Sisters. She stared directly at Anna, chin up.

"Honor," she mouthed to Anna. Her eyes flashed fearlessly.

Anna gave her an almost imperceptible nod.

Little Wendi leaned against Mother's side, dazed, her tiny right hand wrapped in a bloodstained bandage. Penelope knelt next to her, head up, one of her eyes blackened, her nose broken, her eyes on Anna, absolutely defiant.

Malachi wasted no time getting started. When he spoke, his voice was resonant and commanding, his words echoing the Square's ancient walls with the irresistible force of a High Lord of Remain.

"We gather this glorious morning," he began, "to celebrate our victory, to mourn our dead, and to dispense our high justice."

Applause rang out, loud and long, whistles and cheers from the crowd. From the group of Tevéss soldiers, Lord Gideon nodded his approval, looking up and over the spectators. From their perches, the enemy dragons growled their satisfaction. The great Irondusk shook his head at the sky and flared his massive, rust-colored wings. Dark green banners swayed in his wind. The applause continued until Lord Malachi raised his hand to quell it, letting the silence reign for a long moment.

Then he raised his fist suddenly and roared: "Once again, the House of Fel is triumphant!"

Bellowing applause. A group of soldiers began banging spear against shield. The dragons shifted on their perches, swaying and muttering.

Lord Malachi's voice dropped lower and the crowd hushed in response.

"But victory is never achieved without cost. We have lost many brave soldiers, many brave riders, and many brave dragons in recent days."

A low, angry rumble ran through the crowd.

Malachi nodded. "But their commitment and their sacrifices were not in vain. For Fel House now holds Dávanor's High Keeps, Dávanor's High Gates, and Dávanor's lasting peace within its grasp!"

Thunderous applause roared out, raging even longer this

time. Almost every soldier had a weapon of some sort out, banging it against any nearby metal or stone. Whistles and cheers. The dragons unfurled their wings, wind gusting through the Square.

"But for peace to live," Lord Malachi shouted, "then war must die!" He drew his hand across his throat and pointed his finger first at Anna, then at the men of House Dradón. "Behold Anna Dyer! Behold the foes of House Fel! Behold the murderer of Lord Oskor! Behold the enemies of the Silver Kingdom! *Behold the enemies of peace!*"

The crowd hissed. "Traitors!" someone shouted. Thousands of eyes glared down at her. The dragons growled and rocked on their perches, becoming even more agitated. Irondusk looked as if he was having trouble controlling himself.

Lord Malachi raised his hand and all went silent.

He looked at Anna for a long moment.

"And behold," he said softly, so softly that the crowd could barely hear him, "behold the dreaded Moondagger!"

No!

Anna's head spun.

There was a low murmur, and the right side of the crowd parted.

"You can save him, Anna," Malachi whispered.

And then she saw him.

Or what was left of him. Four big soldiers in dark green livery pulled a wooden cart toward the center of the Square, iron-bound wheels scraping the stones. Dagger was strapped to the cart with thick leather bands, his wings bound to his sides, hind legs stretched and splayed out behind him. The bands were tight, making him look more like a trussed snake than a dragon of war. The broken remains of an elaborate splint for his right wing had been torn away and cinched down beneath the straps. His scales were dull, dirty, and grey, their usual white brilliance gone, replaced with filthy scrapes and smears of dirt and grime. A deep gouge on his neck had been stitched up—but the stitches had been freshly torn out.

Anna shut her eyes. Then she opened them. She owed him that much. They all owed him that much. That and so much more.

His jaws had been elaborately chained shut with straps and chains, his tongue caught between his own teeth, punctured by one of his own fangs. A single tear of red blood hung from its tip. His eyes were shut, caked with grime.

Oh, Dagger.

His torn nostrils flared as he sensed her presence. He made some effort to turn his head toward her, but he couldn't do it—his neck was chained to the cart with a collar ringed with spikes, points digging into his flesh.

"Behold," Malachi said, his voice still soft. "The infamous blind dragon. A freak of nature and sorcery, bred by criminals bent on bringing war and savagery and violence to our family, our house, and our world."

Thousands of soft hisses, the malice sweeping the crowd like a wave.

Lord Malachi soothed it with a raised hand.

"And behold," he said, beginning softly, his voice rising. "Behold the price of lies, schemes, and violence. Behold the price of treason, betrayal, and aggression. Behold the price of fear, terror, and tyranny." Then he roared and pointed: "*And behold our justice!*"

A huge soldier wearing a massive suit of plate mail and a dark green executioner's hood stepped from the left side of the crowd. He carried a huge headsman's ax. Behind him, four black horses in dark green tackle waited, their horse-shoes scraping the flagstones. Behind each horse stood a pair of squires in dark green livery, each carrying wickedly hooked chains.

"*Behold our high justice!*" Lord Malachi bellowed again.

The crowd went wild, the cheering swelling like an avalanche. A ringing clash of swords on shields. The furious roar of dragons. Irondusk's rage shook the High Square at its roots, bits of rock trembling on the flagstones, the High Gate responding somehow to the crowd's energy, its silver light flickering and scintillating with soundless white flames.

The thunder washed over Anna like a wave and she saw the blue-clad soldiers of House Dradón wilt against it.

She must be strong.

It was her or it was no one.

So she braced herself, chin up, eyes wide, staring at them all, daring them to meet her gaze, daring them all to look her in the eye.

"She threatens our lives." Malachi pointed at her. "She threatens our High House, and she threatens our High Laws!

But—like *all* those who would bring war to our people—*she has FAILED!*"

Total chaos. The walls of the High Square seemed to buckle beneath the noise, the crowd raving, red-faced, shrieking, stamping. The dragons' bellows were deafening. The High Keep itself seemed to shudder on its foundations. Dark green banners shook against the walls. The High Gate's light blazed like star fire, its weird, silent music seeming to swell and rise in a numinous, noiseless crescendo in response to the crowd's furor.

"But," Malachi whispered, "the House of Fel is *merciful*."

And just like that, all noise ceased. Everyone, soldiers, crowd, dragons—even Irondusk—went quiet.

"And the House of Fel is *righteous*."

Complete silence. The only sound the flap of dark green banners in a faint stirring of breeze.

"And above all, the House of Fel is *wise*."

The people nodded, utterly absorbed.

"Why destroy an enemy, when you can embrace a friend? Why kill and maim and burn, when you can live and thrive and love? Why make endless war, when you can craft lasting peace?"

Malachi looked at Anna directly.

"You can save him, Anna," he said, so that only she could hear.

She returned his gaze with what she hoped was defiance. But she was dizzy. Confused. And she wondered suddenly for whom this entire performance was truly being staged. The crowd was nodding together now, murmuring assent.

"A just peace," someone said, tentatively.

"A just peace!" a woman cried out.

"Peace!" a man yelled.

"Peace!" the crowd began to shout. "*Peace!*"

"A just peace." Malachi nodded. He held his hand up for silence and the Square went quiet.

He looked her in the eye. "What say you, Anna Dyer? Will you end this war? Will you save our blood and our sorrow?"

He gestured gently to her Masters, to Mother, to her sisters, to the line of House Dradón prisoners, and finally to Moondagger. "Will you save your friends? Will you save your family? Will you save your dragon?"

The crowd was utterly still. Total silence. Even the faint breeze had ceased.

Anna's lips trembled. She looked at Moondagger. His ragged eyelids cracked open, the caked blood splitting apart. He blinked sluggishly, weakly, turning his head this way and that, trying to blink through the crust around his eyes.

Anna clamped her lips together. Tried to keep her chin up.

Even now—shattered—her dragon still felt her eyes on him. He still tried to see her. To find her. To protect her.

Dagger's sides shuddered, and he pulled feebly against the constricting straps and chains. His bloody nostrils flared. A low whine escaped his bound jaws.

"I'm here," Anna whispered. "I'm here."

Dagger went still. Then he twisted his head as far as he could toward her, trying to meet her eyes. But the spiked collar dug into his neck and stopped him, a line of blood running down his dirty scales.

"No," Anna groaned and shook her head.

Don't fight.

Their fight was over. They'd done their duty.

You can rest.

A low moan rose somewhere near the center of things.

With sudden strength, Moondagger thrashed his head side

to side, back and forth, blood spurting around the spiked collar at his neck as he craned his head toward Anna, trying to find her, to see her.

65

THEN A CHAIN broke somewhere, and their eyes met, and they were alone.

The crowd, the people, the soldiers, the prisoners, the dragons, the pain—all were gone.

They saw nothing save each other.

And in that vision, something pure opened, and they saw that their faith, their trust, and their love was stronger than ever.

Indeed, it was all that remained.

66

"DAGGER," ANNA WHISPERED. Her lips trembled as she spoke.

His head cocked slightly.

And then his eyes—those huge, strange, beautiful, silver moons—closed with a gentle, final sigh.

67

IT WAS DARK. He could not see. He did not want to leave. But he could not stay. He could not save her. And his heart ached with the totality of his failure.

You see me.

You see . . . .

68

"DAGGER?" ANNA WHISPERED.

"Will you save him?" Lord Malachi asked again.

"Dagger?"

"Will you save us all?" Lord Malachi asked.

Anna couldn't have answered, even if she'd wanted to. Her throat constricted, her head ached, and her vision hazed, tears coming at last, clouding everything with their hot blur. The sadness and the anger, the furious sorrow, every-where—everything. It was as if the anger had *become* her, as if her body was nothing but a shell of wrath and grief. Oh, Great Sisters!

Your dragon is dead.

"Will you save him?" Malachi asked. Somewhere, the crow cawed.

And then—total clarity.

"No," she said.

The word came out simply, without ceremony, almost without thought.

She looked up at Lord Malachi, tears hot in her eyes, her voice thick but true: "No."

The word rang in the silence.

Lord Malachi looked at her for a moment, then made to speak, but she interrupted him.

"We are Davanórians," she said, clearing her throat. "We keep our promises. When I was nine years old, my Lord, in this very Square, I swore an oath to protect the High House of Dávanor, to serve House Dradón, and to honor the High Laws of Remain. I made a *promise*." She raised her eyes defiantly at the crowd. "As did each of you. You might have forgotten. But I remember. I *remember*. I am a soldier of House Dradón, a dragon rider of Dávanor, loyal subject of High Lady Abigail and the true High King, Bellános Dallanar. I don't know who you people are or who you serve, but I do know this: A soldier

317

never betrays her word. A soldier *never* forgets her promises. My answer is no, my Lord. Forever, *no*."

A flicker of anguish in Malachi's eyes, then he turned away and looked up and over the silent crowd.

"'No,' she says. 'No.'" He cleared his throat.

Dead quiet.

Then Malachi turned and pointed at Anna and cried hoarse-ly, "Do you *see*!? This is no soldier! This is a *fanatic*! This is not civilization. This is *savagery*! This is not good. This is *evil*! An evil that must be *cleansed*! And that cleansing begins *now*!"

The crowd roared, and the headsman stepped toward the center of the Square. The butt of his ax tapped the flagstones. Behind him, the four dark horses clacked and jingled forward, their attendant squires carrying their wicked chains. Behind the squires, two infantrymen ran up, carrying an iron brazier of hot coals on a wrought stand. They set it beside Malachi. From his belt, he withdrew the short, iron poker and lifted it for all to see.

"See well, Anna Dyer! See well the cost of *your* treachery, *your* evil, and *your* war!"

He held the poker up for another long moment then

plunged it crunching into the hissing coals.

"But first, we bring final justice to this traitor's 'blind dragon.'"

He nodded to the headsman and his horses and pointed at Moondagger. "Destroy it."

The crowd roared its approval and——.

And then the air in the High Square seemed to *swell*, as if charged before a storm.

The skin on Anna's arms chilled to gooseflesh. A tingly pulse throbbed behind her eyes.

At the center of the Square, the High Gate seemed to hum.

A song felt but not heard.

Somewhere, an alarm gong sounded.

Lord Malachi turned to the High Gate.

It flashed to life, silver radiance spilling across the Square.

Anna stared.

Someone was coming through.

But how?

Silent, silver light pulsed from the Square's center, the Gate's radiance washing over the crowd, the space framed by the Gate's arch going hazy, as if filled by silvery mist.

A massive pulse shook the Square like a silent thunderclap and the four adepts of House Fel at the Gate's legs fell backwards, knocked senseless by soundless force.

"House Fel, House Tevéss—form ranks," Lord Malachi ordered calmly. "Clear the High Square."

His men reacted professionally, as did the crowd, everyone hurrying to obey. There was no way they would get out, but they were doing their best. Green and maroon clad platoons came up quickly and surrounded the Gate in a standard square formation. The soldiers' faces were grim and determined, their carbines held at the ready. Irondusk and the rest of the dragons peered forward, growling with hungry expectation.

"Defense cannon, if you please, Sergeant Lodáz," Lord Malachi ordered.

The big Tevéss soldier turned and bellowed, "Defense cannon!"

There were five large windows set in each of the walls parallel to the opening of the High Gate. Each of these windows was secured with a pair of iron-bound shutters. At Lodáz's order, the shutters fell open and the noses of ten cannon emerged from the windows' darkness. All pointed at the High Gate.

Another silent thunderclap.

The lead adept at the Gate's center looked at Malachi for a moment, her mouth still moving, veins swelling and pulsing at her temples, eyes wide with desperation, her arms crossed fiercely across her chest as she tried to block the intruder—and then she was gone with a soundless zap into the silvery fog.

From the High Gate itself—as if from the very center of its structure—a deep wail sounded. An ancient war horn, a timeless cadence of power and majesty. Anna could still see the other half of the High Square through the arch, but even less clearly than before. The Gate was filled completely with glowing mist.

A flickering silhouette appeared at the center of the shimmering fog—the shape of the head adept from whatever world now forced the Gate open.

But no, Anna looked closer.

How could that be?

The figure was *tiny*. No larger than a small child.

The High Gate flared brighter than ever, the silhouette

vanished, and a young man stepped through the spot where the small shape had been, the Gate's mist clinging to his hair and shoulders like steam.

The young man was tall. But also quite thin and rather *odd* to behold. He wore a fitted breastplate of high silver, but the armor seemed just a touch large for him. A slender saber was belted to his waist, but not properly. When he walked, it banged awkwardly against his thigh, almost but not quite tripping him with every step. He wore beautifully made breeches of Abúcian leather, sky blue and trimmed with silver sable, and a pair of matching boots. A heavy, blue cloak was thrown over his narrow shoulders. The cloak was covered with snow. His hair was dark and cut in a soldier's crop. But the haircut looked peculiar on him, perhaps because of his head, which seemed just slightly too large for his slender neck. His eyes were large, dark, and faintly crossed, an effect magnified by the incongruous reading spectacles he wore halfway down his aquiline nose. His lips were full and turned in a kind of naïve grin, as if he were thinking of a dozen jests he could never tell. Fresh snow powdered his shoulders and his hair.

But the most astonishing thing about the young man was this: he held little Gregory, Master Zar's old messenger dragon, in his arms. But how could that be? Because this little dragon was a brilliant, bright blue, its wings supple and young. Anna stared. But it *was* Gregory, no question. The little dragon looked at her and hissed. His eyes were brilliant yellow, the milky cataracts gone. His little mouth was full of extremely white, exceptionally sharp little fangs.

"Ah," the young man said with that puzzling half-smile. "Good morning."

He squinted into the sun and held his hand up to shield his eyes, taking a look around. He nodded and stamped his feet a couple of times, shaking the snow off.

Little Gregory squeaked, leapt from his arms, and flew straight to Master Zar, nuzzling his snout against the battered Anorian's neck. Zar's eyes were smashed shut, but he managed to lift his bloody hand and hold little Gregory to his chest. Beside him, Master Khondus nodded. Master Borónd and Mother stared at the High Gate and the young man standing before it, a strange combination of disbelief and hope in their eyes.

The young man furled his cloak, shaking more snow loose from his clothing. He took off his spectacles, polished them on his cloak hem, and put them back on. But he'd gotten more snow on them, so they were no cleaner. He took them off again and looked around, casting about for something on which to clean them.

Lord Malachi had gone pale. But there was something else in his face.

Is it relief?

Then he seemed to remember himself, pulled a handkerchief from inside his leather breastplate, and handed it to the young man.

The High Square was absolutely silent. Everyone had stopped mid-exit and turned to watch the scene unfold.

The young man cleaned his spectacles, put them back on, and peered through them, momentarily cross-eyed, making sure they were clean.

"My thanks," he said.

"An honor, Lord Garen." Lord Malachi bowed, taking the handkerchief back.

A murmur ran through the crowd.

Anna stared.

Could it be?

Lord Garen Dallanar. The Under-Duke of Jallow. Lord Librarian of Remain. A spy-master, healer, and scholar whose cunning was known throughout the Realm. The son of High Lord Bellános Dallanar, the true King of Remain.

Lord Malachi cleared his throat. "I am—that is, I am—we are surprised to see you, my Lord."

"I expect so, Malachi. I expect so." Lord Garen raised his chin at Gregory. "That little dragon arrived at the Tarn some days ago carrying some disturbing information. I won't pretend with you, Malachi. Father didn't like it. Michael also was . . . well, how do I say it? *Displeased*? Yes. That's the best way to describe it. Displeased. He and Lord David were good friends, you know. Father shares some interesting history with those poor fellows, too." Lord Garen inclined his head at Master Khondus and Master Zar.

From his perch above the Square, Irondusk gave a low growl.

Lord Garen paid the great dragon no mind.

"Let's get straight to it, shall we?" he asked. "You've seized this Keep in violation of the High Laws. Dávanor is ruled by House Dradón—not House Fel. This means that High Lady Abigail is your rightful liege. She is also the rightful liege of every inhabitant of this duchy. 'Truth and honor.' Is that not right, Malachi? Is that not a common Davanórian salute?"

Dead silence.

"Well, to us, those words count." He took off his spectacles and inspected them again. "We thought Lord David had made this clear three years ago. But apparently the lesson didn't take. So here we are, once more."

"My Lord——."

Lord Garen raised a hand. Malachi's mouth closed with a soft click. "I've convinced Father that our direct involvement isn't necessary. That this is a 'misunderstanding,' nothing more. That this can be resolved without violence. That the House of Fel honors its word. That the House of Fel keeps its promises. What say you?"

Lord Garen spoke as if he was oblivious to the Fel crossbows, guns, cannon, and dragons that were pointed at him from every direction. Instead, it was as if he was speaking to a poorly behaved servant boy regarding an improperly groomed hedge.

"What say you?" Lord Garen asked again.

Malachi said nothing.

But Anna could see his mind spinning.

The new lord of House Fel could not bow to Lord Garen's will without betraying his family's alliance with Lord Gideon and with the Pretender King. Nor could he bend knee without completely losing face in front of his people and soldiers. But to challenge High King Bellános and his sons directly? Publicly? Without preparation? That was almost equally impossible. Perhaps more than that—it was insane.

"Time's short, Malachi," Lord Garen said, pushing his spectacles up onto his nose. "You'll come with me to the Tarn, of course. Gideon? Where are you? There you are. You'll come, too."

From the opposite side of the High Square, Lord Gideon stared, his chubby face red with fury.

Lord Garen paid him no mind. He turned back to Malachi. "Philip will be installed in your place. Oh, don't look so upset, Malachi. Brothers always squabble. And it won't be long. When this unpleasant business between Father and my uncle is resolved, we'll return you home. These soldiers and dragons will need to be gone from the High Keep immediately. Right after they—and you—renew your oaths to High Lady Abigail and to House Dradón. In my presence, of course."

Every eye was on Lord Malachi. Above it all, Irondusk's claws dug rhythmically into his perch, a trickle of debris and splinters streaming down the Square's wall. Lord Malachi looked at his men for a moment, swallowed, then shot a barely noticeable glance at Anna. His shoulders sagged. "As you wish, Lord Garen." He bowed.

Irondusk's growl deepened, low and ominous.

"Excellent!" Lord Garen said with a bright smile. "Splendid! Now, make your will known, and we'll get on with this."

Lord Malachi looked up over the crowd. The people returned his gaze; some with relief, some with scorn, some with wonder. Lord Gideon and most of the Tevéss soldiers stared at Malachi with outright disgust.

"In accordance with——," Lord Malachi began.

Without warning, Irondusk roared and launched from his perch straight at Anna and Moondagger, his enraged bellow thundering the walls, massive jaws wide and slavering, rust-colored scales glimmering like bloody bronze, a falling star of hate and vengeance.

Simultaneously, something else moved inside the High Gate.

It was a man. He stepped from the Gate with liquid, unstoppable grace, clad in black armor, holding a massive, black sword before him in both hands. Irondusk saw him, roared his fury, and drew a deep breath, chest glowing hot with unleashed wrath. The man seemed to leap from the Gate straight into the dragon's maw, flying black sword a tongue of dark flame, slashing downwards, stopping the dragon mid-flight, splitting its huge skull lengthwise like a razored ax through rotten wood, blood and brains exploding across the flagstones, hissing water on hot rock. Screams of fright and terror. The dragon's enormous body flipped, plowed into the side of the High Gate, stopping up against the Gate's indestructible surface. Horror and shock shuddered through the crowd. Even the soldiers seemed to cringe, frozen in place by some unseen force.

The finer details of the armored man coalesced, the Gate's silvery mist clinging to his arms and shoulders.

He was a young man. Taller than Lord Garen and wider, a body built for war. His neck was like a young bull's, thick and corded with muscle. His eyes were dark, almost black, a pair of seething pits. His dark hair was shorn short in a soldier's crop, his square jaw clean shaven. He wore full plate of high silver, but it was tinted black somehow, as if fashioned of dull obsidian. He wore a thick cloak of silver wolf pelts, a dozen tails brushing the backs of his ankles. Fresh snow covered his shoulders and hair. His sword was a shard of starless night, its pommel a black, egg-shaped stone in which light did not reflect. A single drop of Iron-dusk's blood marked his smooth cheek.

"Lord Michael!" someone screamed with pure, naked terror.

The name rippled through the crowd like a dread wind.

Michael Dallanar. The Dark Lord of Kon. General of the Tarn. Older brother to Lord Garen and second born son of the great Bellános Dallanar, High King of Remain.

Lord Michael did not speak.

Instead he stood motionless in the spreading pool of dragon's blood and looked over the crowd, his massive sword held loosely in one hand.

We thirst . . . all of us.

A weird voice. A woman's voice. The words blending and

warping together as if whispered from a hundred mouths. To Anna, the voice seemed to come from the black blade itself. Familiar, somehow. Yet no one else seemed to hear it.

Then Lord Michael spoke. His voice was soft, but carried across the Square with total, royal authority. It was unlike anything Anna had ever heard.

It was the voice of absolute violence.

"You men of House Fel there," Lord Michael said, "stand down. Fel riders, get you and your dragons gone to the Felshold. Gideon, get your men back to Tévesshold."

"But I was just about to—," Lord Garen began, raising his hand as if to protest. Lord Michael shot him a look and Lord Garen put his hand down, shut his mouth, and adjusted his spectacles.

A shuffling murmur ran through the crowd. The riders and soldiers of House of Fel and House Tevéss looked from each other to Lord Michael, then from Lord Michael to Lord Malachi and Lord Gideon. Their faces were worried and confused. Captain Corónd looked down from his perch at Lord Malachi, his face a mask of contempt. His bronze dragon hissed.

"Gentlemen," Lord Michael said softly, his voice somehow present in every ear, his dark eyes catching the light. Anna shuddered in spite of herself. "I'll not ask again."

Simple, silent obedience.

The soldiers of House Fel and House Tevéss lowered and sheathed their weapons, heads bowed, while the Tevéss and Fel dragon riders—all of them, Corónd included—immediately turned their mounts away from the Square and launched toward their homes, maroon and green war banners coursing behind them.

Lord Michael glanced at Lord Garen, a strange look in his eye, a mix of fondness and exasperation. Lord Garen shrugged apologetically and adjusted his spectacles.

Lord Michael shook his head and sheathed his black blade with a click. He held the massive sword beneath its cross guard. Then he turned to Lord Malachi, his boots sucking at the blood beneath his feet. The gory pool continued to spread, the deep red channeling down between the flagstones before overwhelming them entirely.

"You're a traitor, Fel," he said plainly, letting the words sink in.

Lord Malachi didn't look up. His eyes were fixed upon the bloody flagstones.

"I'd butcher you like a newborn piglet and burn the Felshold to the ground this day, this moment—if the decision were mine. But it's not. And, fortunate for you, I honor my vows and my orders. The High King of Remain will suffer no more noble-born blood needlessly spilt. Instead, you and Gideon will follow my brother to the Tarn. There you'll beg my father's forgiveness—what? Did I see you mutter something there, Lord Gideon? My offer displeases you? You have something to say? You think it unfair?"

Across the square, Lord Gideon's plump face went pale. He bowed his head.

"As I was saying," Lord Michael continued. "You'll both come with us. You'll both beg my father's forgiveness. And then you'll both stay with us, as honored guests, until the war is done. Before you go, however, you'll write one letter to each of your most trusted captains. There you shall make clear: If one further sword on Dávanor is drawn against High Lady Abigail, if one further word of treason is spoken against House Dradón, I will return—and I will be free to act as I choose. Where is the High Lady?"

"In her chambers, my Lord," Lord Malachi bowed.

Lord Michael nodded. "I'll speak with her in a moment. Great Sisters save you, Malachi, if she's in any way harmed."

Malachi seemed to shrink into himself.

Lord Michael nodded. "Is everything understood? Is the will of the High King clear to you?"

"Yes, my Lord." Lord Malachi did not lift his eyes.

Lord Michael looked across the High Square. "And you, Gideon?"

Lord Gideon bowed. "Yes, my Lord."

"You will obey the High King's commands?"

"Yes, my Lord," Tevéss and Fel said together.

"Louder please. There are many ears here. We want no confusion."

"Yes, my Lord!" they cried.

But Lord Michael had already turned away, as if the High Lords weren't worth his breath. "Garen, please remove Zar, Khondus, and Boród to the Tarn for treatment." He glanced at Moondagger, lifting his sword in Dagger's direction. "Take this dragon as well." He turned to the line of kneeling House

Dradón soldiers. "You men, free your imprisoned fellows, disarm these soldiers, and escort these good people from the Drádonhold. But hear me well: The High King shall broach no further fighting. No reprisals, no vengeance, *nothing*. If one drop of blood is shed—one drop, be it Fel or Tevéss or Dradón—then all will face *our* justice. Understood?"

"Yes, sir!" The soldiers of House Dradón saluted and got moving.

Lord Michael turned to Anna, stepped up behind her, and unlocked the manacles at her back. She stood, rubbing her wrists. Mother, Penelope, and Wendi walked toward her, their eyes wide with wonder.

"You are Anna Dyer," Lord Michael said softly. It was not a question.

"Your servant, my Lord." She bowed.

"I got your message."

She bowed, low and long. When she looked up again, he was looking her over. His eyes were dark, intelligent, and utterly fierce. He looked into her face, their eyes met—and something electrical passed between them. He cleared his throat. "Your injuries, they're not severe?"

"No, my Lord." Her face flushed, in spite of herself. "My dragon——."

"Leave your mount to Lord Garen." Lord Michael cocked his head at his brother. "He may not know a sword from a stick in the mud, but he's the finest healer in all the Remain."

69

A MONTH LATER, the High Square was once again packed with people: a jubilant, celebrating crowd laughing and milling under a glorious noon sun. They crammed the walls, every window and balcony filled with lords and ladies and soldiers and merchants from across Dávanor, high houses and low, House Dradón banners flying from every wall and hand, each man, woman, and child bedecked in their finest sky blue. High above it all, perched on the Square's uppermost ramparts, House Dradón's strongest remaining dragons rested, Nightlove at their pinnacle, huge and refreshed, her brilliant white scales blinding in the sun, eyes shining like liquid sapphire.

Along the Square's eastern side, on axis with the High Gate and its blue-robed adepts, High Lady Abigail sat on a throne of silver wood. She wore a tiny gown of Eulorian silk; a simple diadem of high silver rested in her blond hair. In her right hand, she carried a miniature scepter topped with a large sapphire enclosed in a sculpted rendering of the Dallanar Sun. Her little feet rested on a sky blue cushion. A huge House Dradón war banner hung from the wall behind her.

The High Lady was flanked by her advisors, councilors, and captains, Master Khondus, Master Zar, and Master Boród first among them.

Master Khondus wore a fresh velvet doublet of sky blue under a greatcloak of heavy, blue wool. The wounds on his head were near gone, his right eye was well on its way to healing, and his nose had been reset, showing only the barest hint of bruise. He wore the high silver revolver he'd taken from Floren d' Rent a month ago in the stable, crossholstered at his leather belt; it glimmered like milky steel, fresh with new polish.

Master Zar stood at Master Khondus's side. The stocky Anorian held little Gregory across his chest and was busy feeding the ravenous little beast bloody scraps of lamb from a silver goblet. Zar would kiss the dragon on the nose, dangle a shred of meat above Gregory's mouth with thick, purple fingers, then repeat. The little dragon's blue scales and white fangs flashed brilliantly. Zar's scalp had been fully healed on Kon; the Dallanar Sun tattooed on his forehead glowed white in the bright daylight. He wore a cloak of purple velvet and a rich doublet of fine Eulorian silk. At his thick neck, a silver amulet in the shape of a book, the token of the Great Sister Aaryn, glimmered. Like those of Master Khondus, Master Zar's other wounds were well on their way to healing. His only care in the world now was making sure little Gregory had a limitless supply of sloppy meat on which to sup.

Master Boród stood next to Zar, his head bowed, his bandaged hands cradled before him. The Master wore a simple robe of blue cotton, the hood cast back around his shoulders, a new pair of wire-framed reading spectacles perched on his nose.

Directly in front of the High Lady's dais, Mother, Penelope, and Wendi waited on a long, ceremonial carpet of sky blue. They wore new gowns of Eulorian silk in various shades of blue along with simple, silver jewelry at their necks and ears. Mother, striking and tall, stood a step behind her daughters, a ravaged Dradón battle flag folded carefully in front of her.

"Here they come!" someone shouted.

There was a blaze of silver trumpets, the Dradón dragons thundered the sky, and the Square's main portal opened to a roar of deafening cheers. Through the door, scores of standard bearers marched, House Dradón's banner first and largest among them. The Dradón banner was followed by dozens more, one from each of Dávanor's loyal minor houses. The Goróns, the Hensporters, the Kyne, the Tallerduns, the Lef, the Berénor, and so many more. Every color of the rainbow, their coats of arms waving in the noon breeze. A column of trumpeters came next, their blaring horns high and true, curled silver gleaming in the sun. Then came Captain Jenifer Fyr, leading a column of perfectly coordinated Dradón guardsmen, steel spears glimmering with spotless polish. She had taken wounds during the battle in the High Square and still wore a silk sling for her right arm, but her smile was fierce and utterly proud.

"Anna!" Wendi cried, pointing at her from across the Square.

Anna Dyer stood in the portal's shadow, waiting for her

cue to enter, looking out into the cheering square.

It didn't seem real.

Everywhere she looked, they were shouting her name.

"Anna! Anna! Anna!"

The trumpets blazed.

That's you.

She took a deep breath and stepped into the sun.

She wore new scout armor and gear, all of it custom fit and fully functional. The high silver dagger she'd received from Master Khondus was sheathed upside down on a polished bandolier marked by silver clasps and studs. The revolver she'd received from Master Zar was slung in a new custom rig beneath her left armpit. Her shoulder pads were modest, the right much smaller than the left, perfectly balanced for the war lance, both dyed sky blue. The right pad was freshly stamped with the coat of arms of House Dradón, a white dragon rampant; the left pad was marked by House Dallanar's six-pointed sun. Her breeches and boots were of the best Abúcian leather, both tinted blue to match the colors of her High House. She wore a thin band of silver in her hair.

Of course, they'd told her to carry a lance in with her,

so she'd done it, even though it was just for show. It was an ancient spear of gleaming high silver from the Drádon-hold's Inner Armory, impossibly light, impossibly strong, a primordial weapon crafted during the first years of the Founding, its strange, fluid design seeming more a product of nature than craft.

When she stepped fully into the sun, the crowd cheered like mad and the dragons roared their triumph. Anna smiled and looked up at them.

"ANNA! ANNA! ANNA!"

And then she couldn't help herself.

She lifted the ancient weapon over her head and cried.

"*For the Remain!*"

The crowd went mad, the dragons bellowed, and the Square trembled. The chant began in earnest.

"Anna! Anna! Anna!"

She looked past the Gate; saw Mother, Penelope, and Wendi. Penelope and Wendi were cheering and yelling their heads off, hands cupped to mouths, and Mother . . . Mother was crying. Anna had never seen it before. Mother's chin was up, her back was straight, but tears streamed down her cheeks. She held the destroyed Dradón war banner tightly to her chest.

Anna looked her in the eye, raised the lance again, for her and for her alone, and the crowd *roared* their approval. Mother laughed, shook her head, then bowed and clapped her hands, grabbing up Wendi, squeezing her to the banner at her chest. "Lemme go! Lemme *go*!" Anna could see Wendi say.

Behind her family, Master Khondus, Master Zar, and Master BoróND smiled. Anna saw Gregory snap at Master Zar's fingers, the stocky Anorian promptly kissing the little dragon on the nose and shoving a gob of bloody meat into his mouth.

High Lady Abigail raised her little scepter and the crowd went immediately quiet. Then she spoke, her voice high, true, and perfectly trained.

"Step forward, Anna Dyer, Dragon Rider of House Dradón, Defender of Dávanor!"

Total, absolute chaos. The entire Square seemed to buckle on its foundations. Sky blue flags waved everywhere. The dragons' roar shook the heavens.

"And step forward, Moondagger, Prince of Dragons!"

Anna's breath caught.

She knew he'd been treated. She knew he was better. But he'd been on Kon the entire time, under the direct care of Lord Garen at the Tarn, or so Master Boród had said. And none of them had said anything about him coming back.

At the High Gate, the House Dradón adepts raised their voices in song, and the Gate flared to life, its brilliant silver shining brighter than the sun, its noiseless sound like a high, clean hymn, totally familiar—eternally unknowable.

And then Moondagger was there.

He stepped through the Gate, scales pure white, wings like sails, huge eyes glowing like silver moons. He wore new gear, as well. A war saddle of molded blue leather trimmed with silver. New reins of soft Abúcian hide. A banner of Eulorian silk crossed his chest emblazoned with the House Dradón crest: a white dragon rampant on a field of high blue. His claws had been polished and his whiskers had been carefully trimmed. His fully-sprouted horns had been burnished until they glowed like white fire, just a touch of black beginning to show at their tips.

And he was *huge*.

Almost twice the size she'd last seen him.

His eyes sought her out immediately, connected, and she walked straight down the blue carpet toward him, trying to be solemn and dignified like they'd told her, but she realized suddenly that she didn't care, that her dragon was home, and that she just couldn't wait.

So she ran, dropped the lance to the carpet, and threw her arms around his neck, pushing her cheek into his scales. The crowd went completely berserk, but the noise seemed not to exist. She pulled back and looked into his eyes. He leaned forward and touched his smooth forehead to hers. Together, they closed their eyes, his warmth filling her mind with everything she'd ever need.

This and only this.

Forever.

70

THERE WERE SPEECHES. And then there were more speeches, and then Anna gave a little speech that they'd prepared for her, and then there were more speeches. Through all of it, Anna kept her hand on Dagger's neck, savoring the feel of the coiled power beneath his warm white scales.

He wanted to *fly*. They both did. The way his broad tongue tasted the air, the way his muscles bunched and shifted, the way his claws dug into the new blue carpet, his eyes rolling with what seemed like exasperation every time yet another speaker would step up onto the dais to commend their bravery and dedication. But then it was done, there was a final cheer, and then the tables and the mead and the food started coming out, the celebration beginning in earnest.

Wendi ran across the courtyard and leapt into Anna's arms.

"*Now* can I ride him?" Wendi giggled as Anna gobbled her ear.

"Of course." Anna smiled.

Mother, Penelope, Master Khondus, and Master Zar came over and surrounded her, hugging her, patting her on the back, squeezing her shoulders. Little Gregory squeaked and Zar gave him some more meat.

"You keep that up, Zar," Master Khondus grinned, "he won't be able to do his job. Be wider than he is long."

They laughed, Gregory snarled, and Master Zar gave him another bloody scrap.

"Can't help myself." The squat Anorian shrugged.

Master Khondus took Anna by the shoulders and looked down into her face. His eyes shone.

"You've made us so proud, Anna. There're hardly words to—."

"What's *this*?!" Penelope cried, from the other side of Moondagger.

Dagger snorted, and they all moved around to his opposite side to see what Penelope was pointing at. There, in a scabbard of blue Abúcian leather, was a short saber of high silver. It was slung on Dagger's left side, so that it could be cross drawn with ease from the rider's right. Its handle was slender and freshly wrapped with a blue leather cord. The circular cross guard had been meticulously shaped as the open mouth of a roaring dragon, the blade extending through its open fangs. With all the fuss, Anna hadn't noticed it.

Tied to the scabbard was a slim, leather message tube. It was capped with a roundel of burnished silver that had been stamped with the six-pointed Dallanar Sun. Everyone looked at each other curiously.

Anna unclipped the sword and held it beneath the cross guard. Ancient, indestructible, priceless; it weighed almost nothing. She handed the sword to Penelope, unfastened the tube, and withdrew from it a single sheet of clean cotton paper. On it, in an elegant, formal hand, was written the following missive:

To Anna Dyer, Dragon Knight, House Dradón—

Few indeed are those willing to live and die for their Honor and Word. Yet here you are, Anna, alive and victorious. The Kingdom owes you a most Solemn Debt, and I salute you, your Dragon, and your Great Achievement. Yet there is more Good Work to be done. Complete your Training—then join us. Let this Letter mark not the End of your Journey, but its Beginning.

Lord Bellános Dallanar, Duke of Kon, High King of Remain

p.s. The last Owner of this Sword was Anna Dallanar, second-born daughter of Hakon the Terrible. I am told that it was crafted early in the Founding, perhaps by the Great Alea herself. Regardless, it has served my House for many Years and on many Worlds, and it is yours, a Symbol of your

Strength, Honor, and Dedication. Use it well, in the Service of
Remain.

p.s.s. If Khondus and Zar are there with you, please do remind
them that they still owe me ten Gold Suns for their Wager on the
Bear, and that I intend to collect—one way or another!

Anna looked from the letter, to the high silver sword, to
her friends and family around her. Dagger growled and shifted his weight, still hungry for the sky. Everyone looked at
her expectantly.

"Well?!" Penelope cried finally. "What's he *say*, for the
Sisters' sake?"

Anna shook her head with wonder. "He says it's the
beginning."

71

THE CELEBRATION LASTED all afternoon and continued well
into evening. But at last, as a huge white moon climbed the
night sky, the final glass was raised, the final toast was given,
and the final song was sung.

Mother, Penelope, and Wendi had left for home several

hours earlier after many hugs and kisses, with Wendi making Anna promise—actually demanding that Anna swear a formal oath—to visit next week with Dagger and to take her on her long-awaited dragon ride. Master Khondus and Master Zar had ended up challenging each other to some kind of bizarre table game that involved several jugs of mead, a brass bowl, and the counting of the moments between little Gregory's hiccups. "An ancient Anorian tradition," Master Zar grinned, his purple eyes bright. Master Khondus had nodded seriously. Now the two of them were loudly recounting some insane adventure they'd had with Bellános fifty years past while Captain Fyr and her men roared with laughter, pounding the tables, shaking their heads in disbelief. Master Boród had pushed his wire-framed spectacles up onto his nose and had respectfully asked Anna if he could take Moondagger down to the lower stables to measure the dragon's growth and to give Dagger the last of his medicine as prescribed by Lord Garen. Anna had agreed, gently holding the scholar's destroyed hands. She knew that Voidbane's son would receive the very best of care.

And now it was time for bed, but she wasn't tired, and she

had something she wanted to do anyway. So she slipped away from the High Square without anyone noticing and walked down to the Dragon Steps with only the moon to light her path. From there, she made her way to the lower stables and crossed that last series of bridges to the main door. She opened it and stepped down the stone staircase into the stable proper.

That's odd.

She cocked her head.

Halfway down the stable's central hallway, she could see Dagger's stall door. It was cracked open and warm lantern light spilled onto the ancient flagstones. She heard him snort at her presence as she approached.

He was waiting for her, curled in the golden straw, his nose resting on his white tail, his huge eyes glowing like twin moons. To the right of the door, directly beneath a suspended lantern, someone had carefully laid out his new saddle, his new tackle, and the rest of his gear on a trio of wooden rigging stands. Someone had known that she'd come.

It took her about half a bell's time to get Dagger saddled and harnessed, and she still wore her new scout gear from the day's festivities, so there were no issues there. Ready to go, she slid his stall door wide and walked him down the hallway, up the far ramp, and out onto the broad flight deck.

The moon was bright and enormous, floating high above the piling clouds to the west. The air was cool but not cold, with just a touch of breeze, just enough to stir her dark hair and to flicker the torches in the far towers.

Perfect flying weather.

She smiled and patted Dagger's neck, closing her eyes, savoring the smell of the wind. Dagger grunted impatiently and bumped his head against hers. She chuckled and opened her eyes. His scales shone white in the moon's pale glow.

She mounted and clipped on, the new saddle soft and sturdy beneath her. It was rather different from their first rig, and it felt great; snug and perfect. She gave herself a solid checking over, tugging and pulling and twisting to make sure everything was in order, put her helmet on, and brushed out her goggles.

You ready?

Dagger snorted and tutted, as if to say that he'd been ready for the last month. She smiled, fit her goggles over her eyes, and put her hands on his neck for a long moment, feeling the rippling power beneath his smooth scales. She settled deeper into her saddle, closed her eyes—and the night opened up before her.

"Go," she whispered.

They launched into moonlight.

Epilogue

"I AM DEFEATED," High Lord Dorómy Dallanar whispered to himself.

He touched the blue-grey disc of polished agate in front of him. The disc represented the world of Dávanor. It was a small but important duchy, ruled by a small but important High House.

Dorómy Dallanar stood in the Chamber of Worlds, the great map room of the mighty citadel of Káladar. He cut a striking figure: tall and broad of chest; full, black beard, carefully trimmed and shaped to a point at his chin; dark eyes, widely set, glittering with strength and cunning. His garb was simple: the standard silver-grey uniform of the Silver Legions, well-worn jack boots of black Abúcian leather, and a black leather belt. A dagger of high silver was scabbarded horizontally across the small of his back and an ancient revolver was strapped beneath his left armpit. He sported no jewelry save a wide band of high silver on his right index finger, a gift from his brother Bellános, long ago. No marks or insignia showed his status. Like his legionaries, he wore his dark hair in a short soldier's crop.

Dorómy cleared his throat. A small, silver token sat atop the blue-grey disc. The silver token meant that the world belonged to him, that the High House of that world was loyal to his cause, that he could count on the ruler of that world to support his war with men, arms, and blood.

All that could have been true. All that *should* have been true.

But it wasn't.

And Dorómy didn't know why.

Dorómy tapped the disc of Dávanor, then turned away, gazing out the windows to the west. The citadel of Káladar loomed high atop the sun-drenched crags of Dothar, the steepest cliff on the great world of Paráden. Looking out over the Sea of the Sun, it was the Kingdom's most ancient High Keep, a soaring mass of tawny stone and golden battlements that heaved itself skyward, towering above the land and waters as if built by titans of old. Primordial, vast, indomitable, the Káladar was the center of the Realm, the site of the Kingdom's first and oldest High Gate, an eternal symbol of the Remain's strength, durability, and power.

"And yet, for all that," Dorómy murmured to the sea, "I *am* defeated."

He'd never speak those words in public, of course. Not even in front of his most trusted advisors, few as they might be. He was the "Silver King," after all. The Gate Master. The Prince of the Sea of the Sun, the Grand Duke of Paráden, Ward of Káladar, the Protector of the Realm, and the High King of Remain. As such, his every word and deed must embody the very essence of authority. Indeed, for the Silver King, there could be no such thing as "defeat."

Right.

Dorómy scoffed at the thought and smoothed his black beard. Years of political maneuvering, court intrigue, and outright war had taught him many lessons regarding moments like these. And one of the most important was this: A man who would keep his power could lie to everyone else forever, but he could never lie to himself. The moment you began to trust your own pretense—the moment you started believing your own lies—was the moment you gave your life and your position to your enemies.

Deceit can live everywhere, save your own heart.

It was wisdom that Dorómy had earned the hard way.

"I am defeated," he said again, letting the words sink in,

letting himself taste their meaning. He turned away from the windows, back to the Chamber.

The Chamber of Worlds was a circular room, sixty paces across, paved with the rich, golden-white marble of Paráden's finest quarries. All its walls, except those that faced west, were hung floor to ceiling with polished bookshelves made of the finest Anorian oak. The western wall was made almost entirely of glass, a wall of leaded windows that opened onto a rock-cut terrace from which you could enjoy unrivaled views of the Dothar cliffs and the Sea of the Sun. The bookshelves were filled with well-ordered atlases, scrolls, maps, navigational tables, and charts—the geographical records of all one hundred and four of the Kingdom's worlds, a library of topographies and landscapes second only to the royal collections of Genonea. Around the Chamber's circumference, lamps flickered brightly, their flames safely caged in fixtures of gilded bronze.

In the Chamber's exact center, where Dorómy stood, rested the Stand of Worlds. The Stand was a large, circular table, ten paces across and meticulously fashioned of the finest materials. Some scholars argued that the Stand was truly ancient, conceived and crafted by the mad Volzabon, friend and sometimes-lover of the Great Sister Alea the First. Others said that it had been commissioned hundreds of years later, by the great scholar-queen Katherine. Regardless, it was a marvel of artistry. Its innumerable, squat legs were made of Anorian oak, all as thick as Dorómy's thighs and carved as powerfully muscled telamons carrying mighty burdens. Their feet were perfectly shaped dragons' claws squeezing bulging worlds in their taloned grips. The table top itself, however, was the true marvel. It was a single, massive slab of dark Marsinion granite, its wide, polished edge painstakingly inlaid with an interlaced pattern of high silver ribbons that braided their way around the table's circumference before winding beneath the table to the Stand's central column. From there, the silver ribbons wound into the guts of the Káladar, terminating at the citadel's mighty High Gate.

But it was the Stand's surface that concerned Dorómy now.

There, inlaid and polished in the most exacting detail, lay a schematized map of the Kingdom's one hundred and four worlds, each duchy represented by a single disc made of some native stone. Each disc was a different size and color. Some were huge, some were large, and some were rather tiny. The disc representing Paráden, for example, was near the middle of the Stand, a huge disc of polished, golden-white marble nearly two palms in diameter. Tóvonok, on the other hand, a duchy from which Dorómy drew some of his most ruthless shock troops, was represented by a blood-red disc no larger than a coin. The great world of Kon, Bellános's wintery home, was represented by a disc nearly as large as Paráden, a scintillating white circle of blue-white quartz. Regardless of its size or color, each disc was connected to several others by a complex pattern of inlaid high silver, hair-fine arcs that represented the High Gates' eternal paths and songs, the songs that bound together the Kingdom's worlds.

Dorómy frowned and put his fists on the Stand's smooth surface. Millennia ago, during the Founding, when the songs of the High Gates had been at the apex of their power, the Stand had been a living thing, able to be spun, adjusted, and focused so that the user's eyes could rest upon any world at will. (Indeed, it was often said that the great scholar-queen Katherine could control the Stand with such dexterity that she could read a book over a man's shoulder anywhere in the Realm.) But those days were long gone. Nowadays, it took all of Dorómy's strength, and sometimes the assistance of an adept or two, to simply rotate the Stand's surface, and even that could be a slow, draining process not often worth the effort.

But it had been worth it today.

In front of him, between his fists, rested that small, blue-grey disc of polished agate.

Dávanor.

"I was defeated *here*." Dorómy touched the edge of the disc with his index finger. The blue-grey stone was cool and smooth.

Years ago, when this silly war first started, Dorómy had placed tactical tokens made of either silver or obsidian onto each of the Stand's one hundred and four discs. The tokens made of silver designated worlds that he certainly—or almost certainly—controlled. Tokens made of obsidian designated worlds that were controlled by his brother, Bellános. Right now, silver tokens outnumbered obsidian by more than two to one.

And yet, I was defeated.

He knew that much. He understood that much. Just as he had understood it many times in the past. Defeat was a part of war. Reversals were to be expected during any campaign. To deny that truth was to deny reality itself.

"War is a savage, chaotic horse," the great Poder Jarlen had once said. "But victory will always go to the general who bridles, mounts, and rides with the most courage, the most ferocity, and the most *conviction*."

Some losses were inevitable.

What matters is perseverance.

But *how* had he been beaten?

He stared at the blue-grey disc of Dávanor. His own ignorance was infuriating. And dangerous.

Both of Dávanor's High Gates were now closed to him. Two of his great cannon had been seized. And the world's unique and priceless dragons were lost to his Legions. He had been totally outflanked.

There was a soft knock on the far door.

"Come," Dorómy said. His baritone was perfectly calm.

One half of the double door in the eastern wall opened. A Silver Guardsman stepped inside, crossed his chest with his fist, and bowed.

"Lord Lessip has arrived, Your Grace."

"Show him in, lieutenant."

"Yes, Your Grace."

The Guardsman shut the door. A moment later, he opened it again, and Lord Corlen Lessip, High General and Grand Duke of Peléa, entered.

Lessip was short, rotund, and impeccably dressed. He wore a jacket of Eulorian silk cut in the latest fashion, a grey doublet, and matching grey pants. He kept his dark red hair a bit longer than was usual in war time, the tips just touching the top of his collar. Both his fleshy ears were adorned with fine hoops of gold. He wore gems on his chubby fingers, a fine ruby on each pinky finger and blood-red garnets on each thumb—all meticulously cut and set by Paráden's best jewelers. He was clean shaven, save a small patch of dark red hair below his plump lower lip. At first glance, you might be tempted to call Lessip a poseur or even a dandy. But you'd be mistaken. Lessip was Dorómy's spy master, his chief tactician, and one of the most ruthless men in the Kingdom. While his dress was flamboyant, to say the least, Dorómy knew that the man wore spring-loaded daggers in each of his silken sleeves and that his boot tips held hidden crescents of poisoned steel. Beneath his doublet lay a vest of high silver, light and indestructible. He was a short, round, eccentric man, yes. But he moved with that smooth grace that marked the Remain's most dangerous fighters. Brilliant, calculating, merciless. He was Dorómy's most trusted confidant.

Lessip spoke a few words to the Guardsman, then turned into the room. He carried a large, ornate bird cage. The cage was crafted of high silver. Inside the cage, a large black crow sat atop a gnarled perch. Lessip approached the Stand of Worlds and bowed respectfully.

"Your Grace," he said. His voice was a mellow tenor.

Dorómy nodded. Lessip set the cage on the floor and glanced over the Stand of Worlds, taking it in all at once. The crow fluttered but was otherwise silent, its only motion a slight cock of head.

"What do we know?" Dorómy asked.

"Alas, I myself have no more news to share, Your Grace," Lessip said.

Dorómy scowled at the crow and raised an eyebrow at

Lessip.

"More vague talk," Lessip continued. "Treachery within either the House of Fel or the House of Tevéss is the most common explanation. Although I just heard now that Lord Fel was killed by two teenage boys and a trained swarm of messenger dragons. The widest range of rumor."

"We need facts, Lessip. Not lowborn gossip." Dorómy's voice was perfectly calm.

"Of course, Your Grace," Lessip said, bowing.

Dorómy shook his head. "How did Abigail—a nine-year-old girl—outmatch both Tevéss and Fel? Fel was no fool. He killed Lord David with ease—and David was a cunning, experienced soldier. Lady Abigail is a child, for the Sisters' sake. A *child*. Yes, she has captains of some worth, but even so. Did Bellános help her? Did Bellános know? How? I find it impossible to believe that House Dradón could've defended itself—alone—against a coordinated effort so carefully conceived. Bellános must've helped her. High General Ruge and a few others agree. Most of the others don't think it possible."

"Of course it's possible," Lessip said, his lips pursed. "It is Bellános Dallanar we're talking about. And yet, the siege on Kon continues in earnest. Your brother is hard-pressed, no doubt. If he did send her aid, it couldn't have been easy for him."

Dorómy frowned. "Would my brother hazard everything for one world? Needlessly expose his High Gate to our adepts? Risk all for one duchy?"

"You know the answer as well as I, Your Grace. Bellános understands the Davanórian mind. He knows what it means should he fail in his promise. 'For this Reason the Dragon Riders of Dávanor are rightly feared throughout the Realm: Nothing is more terrifying than a Warrior willing to die for his Word.' Or so it's written."

Dorómy nodded at the reference.

"Moreover," Lessip continued, "if Bellános did send Lady Abigail aid, it could only have been for the briefest of moments. Our adepts have sensed no major changes in the High Gates' songs."

"And yet." Dorómy scratched at his nose. "His adepts have proven most proficient in screening his movements, not to mention deflecting and circumnavigating our own assaults."

"He is called the Silver Fox for good reason, eh?"

"Great Sisters curse the man." Dorómy shook his head, but he smiled. It was hard not to admire his brother's skill. Dorómy had Kate, yes. But what he wouldn't give to have one of his *nephews* serve beneath him as High General . . . .

"I have half a mind to force Dávanor's gate, to send in the Legions *en masse*," Dorómy said.

Lessip nodded. "Indeed. But even if our adepts could penetrate their defenses—which, quite honestly, I doubt—what would we meet? A few squads of House Dradón guardsmen? Or two of our own great cannon supported by a hundred irate dragons and a company of Michael's ogres?"

"Too true." Dorómy grinned. "Can I offer you refreshment?"

"Honored, Your Grace."

Dorómy walked to the wall and pulled the golden rope that hung there. A moment later, the far door opened and the attendant Silver Guardsman entered, bowed, and saluted.

"Mead for Lord Lessip and myself, if you please, lieutenant," Dorómy said.

The Guardsman bowed and closed the door behind him.

"I've been dwelling on another possibility," Dorómy said.

"Is it possible that Bellános anticipated our move from the beginning? Surely he saw the vulnerability there. We certainly did. Is it possible that he'd already assembled forces? That he was waiting for *us* to strike? Did Fel and Tevéss walk into an ambush? Were we caught in our own trap?"

"If so," Lessip said, "it was masterfully done."

"Agreed."

"And if so," Lessip continued, "not only were we defeated, but we were defeated in what appears to be defiance of the High Laws. There were several missives on my desk this morning asking—rather indirectly, of course—if Fel and Tevéss acted under our orders. Toromon Jor of Hakonar is saying—quite publically and to anyone who will listen—that we were the aggressors here."

"Great Sisters curse that man."

Lessip cocked his head in assent.

"Did Bellános lure us into this?" Dorómy looked at Lessip directly. "Is it possible?"

"It's possible, of course," Lessip said. "But the rumors I've heard give no hint of organized or planned resistance. Perhaps bad luck, rather than the skill of your brother, was the real enemy here."

"You don't believe that."

"No." Lessip shrugged and looked at the crow. "Take it as testament to my own ignorance."

Dorómy nodded. Lessip was the only man he'd ever known to speak thus in his presence. No lies. No pretense. No flattery. Just the truth, as he saw it.

"And what of our spy?" Dorómy looked at the crow, a slight frown on his face. The bird cocked its head. Its black eyes glittered intelligently.

"I've not yet asked him," Lessip said. "Indeed, he has only now arrived, not one bell past."

A soft rap on the door.

"Come," Dorómy said.

The Silver Guardsman opened the door and let a servant wearing formal palace garb into the chamber. The servant carried a golden tray that held a tall beaker of mead and two golden cups. He placed the tray on an ornate serving table, carried the table to the Stand of Worlds, and set it down beside it. He poured two cups, bowed, and left. The Silver Guardsman shut the door behind him.

Dorómy handed a cup to Lessip, then raised his own and sighed. "To Bellános Dallanar."

Lessip raised his cup. "To lessons learned."

They nodded, looked each other in the eye, and drank deeply.

Dorómy set his glass down. He took the silver tactical token that had rested atop Dávanor's disc for the last year and replaced it with one made of obsidian.

"Dávanor belongs to Bellános now," Dorómy admitted.

"For the moment." Lessip inclined his head.

"Shall we hear what this thing has to say?" Dorómy glanced at the crow. He made no effort to keep the distaste from his voice.

Lessip nodded, turned, and walked to the chamber's door. He locked the door and withdrew a silver box from his pocket. He opened the lid and took from the box a small, clicking mantis of high silver. The mantis had shiny black eyes, like tiny shards of obsidian. Lessip pricked his finger, whispered something to the mantis, and dripped two drops of blood into its ticking mandibles. The mantis shivered and rubbed its front claws together. Lessip placed it on the door handle and whispered a final word. The mantis went still as stone.

Lessip returned to the Stand and lifted the crow's cage from the floor. The crow squeezed its perch, black eyes silent and gleaming. Dorómy noticed a strange bend in its right wing.

Lessip opened the cage's door. The crow dropped from its perch, cocked its head, and hopped to the Stand. It gave the map and the tactical tokens a glance, then leapt to the air, circling the Stand twice before splitting into two dark shapes, the shapes dropping to the Chamber's floor, becoming large, billowing up like black smoke, taking human form in a swirl of dark fog, shadowy feathers dropping from arms and fingers, tendrils of murky vapor circling and gathering into the coils and loops of hooded robes. One of the shapes was tall. The other was tiny, like a child. The tiny one reached up and took the tall one's hand. The tall one carried a sword of black iron, holding the blade under the hilt, tip pointed behind it, its shoulder sagging with the weight, as if the weapon was too heavy to bear. Its face was hidden in a deep cowl, but its hands were black claws, its fingers like skeletal talons.

Kalaban. Dorómy frowned. Or so such a thing would've

been known in ancient times.

The tiny one threw back his hood and revealed a pale, child-like face. He was completely bald, his eyes heavily lidded and colorless. His skin was almost white, like an albino's. A flat, black stone—the size of a bird's egg—was set into the center of his pale forehead amidst a cluster of purplish veins. The stone reflected no light. The veins seemed to radiate from the stone, fanning back over the tiny man's skull. A band of black ink was tattooed directly beneath his tiny bottom lip, running down his tiny chin and disappearing beneath his jaw. The little man had a soft overbite, like a baby might have. He bowed and raised his right hand in formal greeting, wincing a bit, as if his arm pained him. When he spoke, his voice was high and lisping, like a child's.

"Hail, High Lord Dorómy Dallanar! Silver King, Master of Gates, Prince of the Sea of the Sun, Grand Duke of Teládon, High Ward of Káladar, Protector of the Realm, and true King of Remain."

Dorómy barely tilted his head. "Sles."

The tiny man bowed again, perhaps too deeply and too long, the faintest hint of sarcasm in his formality. "We appreciate your willingness to converse with us. Truly honored." Sles lisped and looked around the chamber. "It has been many years since our people walked the halls of the mighty Káladar. Truly, the tales are nothing to the thing itself. It is said that its great walls were planned by the great Acasius himself, is it not?"

"So it is said," Dorómy said, frowning.

"Ah!" Sles said, his lisp becoming more pronounced. "Did the Great King see his full plans come to pass? Or, perhaps, one of his High Sisters completed his great work? We are, you might say, *students* of your long history. Perhaps we could see the Great King's Gate? There is none grander, none more powerful in all the Kingdom. Or so it is said. Oh, what a sight it must be!"

"You have something for me, voidling?" Dorómy asked. "If not, then Lord Lessip will see you out."

Beside Sles, the kalaban growled. Dorómy saw Lessip pivot at the sound and take a step toward the creature, placing himself slightly between Dorómy's person and the cloaked beast. Dorómy wasn't worried, not in the slightest. But he did realize that he was glad Lessip was there. Sles glanced from Dorómy to Lessip and back to Dorómy again. His eyes were glittering and black. The eyes of a crow. He did not blink.

"Of course." The little man said finally, bowing long and deep. His lisp was pronounced. "Please forgive us, Your Grace. We do indeed come with intelligence and news. Remarkable things. Incredible things. Things we have witnessed with our own eyes. And, if you will give us but a moment, we shall tell you truly all that we have seen."

APPENDIX 1

The Duchies of Remain
as Recorded by Susan Dallanar

High Lady Susan Dallanar composed the following list of the Realm's fiefdoms in the Third Year of Dorómy III, Founding Year 12,040. At that time, she was four years old. Lady Susan's roster is a succinct account of the Kingdom's constituent duchies. Her record consists of a catalogue of the Remain's worlds in alphabetical order, organized by founding Great Sister. (All names are given in the Kingdom's Common Tongue rather than the duchy's local dialect.) Each entry begins with a brief description of the character and/or the notable features of the named principality. This is followed by the year in which the duchy was annexed (its so-called "Founding Year"), the number of High Gates known to have been established on the world, and the name of the duchy's current ruling family. The colors and sigil of the current High House are also included. (While the illustrations printed here are based on Lady Susan's original drawings, they have been adjusted and cross-checked to precisely reflect the specifics of each duchy's coat of arms.) The world of Paráden is not included. As the Remain's Founding World, humanity's First Home, and the royal seat of Acasius Dallanar, it is the only world known to have been inhabited before the Five Sisters began their Great Expedition. Five High Gates were established on Paráden in F.Y. 1, by Acasius Dallanar. These five High Gates are the only Gates known to have been created by the Great King.

— Nordo Ness, Chief Librarian of the Tarn
Fourth Year of Dorómy III, F.Y. 12,040

The First Great Sister, Eressa the Lost
53 worlds recovered

Amágos

A world of vile pits, stench, and decay; violent hills and castles of iron.
Founding Year: 11; two High Gates.
Ruling House: Gokór.
Color and Sigil: A scimitar of bronze on a split field *(par fess embattled)* of red and black.

Anis

A world of frost with three moons of fire; the toughest soldiers in the Realm.
Founding Year: 21; one High Gate.
Ruling House: Kellson.
Color and Sigil: Three red discs on a field of pale silver.

Anótos

A world of dreams, dreamers, and magic; soundless, mystical, and enchanted.
Founding Year: unknown; one High Gate.
Ruling House: Wanten.
Color and Sigil: A silver crescent over a lavender mountain on a field of deep purple.

Asarnór

A world of clean, green waters and seas; glass cliffs, diamond shores, and scintillating coasts.
Founding Year: 12; two High Gates.
Ruling House: Moráldan.
Color and Sigil: A jumping, silver fish on a split field *(per fess engrailed)* of lime green and aqua blue.

Árcdoth

A world rich in gold, silver, and copper; productive mines and cunning engineers.
Founding Year: 5; three High Gates.
Ruling House: Dérenno.
Color and Sigil: A golden miner's pick on a split field *(party per pale)* of dark brown and dark tan.

Atlósios

An unsoiled world of green plains, vast trees, and windy steppes; home of the tree shamans.
Founding Year: 9; two High Gates.
Ruling House: Barnard.
Color and Sigil: A silver tree of many branches on a field of high green.

Batládea

A night world of thieves and assassins, bathed in perpetual twilight.
Founding Year: 27; three High Gates.
Ruling House: Torg.
Color and Sigil: A silver bull's skull on a black field.

Callón

A world of foggy swamps; low sad hills.
Founding Year: 1; one High Gate.
Ruling House: Veticar.
Color and Sigil: Two copper snakes entwined on a split field *(party per pale)* of sad green and melancholy lime.

Cathanósa

A world of turbulent storms; lightning fields of sparks and chaos.

Founding Year: Unknown; one High Gate.

Ruling House: None (Contested).

Color and Sigil: None. At least four "high houses" currently claim dominion of Cathanósa.

Colodóx

A near dead world; a ruined husk of blighted misery and sorrow.

Founding Year: Unknown; one High Gate.

Ruling House: Landown (Contested by Jahoryn).

Color and Sigil: A white disc crossed by a black sword on a field of red.

Danarcion

A world of orange and brown sunsets; the merchant's nest and trading center of the Realm.

Founding Year: 11; four High Gates.

Ruling House: Tacir.

Color and Sigil: A crescent harp of gold on a field of brilliant orange.

Dunsáor

A flooded world with eternal seas and oceans; home of the sea folk and their kin.

Founding Year: 22; one High Gate.

Ruling House: Garosh.

Color and Sigil: A silver sea-beast with eight tentacles on a field of deep blue.

Exarkiha

A world with deserts of obsidian sand; sharpest blades in the Kingdom.

Founding Year: 26; two High Gates.

Ruling House: Saan.

Color and Sigil: Crossed silver daggers on a split field *(party per fess)* of black and emerald green.

Ebum

A world of madmen, fanatics, and criminals; low, whispering hills; silent, cold mountains.

Founding Year: Unknown; one High Gate

Ruling House: None (Contested).

Color and Sigil: None. At least six "high houses" currently claim dominion of Ebum.

Egáton

The largest and most bountiful world in the Realm; a farmer's paradise.

Founding Year: 15; three High Gates.

Ruling House: Nelleron.

Color and Sigil: Crossed pitchforks in gold on a field of light green.

Egókontos

A world with ageless mountains of iron and granite; the most ancient forges in the Realm.

Founding Year: 4; two High Gates.

Ruling House: Von.

Color and Sigil: A jet black hammer on a field of pale grey.

Ekor

A frozen, barren rock inhabited almost entirely underground; home of the tunnel men.

Founding Year: Unknown; one High Gate.

Ruling House: None (Contested).

Color and Sigil: None. At least three "high houses" currently claim dominion of Ekor.

Escódon

A luminal world of eternal twilight; second only to Anótos with regards to the arcane.

Founding Year: Unknown; one High Gate.

Ruling House: Porró.

Color and Sigil: A silver quarter moon and two stars on a field of pale lavender.

Espónyo

A world with cavaliers and ladies; the best drink in the Kingdom.

Founding Year: 7; two High Gates.

Ruling House: Dontaigne.

Color and Sigil: Crossed golden rapiers on a split field *(party per fess)* of crimson and white.

Elágios

A world of song, dance, and merriment; the musician's haven; a world of eternal sunshine.

Founding Year: 15; two High Gates.

Ruling House: Zappata.

Color and Sigil: A lyre of white on a split field *(party per bend)* of dark orange and dark yellow.

Eupóseol

A merry world, with primitive shores of crystal and gold.

Founding Year: 16; one High Gate.

Ruling House: Lan.

Color and Sigil: A golden fish on a split field *(party per pale)* of white and green.

Eureok

A world with black seas, blood red moons, and vast, blank continents.

Founding Year: Unknown; one High Gate.

Ruling House: None (Contested).

Color and Sigil: None. At least eight "high houses" currently claim dominion of Eureok.

Evalok

A world of wind storms and typhoons; a tropical maelstrom.

Founding Year: Unknown.

Ruling House: Liau (Contested by Tak).

Color and Sigil: A black crane over a black mountain on a field of blood red.

Farámor

A world of vast, grey oceans and huge, grey skies; clever sailors and navigators; best boat builders in the Realm.
Founding Year: Unknown; two High Gates.
Ruling House: Hannér.
Color and Sigil: A grey kraken on a field of black.

Gellátek

A dying world near the Kingdom's edge; supposedly visited by the Voidfolk.
Founding Year: Unknown; one High Gate.
Ruling House: None (Contested).
Color and Sigil: None. At least two "high houses" currently claim dominion of Gellátek.

Golladós

The frozen moon of a massive gas giant; vicious; last world to be reclaimed in the Founding War.
Founding Year: Unknown; one High Gate.
Ruling House: Svonsorn.
Color and Sigil: a white bear on a split field (party per bend sinister) of black and grey.

Gunorica

A world of huge, flat hills; huge, broad men; some of the best infantry in the Realm.
Founding Year: 17; two High Gates.
Ruling House: Yordán.
Color and Sigil: A dark brown war hammer on a split field *(party per pale)* of tan and crimson.

Hakonar

A world of savage, brutal cliffs and mountains; relentless, ruthless, and cunning.
Founding Year: 14; two High Gates.
Ruling House: Jor.
Color and Sigil: A double-bladed axe of blood red, lined with silver, on a field of black.

Helvanthíos

The high sky land of the floating folk; rainbow dawns and polychromatic seas.
Founding Year: 13; one High Gate.
Ruling House: Holte.
Color and Sigil: A silver falcon *(rampant)* on a field of high blue.

Indónok

A world of razor blade storms; uninhabitable save the mountains at the southern pole.
Founding Year: Unknown.
Ruling House: None (Contested).
Color and Sigil: None. At least three "high houses" currently claim dominion of Indónok.

Itáteos

The smaller library world; second only to Genonea for the size of its collections.
Founding Year: 4; four High Gates.
Ruling House: Cuon Sach.
Color and Sigil: A copper chalice on a field of brown.

Jaga

The world of the snake lords – and their pets; pale green sunsets; eternal marshes.
Founding Year: 14; two High Gates.
Ruling House: Soness.
Color and Sigil: A coiled silver serpent on a split field *(party per bend)* of pale and emerald green.

Jun

A world of burning, dry, red sands; an untamable wasteland governed by violence.
Founding Year: 20; two High Gates.
Ruling House: None (Contested).
Color and Sigil: None. At least eight "high houses" currently claim dominion of Jun.

Lábbarkos

A world of strange animals, melted mountains, and ashen fields.
Founding Year: Unknown; one High Gate.
Ruling House: Vyre.
Color and Sigil: A black wolf on a field of dead grey.

Lythéntor

The mercenary world; a land of professional soldiers, scouts, spies, and saboteurs.
Founding Year: 6; three High Gates.
Ruling House: Rorvik.
Color and Sigil: A blood red, spiked mace on a field of white.

Marsinion

The land of eternal war; also known as "Acasius's Folly."
Founding Year: 2; seven High Gates.
Ruling House: None (Contested).
Color and Sigil: None. At least nineteen "high houses" currently claim dominion of Marsinion.

Mercal

A world of death, graves, tombs, and dark scholarship; rumored alliances with the Voidfolk.
Founding Year: Unknown; one High Gate.
Ruling House: Fando Myre.
Color and Sigil: A skull crowned in red on a field of black and mustard *(per saltire)*.

Nelor

A world of green, soft fields; high harvests; honorable customs; "Acasius's Rest."
Founding Year: 15; one High Gate.
Ruling House: Nellerman.
Color and Sigil: A white lion *(passant regardant)* on a field of high green.

Norága

A world with a sky of a thousand colors; the nursery of stars and suns. Once bred dragons.
Founding Year: 7; two High Gates.
Ruling House: Mong.
Color and Sigil: A golden dragon *(rampant regardant)* on a split field *(party per pale)* of red and purple.

Olóros

A world of pure white ice; blinding skies; frozen tundras and steppes.
Founding Year: Unknown; one High Gate.
Ruling House: Ty (Contested by Tuk).
Color and Sigil: Crossed black axes on a split field *(party per fess)* of grey and white.

Peléa

A world of hard warriors and sly slavers; steel grey skies and blood feuds.
Founding Year: 6; two High Gates.
Ruling House: Lessip.
Colors and Sigil: Crossed, curved falcions in silver on a field of iron grey.

Somákos

A world of liars, thieves, and assassins; violet skies and sunsets; four moons.
Founding Year: Unknown; one High Gate.
Ruling House: Bostrok.
Color and Sigil: A straight, black dagger on a field of bruise purple and black *(quarterly)*.

Swozox

A world with dark caverns of glowing stones and skies with dark moons.
Founding Year: 4; two High Gates.
Ruling House: Mordán.
Color and Sigil: A crescent in silver on a field of dark purple.

Tarcéron

The world of the flying cities; winged men of white and gold and copper.

Founding Year: 9; two High Gates.

Ruling House: Clarán.

Color and Sigil: Acasius's Star in deep gold on a field of pale ivory.

Terelag

A world with high brown grasses and deep, eternal fields; endless plains and rolling hills.

Founding Year: 3; one High Gate.

Ruling House: Xiang.

Color and Sigil: A golden stag *(rampant)* on a field of light brown.

Terótan

A word with twelve weird moons; bizarre, dark creatures unlike anywhere else in the Realm.

Founding Year: Unknown.

Ruling House: None (Contested).

Color and Sigil: None. At least three "high houses" currently claim dominion of Terótan.

Tóvonok

A small red moon, like a demon's eye; some of the cruelest soldiers in the Realm.

Founding Year: Unknown; one High Gate.

Ruling House: Xath (Contested by Modán).

Color and Sigil: A blind red eye on a solid field of midnight black.

Ugásur

A world of eternal forests; high cities of the trees; home of the tree folk.

Founding Year: 3; one High Gate; sister world to Ugátria.

Ruling House: Sur.

Color and Sigil: An oak of black on a field of silver.

Ugátria

A world with low hills; grey plains; dreary and primitive, but full of undiscovered secrets.

Founding Year: 3; one High Gate.

Ruling House: Gatron.

Color and Sigil: A silver-grey sun with seven rays on a field of black.

Ursobór

A massive and dark world; giant brown sun; ancient warrior traditions.

Founding Year: 12; one High Gate.

Ruling House: Anor.

Color and Sigil: A disc of deep brown, crossed with two blades in white, on a field of tan.

Wasondí

A world with caravans of spice, bronze, and sand; pale green moons.

Founding Year: 6; four High Gates.

Ruling House: Faraní.

Color and Sigil: Two green discs over a bronze griffin *(rampant regardant)* on a field of tan.

Wenevron

A world of ashy darkness; painfully grey and bloody.

Founding Year: 10; one High Gate.

Ruling House: Shakán.

Color and Sigil: A double headed lion in red *(rampant)* on a field of dark grey.

Zeloros

A burning world on the farthest edge of the Void.

Founding Year: Unknown.

Ruling House: None (Contested).

Color and Sigil: None. At least three "high houses" currently claim dominion of Zeloros.

The Second Great Sister, Alea the True

22 worlds recovered

Akrivor

A world of nightmare skies and demons, blood red suns, and warrior clans.
Founding Year: 7; one High Gate.
Ruling House: Tallyn.
Color and Sigil: A hawk's head in black over a disk of red, on a field of dark grey.

Albotos

A world with cool waves and sunny islands; an idyllic haven for hedonists and philosophers.
Founding Year: 12; two High Gates.
Ruling House: Bonón Tor.
Color and Sigil: A dark blue sea turtle on a field of silver.

Amá

A world of grey wastes; tough, melancholy, and dire; home of the beast men.
Founding Year: 40; two High Gates.
Ruling House: Konter (Contested by Dor).
Color and Sigil: A grey lion's head on a field of brooding black.

Amótros

A world with friendly hills, blue flowers, and a huge, silver moon.
Founding Year: 8; one High Gate.
Ruling House: Hylor.
Color and Sigil: A silver circle on a split field *(party per bend)* of light blue and deep blue.

Anortion

A world of hard edges and broad, pale mountains; great hunters, trackers, and scouts.
Founding Year: 21; one High Gate.
Ruling House: Maeleon.
Color and Sigil: A black boar on a split field *(party per pale)* of white and grey.

Anor

A world of iron hills and strong, stocky, broad trees; home of the purple dwarves.
Founding Year: 14; one High Gate.
Ruling House: Nor.
Color and Sigil: A broad plain tree in iron grey against a field of deep purple.

Asada

A world of smiling clouds and skies; a sandy, open world of merchant princes and traders.
Founding Year: 25; one High Gate.
Ruling House: Asanar.
Color and Sigil: A radiant, silver star on a field of brilliant, light green.

Básadon

A world with a wide archipelago; teal seas and shores; great beasts of the lurking deep.
Founding Year: 37; one High Gate.
Ruling House: Kerek.
Color and Sigil: A copper octopus on a split field *(party per fess engrailed)* of teal and dark green.

Brotunaeon

A world of volcanic chaos and lava flows like the veins of a molten giant.
Founding Year: 7; one High Gate.
Ruling House: Lorno.
Color and Sigil: A black mountain peak crossed by a double tipped spear on a field of orange.

Corícea

A world of honor and principle; fine cities and towers; the finest steel in the Kingdom.
Founding Year: 38; one High Gate.
Ruling House: Reneé.
Color and Sigil: A high silver tower on a field of clean, radiant blue.

Dalíos

The most tragic world in the realm, haunted by memories of lost loves and dreams.
Founding Year: 42; one High Gate.
Ruling House: Dalían.
Color and Sigil: A circle of braided black and silver on a field of blue.

Dalonás

A world with lonely, pale shores; seven pearl moons, also inhabited; intricate politics.
Founding Year: 39; two High Gates.
Ruling House: Han (Contested by Tros).
Color and Sigil: Seven circles of silver over a mountain of gold on a field of pale blue.

Ebavia

A world of fierce warrior women; fertile plains, fields, and streams.
Founding Year: 40; one High Gate.
Ruling House: Bavian.
Color and Sigil: Five crossed war spears in red on a field of dark blue.

Eborium

A world of underwater cities, island ports, and deep coral islands of glass.

Founding Year: 7; one High Gate.

Ruling House: Ebor.

Color and Sigil: Acasius's Star on a split field *(party per pale)* of deep blue and healthy green.

Ephak

A world with wide clouds of pink and gold; seas of grass; home of the roc riders.

Founding Year: 10; two High Gates.

Ruling House: Phak (Contested by Lenow).

Color and Sigil: A falcon *(rampant)* in silver over a field of ruby pink.

Ferragias

A world with a mother-of-pearl moon; towers of light and diamond. Once bred dragons.

Founding Year: 23; two High Gates.

Ruling House: Jang.

Color and Sigil: A silver dragon *(passant)* crossing a silver crescent on a field of mother-of pearl.

Genonea

The world of scholars, philosophers, historians, and poets; eternal, grand libraries.

Founding Year: 22; two High Gates.

Ruling House: Scolum.

Color and Sigil: The ancient letter "A" in silver on a field of high blue.

Okógon

The land of the giants; vast mountains, deep rivers, and ancient seas.

Founding Year: 40; two High Gates.

Ruling House: Gorók.

Color and Sigil: A war hammer in silver on a split field *(party per pale)* of high white and blue.

Panávion

The Realm's only truly divided world; lavender skies and cities; land of the eternal men.

Founding Year: 15; two High Gates.

Ruling Houses: Jyran and Kylon; contested since the Founding.

Colors and Sigils:

House di Jyre – A circular silver shield on a field of high blue.

House di Kylo – A golden, double-bladed battle axe on a field of blood red.

Spárunok

A world of grunting beasts and brutal villages; a freakish, primordial hell.

Founding Year: 6; one High Gate.

Ruling House: None (Contested).

Color and Sigil: None. At least six "high houses" currently claim dominion of Spárunok.

Teládon

A world of high blue glaciers; deep, clean rivers and pure mirrored lakes.

Founding Year: 5; one High Gate.

Ruling House: Serán.

Color and Sigil: Acasius's Star in white on a field of glacial blue.

Yor

A raspy, harsh, barren, and hot world.

Founding Year: 10; one High Gate.

Ruling House: Krodan.

Color and Sigil: Twin, curved daggers in black, crossed on a split field *(party per fess)* of burnt orange and blood red.

The Third Great Sister, Aaryn the Chronicler

14 worlds recovered

Abúcia

A world with rich soils, strong men and women, and dark, bountiful earth.
Founding Year: 10; one High Gate.
Ruling House: Ción.
Color and Sigil: An ox in white *(passant)* on a split field *(party per pale)* of brown and tan.

Dávanor

A world with high, white peaks, stony vales, and eternal forests; home of the dragon riders.
Founding Year: 21; two High Gates.
Ruling House: Dradón (Contested by Fel).
Color and Sigil: A roaring white dragon *(rampant)* on a sky blue field.

Dorn

A world with huge mountains, tan fields; strong and implacable; home of the iron dwarves.
Founding Year: 10; two High Gates.
Ruling House: Beln.
Color and Sigil: A broad mountain of deep brown on a field of tan.

Ethené

A world of healing lakes and trees; gentle farms and plains.
Founding Year: 23; two High Gates.
Ruling House: Benford.
Color and Sigil: A silver plow on a field of gentle blue.

Farák

A world of wailing winds and frozen rains; merciless and unforgiving.
Founding Year: 22; one High Gate.
Ruling House: Nyr.
Color and Sigil: A silver lightning bolt across a split field *(party per fess)* of bruise blue and black.

Gelánen

A world with great rivers, green grasses; clean, bountiful, and pure.
Founding Year: 17; one High Gate.
Ruling House: Julane.
Color and Sigil: A braided circle of white on a field of high green.

Horizon

A world with fine sands; wind farms; silk trade and unsurpassed hospitality.
Founding Year: 13; two High Gates.
Ruling House: Dallanar.
Color and Sigil: Acasius's Star in silver on a split field *(party per fess)* of high blue and golden yellow.

Ibittion

A world of madmen and lunatic moons; longest continuous High dynasty in the Realm.
Founding Year: 28; one High Gate.
Ruling House: Goylen.
Color and Sigil: Four crescents *(white, blue, silver, and grey)* on a field of black.

Jallow

A hard and honest world; deep lakes and rivers; mighty mountains; home of the ogres.
Founding Year: 31; one High Gate.
Ruling House: Dallanar.
Color and Sigil: Acasius's Star in silver on a split field *(party per pale)* of high blue and deep brown.

Kon

A world with icy seas; snowy forests and mountains; a world of perpetual winter.
Founding Year: 9; one High Gate.
Ruling House: Dallanar.
Color and Sigil: Acasius's Star in silver on a field of high blue.

Pénulen

A world of gritty dust and yellow hills; low valleys of shame and hauntings.
Founding Year: 32; one High Gate.
Ruling House: Len.
Color and Sigil: A dog *(rampant)* on a field of dusty, burnt yellow.

Póntokos

The home of the star sailors; a world with rainbow river boats and prismatic sunsets.
Founding Year: 12; three High Gates.
Ruling House: Evenór.
Color and Sigil: A golden boat on a split field *(tierced per pall)* of red, orange, and purple.

Rigel

A world with platinum sands and lakes; fish of silver and gold and copper.
Founding Year: 33; one High Gate.
Ruling House: Ruge (Vymon).
Color and Sigil: Acasius's Star in brilliant white on a field of dark blue.

Sparáton

A world of stern hills and fortresses; pale, cruel warriors of the most lethal cunning.
Founding Year: 36; one High Gate.
Ruling House: Stenegard.
Color and Sigil: Two crossed scimitars of silver against a field of pale grey.

Utarcton

The Kingdom's prison world; a baked husk; completely subterranean.
Founding Year: 9; one High Gate.
Ruling House: Konnór.
Color and Sigil: A flat black key on a field of pale, lifeless silver.

The Fourth Great Sister, Kora the Just

9 worlds recovered

Aradan

A world of soft hills and fields; flowers of silver, yellow, orange, and pink.
Founding Year: 15; five High Gates.
Ruling House: Aradak.
Color and Sigil: Acasius's Star in white on a split field *(party per fess)* of deep pink and gold.

Borádon

A world of violent caves; underground lairs of the deepest and strangest dark.
Founding Year: 27; one High Gate.
Ruling House: Rondan.
Color and Sigil: A battle axe in black on a split field *(tierced per pall)* of purple, red, and green.

Bentór

A world with eternal stonewood forests; towering jade peaks.
Founding Year: 13; one High Gate.
Ruling House: Kentón.
Color and Sigil: A green serpent wrapped around a silver mountain on a field of light green.

Kesst

A world of high waves; blue-green skies; eternal breezes; timeless sunsets.

Founding Year: 26; two High Gates.

Ruling House: Ruge (John).

Color and Sigil: Acasius's Star in silver on a split field *(party per fess)* of cobalt and white.

Nordán

A beautiful, azure world with an ocean-white moon and castles of cloud.

Founding Year: 16; two High Gates.

Ruling House: Dallanar (Dorómy).

Color and Sigil: Acasius's Star in ice white on a field of dark blue.

Nod

A world of black, wet jungles and weird, moaning cliffs; undoubtedly haunted.

Founding Year: 29; one High Gate.

Ruling House: None (Contested).

Color and Sigil: None. At least three "high houses" currently claim dominion of Nod.

Sodemar

A world of decayed cityscapes and skeletal, dark castles long since destroyed.

Founding Year: 26; one High Gate.

Ruling House: Sode.

Color and Sigil: A black tower against a split field *(party per pale)* of grey and red.

Selánon

A world of dread ice; deadly blue-grey glaciers and giant war-bears.

Founding Year: 14; two High Gates.

Ruling House: Jellenyr.

Color and Sigil: A giant silver bear *(rampant)* on a field of ice blue.

Weron

A world with high towers of air, color, grace, and clarity.

Founding Year: 30; one High Gate.

Ruling House: Weron.

Color and Sigil: A blue spear on a split field *(party per pale)* of high yellow and high white.

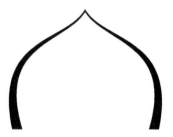

The Fifth Great Sister, Margot the Gentle

5 worlds recovered

Baleen

A world of dusty plateaus, faded trees, and leeched soil; all but barren.
Founding Year: 45; one High Gate.
Ruling House: Jomónoz.
Color and Sigil: A barren, lifeless tree in black on a field of dead grey.

Dayáden

A bountiful world with honey farms, cheerful winds, and sweet clover.
Founding Year: 16; three High Gates.
Ruling House: Dayon.
Color and Sigil: Acasius's Star over a field of sweet green.

Escena

The land of eternal night; inhabitable only at the northern-most pole.
Founding Year: 27; one High Gate.
Ruling House: None (Contested).
Color and Sigil: None. At least three "high houses" currently claim dominion of Escena.

Jenysyn

A rainy world; blue-grey; high cliffs; home of the best horse cavalry in the Realm.

Founding Year: 33; one High Gate.

Ruling House: Tworn.

Color and Sigil: A silver horse *(rampant)* against a rain cloud of grey on a field of high blue.

Targus

A world with nine quick, golden moons; skillful and sharp; home of the Guild of Assassins.

Founding Year: 19; one High Gate.

Ruling House: Targon.

Color and Sigil: A crescent of deep gold on a field of dead white.

APPENDIX 2

The Canon of Tarn and the Dallanar Kings

The Canon of Tarn—also called The Tarn's Canon and, less commonly, The Silver Book—is an epic prose work begun by the Third Great Sister, Aaryn Dallanar ("The Chronicler") during the Second Year of Alea the First (F.Y. 29). The descendants of Aaryn, and many others, continue the composition of the Canon to the present day.

The original copy of the Silver Book is located on the world of Kon, in the central library of the fortress of Tarn. It has been protected there (with two brief interruptions) since its inception. There are five other "primary copies" of the Canon—all endowed with unique properties. Three thousand and twelve other "official manuscript copies" of the Canon are known. Many of these copies are housed on the worlds of Kon, Genonea, Itáteos, and Paráden. Countless other printed copies, of various quality, are available throughout the Kingdom. At present, the Canon consists of 128 main entries (one for every Dallanar monarch) and well over ten thousand appendices that treat various heroes, villains, mercenaries, warlords, merchant-princes, healers, adepts, explorers, brigands, poets, and scholars. Also included in the appendices are stories that pertain to notable events in which otherwise unknown characters play prominent, if brief, roles.

The Canon is the founding literary monument of the Silver Kingdom. It has been considered a work of history, an epic poem, and a historiographic treatise. It is all of these and more. Throughout the Realm, the Canon is regarded as the foundation of a liberal education in both the practical and scholarly sense. To "know one's Canon" is a mark not only of basic literacy but also of cultural and historical fluency.

At its core, the Canon is a history of the Kingdom of Remain, beginning with the creation of the Realm by Acasius Dallanar and his five Great Sisters and continuing to the present moment. The Silver Book is constantly being updated, copied, and transcribed. It is a living, breathing document. The work is not precisely chronological (especially when the magical "primary copies" are "consulted") but, even in those instances, there is a clear sense of movement through time. While the organization of the work is bound to the reigns of the Dallanar monarchs, the Canon's sustaining theme is that of the Silver Kingdom itself. This is important to remember, since some scholars continue to claim that the Canon is nothing more than Dallanar propaganda. This debate need not be treated with much seriousness here. (Indeed, the Canon's accounts of Christopher I "The War Bringer," Christopher II "The Cursed," Simon I "The Silver-Hand," Michael I "The Peacemaker," and—above all—Hakon I "The Terrible," are so unflattering as to make any notion of royal interference in the Silver Book's composition near impossible.) The Canon does include accounts of the Dallanar monarchs, but those are hardly the full measure of its contents. Indeed, if there must be one, then the true protagonist of the Tarn's Canon is not the Dallanar family, but rather the Eternal Kingdom itself.

The Canon is divided into three parts: the heroic, the historical, and the contemporary ages. I have treated the debates regarding the nature and origins of these divisions at length in my *Introduction to the Study of the Canon of Tarn*. Although some controversy remains, it is almost certain that these divisions were created in the second year of Hakon I, by Hakon's Chief Librarian, Kator Xu. Academic opinion is divided on the reasons for Xu's move, but most scholars now believe (as do

I) that it was an attempt to mark Hakon's reign as the end of an era. In at least one sense, then, the Canon's organization is entirely arbitrary.

Two final notes on the List of Dallanar Kings, below:

First, Founding Year designations are given here for convenience only. In educated parlance, the dates in question are known exclusively by the names of the ruling monarch. Thus, Founding Year 10,315 (F.Y. 10,315) would be called "The Third Year of Michael I." This convention was dictated by the practice of Great Sister Aaryn; it has been adhered to here.

Second, following the murder of the Fifth Great Sister, Margot I, in the Third Year of Her Reign (Founding Year 45), all Dallanar rulers until Hakon the Terrible belonged to the House of Alea. Following Hakon's Purge, all Dallanar rulers belonged to the House of Aaryn. Since all ruling families, on all one hundred and four of the Kingdom's worlds, are of "Dallanar" descent, only those High Dallanar belonging to the ruling House of Aaryn now employ the Dallanar family name.

– Nordo Ness, Chief Librarian of the Tarn
Third Year of Dorómy III, F.Y. 12,040

The Dallanar Kings

The Heroic Age

The Founding — The Founding Monarchs
>Acasius I "The Great" or "The Great One" (01-27)
>Alea I "The Cruel" (27-42)
>Margot I "The Generous" (42-55)
>Garen I (55-67)
>Julia I (67-79/80)
>Adara I "The Kind" (79/80-101)

The Founding War — The Warrior Monarchs
>Christopher I "The War Bringer" (101-102)
>Poder I "Poder Jarlen" also "The Invincible" (102-109)
>Bellános I (109-110)
>Katherine I (110-112)
>Terence I (112-113/4)
>Dorómy I (113/4-120)
>James I (120-129)
>Jessica I "The Trickster" (129-131)
>Samuel I (131-133)
>Diégan I (133-167)
>>— The First Peace —
>Emily I (167)
>Jordun I (167-169)
>Kelian I (169)
>Julia II (169-171/2)
>Korlen I (171/2-173)
>Katherine II "The Scholar Queen" (173-191)
>>— The Second Peace —
>Jon I (191-192)

Derek I (192-193)

Margot II "The Strong" (193-195)

Samuel II (195)

Christopher II "The Cursed" also "The Blight" (196)

— Dawn of the Plague Years —

The Plague Years (196 - 10,211)

Also known as the "10,000 Year War."

The Restoration — The Avenging Monarchs

Marden I (10,211)

Jason I (10,211)

Peter I (10,211)

Heath I (10,212-10,213)

Samuel III (10,213-10,216)

Kelian I (10,216-10,218/19)

William I (10,118/19-10,222)

Jane I (10,222)

Daniel I (10,222-10,217)

Simon I "The Silver Hand" (10,217-10,245)

Jon II (10,245-10,266/7)

Peter II (10,266/7-10,278)

Margaret I (10,278-10,282)

Derek II (10,282-10,284)

Kendal I (10,284-10,289)

Jeremy I (10,289-10,298)

Hugo I (10,298)

— The Siege of Paráden —

George I (10,298)

Korlen II (10,298)

Gregg I (10,298)

Richard I (10,298)

Karen I (10,298)

Julia III "The Siegebreaker" (10,298-10,300)

Falmon I (10,300-10,301)

Susan I "The Silver Whore" (10,301-10,312/13)

Michael I "The Peacemaker" (10,312/13-10,349)

 — The Final Peace —

Peter III (10,349-10,367)

Katherine III (10,367-10,401)

Hugo II (10,401-10,433)

George II (10,433-10,458/9)

Doldon I "The Eternal" (10,458/9-10,519)

The Historical Age

Délen I (10,519-10,522)

Délen II (10,522-10,568)

Fen I "The Silver Dog" (10,568-10,590)

Samuel IV (10,590-10,604)

Susan II (10,604-10,616/7)

Filip I (10,616/7-10,643)

Peter IV "The Just" (10,643-10,699)

David I (10,699-10,717)

James II (10,717-10,726)

Marden II (10,726-10,744)

David II (10,744-10,825)

Alea II "The Virgin Queen" (10,825-10,868)

Terence II (10,868-10,874)

Roger I (10,874-10,901)

Kendal II (10,901-10,916)

Mikal I (10,916-10,924)

Xavier I (10,924-10,943)

Órtha I "The Explorer" (10,943-10,975/6)

James III (10,975/6-11,003)
Fen II (11,003-11,012)
Vymon I (11,012-11,045)
Tomas I (11,045-11,046)
Marcus I (11,046-11,058)
Peter V (11,058-11,069)
Deborah I (11,069-11,081)
Heather I (11,081-11,085)
Acasius II (11,085-11,110)

The Contemporary Age

Hakon I "The Terrible" (11,100-11,132)
— Hakon's Purge —
Michael II (11,132-11,146)
Dorómy II (11,146-11,158)
Jessica II (11,158-11,190)
Roger II (11,190-11,208)
Elizabeth I (11,208-11,222)
Kyla I "The Pale" (11,222-11,270)
Króan I (11,270-11,271)
David II (11,271-11,301)
Charles I (11,301-11,345)
Filip II "The Wandering King"(11,345-11,402)
Roger III (11,402-11,431)
Andrew I (11,431-11,467)
Peter IV (11,467-11,489)
Xavier II (11,489-11,520)
Hakon II "The Beast" (11,520)
James IV (11,520-11,534)
Délen III (11,534-11,572)
Sophia II (11,572-11,604)

Derek III (11,604-11,616)

Marcus II (11,616-11,660)

Marcus III (11,660-11,663)

Hugo III (11,663-11,687)

Susan III (11,687-11,706)

Tarlen I "The Finder" (11,706-11,770)

Garen II (11,770-11,794)

Orlen I (11,794-11,809)

Hana I (11,809-11,832/33)

Sophia III "The Deceiver" (11,832/33-11,840)

Sabella I (11,840-11,845)

Michael III (11,845-11,867)

Susan IV (11,867-11,884)

Filip III (11,884-11,905)

David IV "The Lonesome" (11,905-11,910)

Marden III "The Silver Shield" (11,910-11,913)

Timothy I (11,913-11,923)

Poder II (11,923)

Peter V (11,923-11,925)

Dana I "The Caregiver" (11,925-11,948)

Adara II (11,948-11,972)

Tomas II (11,972-11,996)

Balmás I "The Frail" (11,996-12,014)

Bellános III "The Silver Fox" (12,014-12,034)

Dorómy III "The Iron Lion" (12,034 – present [12,040])

ACKNOWLEDGMENTS

Deepest thanks are due Amy S., Andrea W., Becky D., Erika F., Erin H.K., Heidi G., Jen K., Kari M., Kelsey D., Lincoln H., Matt C., Marilyn D., Mark E., Nikoli F., Nina M., Robert K., Robert R., Tamara W., Vanessa H., and Zoey S. for their generosity, criticism, support, encouragement, and faith. High Ladies and Lords of Dávanor, the Kingdom and its peoples salute you.

Extra special thanks are also owed a tough squadron of young dragon squires who reviewed this book at an early stage: Anna L., Ainsley N., Amanda H., Aubrey G., Bennett W., Elissa C., Gentry N., Giovanni N., Grace S., Joey B., Lindsey H., Maddie B., Mason C., and Thomas W. Let it be known throughout the Realm: the next generation of dragons is blessed with riders of the highest quality—smart, dedicated, and fierce.

Finally, the Kingdom of Remain would not exist without the love and friendship of the following warriors and poets: Anna S., Aurora M., Cady M., Christopher M., Darcie D., Jesse H., Kan L., Kristin L., Liz N., Mari H., Olga P., Roger S., Ruth S., Tianhua X., Tom M., Travis K., William S., and Zach F. I have not the words—so these, I borrowed: Πᾶς γοῦν ποιητής γίγνεται οὗ ἂν ἀγάπη ἄψηται.

About the Author

Peter Valerianos Fane served in the Silver Legion's artillery corps for over forty years, rising to the rank of Peer Colonel under High Lords Bellános and Dorómy Dallanar. His most well-known actions took place on Colodóx, Batládea, and Ebum—all in the service of the High House of Remain. In retirement, Colonel Fane spends the majority of his time on the great library world of Genonea, where he lectures on military theory, ancient Davanórian war poetry, and moral philosophy. He winters at his clan's hereditary estate on Egáton with his wife, his family, and a small flock of messenger dragons.

The Silver Kingdom awaits your thoughts regarding the latest tale from the Canon of Tarn. Indeed, Colonel Fane dispatches messenger dragons weekly to retrieve the latest reviews from Amazon and Goodreads, which he then archives along with other material from the Canon. So don't be shy—let your voice be heard. For the Remain!

amazon.co.uk

A gift from **Dave**

Enjoy your gift! From Dave

Gift note included with **The Blind Dragon: A Tale from the Canon of Tarn: 1**

Printed in Great Britain
by Amazon